The BLACKHOLE KIDS

ESSENTIAL PROSE SERIES 227

Canada Council for the Arts
Conseil des arts du Canada

ONTARIO ARTS COUNCIL
CONSEIL DES ARTS DE L'ONTARIO
an Ontario government agency
un organisme du gouvernement de l'Ontario

Guernica Editions Inc. acknowledges the support of the Canada Council for the Arts and the Ontario Arts Council. The Ontario Arts Council is an agency of the Government of Ontario.

We acknowledge the financial support of the Government of Canada.

The BLACKHOLE KIDS

J.L.ONEILL

GUERNICA EDITIONS
TORONTO • CHICAGO • BUFFALO • LANCASTER (U.K.)
2025

Guernica Founder: Antonio D'Alfonso

Michael Mirolla, editor
David Moratto, interior and cover design

Guernica Editions Inc.
1241 Marble Rock Rd., Gananoque, ON K7G 2V4
2250 Military Road, Tonawanda, N.Y. 14150-6000 U.S.A.
www.guernicaeditions.com

Distributors:
Independent Publishers Group (IPG)
600 North Pulaski Road, Chicago IL 60624
University of Toronto Press Distribution (UTP)
5201 Dufferin Street, Toronto (ON), Canada M3H 5T8

First edition.
Printed in Canada.

Legal Deposit—Third Quarter
Library of Congress Catalog Card Number: 2025936576
Library and Archives Canada Cataloguing in Publication
Title: The blackhole kids / j.l.oneill.
Names: O'Neill, J. L., author.
Series: Essential prose series ; 227.
Description: Series statement: Essential prose series ; 227
Identifiers: Canadiana (print) 20250190834 |
Canadiana (ebook) 20250191717 | ISBN 9781771839518 (softcover) |
ISBN 9781771839525 (EPUB)
Subjects: LCGFT: Novels.
Classification: LCC PS8629.N442 B53 2025 | DDC C813/.6—dc23

… this first one's ours.
sáhm. sláinte. cois.

[first set]

Old Boy.

She stepped into traffic with snotty defiance, a morose smirk waxing her lips as she danced between oncoming vehicles, a damp squeegee trailing behind her. I braked. Tires squealed as I cut the curb and avoid splattering her over the battered asphalt as she crossed onto Hastings.

My evening coffee jumped onto my dashboard, scalding my hands and lap. I cursed. A hooded youth beside her, with a thin fox nose, cackled behind his ruddy beard as he collected coins from faceless commuters.

Squeegee girl pointed, said something, and the fox boy held his chest as they laughed. I turned away. Eyes rolled. Strung out. Shame.

Be careful, I mouthed, losing my place in my podcast.

Her braceleted hand pointed at her scuffed combat boots. Crosswalk. My fault. I wanted to scold her for telling lies under the red light, but recoiled at the thought of confrontation.

I've been lost these days. Avoiding home, circling the city like an aimless arrow, wishing for something to collide with and rend me from malaise. Aunty Donna, my therapist calls it. Wife says PTSD. I didn't know youth could traumatize you.

I waved squeegee girl to continue, uncertain if I knew her, or the fox boy. A vague sense of sorrow pulled at my face from the inability to place them within my cluttered life.

She refused to leave my lane. Pulled back her pink tatty hair from her long face, and said something as wild as her torn pants with haphazard band patches. I didn't recognize the slang. A first for me. Signs of a sellout. She couldn't have been older than my daughter, waiting to grow into her nose.

I honked. Not loud or long, but short bleats asking squeegee girl to continue on with her life so I could move on with my own.

She gave me the finger. Boney. Pale. Chipped black nail polish with grime caked along bitten tips. Then I saw her for her. The reason why she looked so damned familiar. Sav. Squeegee girl was Sav reincarnate. Scrawny. Dyed hair. Sides shaved. Skinny jeans with scabbed knees poking underneath and faded brown from seasons of sidewalk surfing.

I wanted to call to her. Ask her name. Would she answer, or call me a nitwit, move on? Probably not.

Another boy darted out from an alleyway. Benji. No doubt. His jean jacket flapped behind him. His back-patch with an illegible logo made from gore was stitched on crooked. He even wore Benji's sun faded toque and soul patch.

Squeegee girl flashed a smile at him, turned back to me and stuck out her hairy tongue, before shouting a warning to the fox boy who gave me his best punk rock sneer from under his hoodie. Threadbare and stitched with safety pins.

I knew him too.

With a fervent guile found only in youth, they scrambled through the traffic as two cops poured from the alley. The fox boy slid over the hood of my car, chucking his squeegee at Officer Friendly, taunting him with curses over his shoulder, and cackling anti-fascist slogans I too had memorized in youth.

He was me. I was the fox boy tripping in the moonlight with my friends.

I stalled on the crosswalk as the chase tore through Hastings. My car lurched with a metallic grunt. Died.

Honk. I pictured Sav, young and wild, howling at the weary middle-aged man fighting with his beater as she lived her fullest life. Honk. My face flushed as I killed the ignition, started over. Honk. My sedan's engine jumped to life and I popped the clutch. Honk. Honk. The car jerked into gear. I left the squeegee kids behind, wishing them all the best.

I didn't go home to my wife and daughter that night. Again. I called her from Fionn's Bar off Melrose, and explained I was decaying with the boys. Again. She told me, with a panged bitterness, to have a nice time.

Reality was I sat alone with a dirty glass. Prodding unwanted fries. Pathetic and soggy and tepid, I debated if I should end my sobriety streak of twenty-some odd years so I could feel the warmth of the forlorn friends I left behind in Green River. I counted on my overworked fingers back from my daughter's birth, trying to settle on a proper number since my last shot. My wife knew the score. I feared asking.

A skinhead ordered a pony bottle of Dean and I had half a mind to join him. Opportunity passed. Gateway closed. Anxiety overcame thirst.

This was a long time coming, I knew.

How many times had I tried to write this out?

I pulled out my phone, thinking of the squeegee kids, of my past life, and tapped away on the cracked screen. Words exploded from my fingertips as I traced my roots from Victoria to Green River, Vancouver to Skunktown. Southern fucking Ontario. I had tried for years to find sufficient words. Once during the long winter overseen by a fat man in the bug house. My time living there was volatile. Worse than the days of my youth, homeless and sketching with Sav and Benji, and Dev and Ryan and Alex. I remembered Alex.

My second attempt to purge the grief came after my wife miscarried. We were going to name him Benji. The irony of another failure, never lost.

But as I sat in that dingy bar on Melrose, listening to sponges, toppers, degenerates, and addicts while sucking in cancer smoke from the open patio, the words came. I could smell the dust from the demolished buildings rotting in Skunktown, taste the chalky pills we openly chewed on the bus before punk shows, feel my knuckle splitting open under that bastard's chin. I needed a catalyst. Squeegee girl, who reminded me of Savannah Anne Moore, triggered something profound inside my dormant soul. She connected my subconscious to conscious with a clarity never experienced in sobriety.

For the life of me I could not stop. I wrote every break alone in my car, nights after work, weekends consumed by past trauma, and when my daughter's disgruntled pouts and angry shouts echoed in the car when I forgot to collect her after band, I knew after all these years I was still possessed by rot. It lingered inside me. Hibernating.

'Sorry, dear,' I said to her when I forgot to help her with a science project. I chose to avoid spring rains singing above the garage. I lied about needing to fix the car.

I wanted to explain everything to her. About the rot. The addiction. I wanted to tell her she'll understand when she's older, but thought better of it.

I hope she'll never understand. That she can avoid my mistakes. Because if she ever does understand, then I've failed her as a father. She will have become everything I ran away from.

I was dope at running away. Real swell. Hawthorn, the strength and conditioning coach my parents sent me to, once said I was Olympic material. I just needed to put in the work. Scrub. Which was why, when I think back to my youth, Hawthorn's training gave me the skill to outrun John Law and Officer Friendly.

Stoned. Legs blazing. Defiant strides. Benji loved this game: measuring distance before capture. There was nothing more punk than spitting in the police's face.

This is what I thought while Benji and I raced over the cracked sidewalks of Green River at 6 in the morning. Steel toes racking concrete. A susurrus of trousers. Cackling with cotton-mouths.

I floated through deep space nine past Town Hall in the half-hearted spring air. Damp wind whooshed through my frayed ends.

I ditched the pipe, hurled it at the pavement. It shattered in a dull rainbow as I sped around Barry's Tirecraft, crunching under John Law's merciless heel.

How did we get here? Called the void consuming chaos thrusting for my neck.

Simple.

Benji wanted to witness dawn.

We had smoked a bowl of blackberry kush, listening to *Chaos is Me* on my Discman, splitting earbuds on the roof of Enrico's Pizza as the rising sun stretched over Green River in lazy pink clouds igniting red as they shrouded the banks, painting silhouettes of the old buildings standing stark throughout the valley. Early morning breathed life into the dilapidated homes. The regal statues and crumbling brick made for a fantastically dismal sight. No wonder Benji had wanted to see it.

Our scrawny legs hung over the side of Enrico's as John Law flashed his lights at us. Fish on a hook. We did the only thing we could. We jumped from the single story, rolled onto the pavement, and bolted towards the sun, running the wrong way down a one-way street.

Officer Friendly joined the chase as we skirted past Hope's Convenience. Benji and I split up at The Horn of Plenty. We knew the layout of the city well, had made a point to find places that weren't heatscore. We memorized the twisting alleyways and burbs like songs of our favourite CDs.

I cut down Parkside, sprinted across the footbridge by the Moose Lodge, and doubled back on Market, using the community centre as a throughway.

I planned to sneak through the trails and gullies winding through Green River to avoid capture. The old Fenian Raid routes would be overgrown, and Shallow Creek would sponge the footpath. I knew exactly where to step, having used those mucky trails on the days my dad refused to pick me up from Runners Club, before turning my brain off in my room, absorbing 'violent' music.

I could be back at my parent's before the cops caught up. Sneak through the window before my dad woke for work and burnout in bed to The Locust.

My footfalls echoed in the community centre parking lot. Heart throbbing. I wiped away the pasties sponging in the crooks of my lips. Looked back.

Alone.

I steadied my stride. Caught my breath before the inevitable second heat. Offroad. My specialty.

Discarded ice from the indoor rink slouched in a heap at the edge of the lot near the trail entrance. Slush melted into the gully, polluted the veins splitting from Shallow Creek.

John Law sideswiped me. The weight of a grown-ass man crosschecking a knobby teenager is the exact force a freight train requires to obliterate a herd of deer. He hit me so hard he smashed up my Discman.

Entombed inside his black uniform, I struggled to free myself. Limbs pinned by his thick arms. The curb bit into my wrist and John Law drove his knee into my guts.

I'll admit it. I resisted.

My eyes caught fire. He maced me again. I tried to swear through my tears, unable to breathe, and clawed at my burning throat as I choked on an inferno.

Jon Law wrestled my flailing arms as instinct and self preservation overrode sentience. I blinked away acidic tears and in a moment of clarity I saw Benji. His boney fist raised in defiance as he soared through the blur. His biker jacket flapped behind him like sanctified wings of a hussar during a calvary rush. He swung for John Law's throat.

Officer Friendly caught Benji's arm before it could connect. It popped.

We were beaten and maced and beaten again for resisting—which I'm sure we rightly deserved, but Benji needed a hospital. Our riot lasted until the station.

When they hauled us out of the cruiser, Benji spat in Friendly's mouth. He and Law pinned Benji against the hood while a beaut of a woman strapped a sack around his head. He looked like Hannibal cosplaying a beekeeper. They tethered him to a wheelchair and rolled him towards their medic monkey.

I no longer blame the cops. We knew what we were doing. We wanted trouble. A reason to break loose of our frustrations at parents, bullies, teachers—which are all the same thing when you boil out the marrow—to release the rage and dysphoria of teen angst. Our counsellors called it 'low self-esteem.'

Through my jaded adult lens, I know the cops were just normals collecting a paycheck. Some are just less honest than others. Like all jobs it's about purging toxicity. ACAB.

The judge who sentenced us was a haggard toad with grey skin and a bowl cut and smelled of dust. We got off easy. 'First Time Offenders.' First time caught.

As minors we got wrist slaps for possession. My father's beating was a worse punishment. But I was lucky, hell thankful, there was nothing about assault of an officer, trespassing, theft—we stole chocolate from Hope's Convenience—not to mention the colossal turds we left on the post office's backsteps. The Green River

Review covered it. Urged citizens to pick up after their dogs. Woof.

I can't help thinking that's all we were. Pit bulls of the Great White North.

Our mothers forced us to dye our hair back to natural colours for court. They believed appearance dictated sentencing. I got 100 hours of community service playing librarian. Benji got 120 playing park janitor, cleaning Peanut's tags from kiddie pools and benches. Unlike me, he was able to talk at work.

He only served 90 hours of punishment. Three weeks after our sentencing, Benji died. A Wednesday. Same day his mother farted him out.

No one in our social circle knew how he passed. The letter from Benji's mom, a devout Irish Catholic, said his heart unexpectedly gave out. I thought that was bullshit.

I received mine after a show at The Cellar—I had snuck out with Sav to celebrate the end of being a book monkey. My mother had set the letter aside in a fruit bowl, an error amongst apples and mangos. A reminder to feed me soap. I read it after my beating for defying my grounding.

I felt guilt for going to the show, not being there when his mother came by with the letter. Between bands Dev and Alex had asked where Benji was. 'Not here,' I joked to the older boys, thinking his parents had caught him sneaking out.

I regretted my words while reading the letter. Tears in my eyes hurt more than my belted ass cheeks. His mother formally invited me to carry his coffin. I was seventeen. I declined. Had to. I nearly missed the whole funeral when I spent a few days in the hospital. Broken finger. I snapped it punching the foundation in my parent's basement.

I hold that night we ran from the police close to my heart. Though I know I shouldn't. When I think about my youth, that's what I remember. Benji. The last time he and I indulged in one of our adventures. The last time I heard his laugh. The last time the world was a beautiful place where—

What I mean to say is, under the morning sun I was never afraid of the rot.

That's all I would like to say about that.

Creature from the Haunted Sea.

Funerals aren't for the dead, they're for the living. The dead don't give a damn about thoughts and prayers. Ease the hurt. Laugh again. Self-serving leeches fear the abyss.

Sav and I, and Crazy Dev, and Ryan, and Alex, among others, came to celebrate Benji's life. Not sulk about or glorify his existence.

It was only natural Sav and I split a joint in the bathroom of St. Pad's Funeral Home before the reception. Benji would have encouraged it.

As she rolled in the cramped mint scented piss-cake stall, we reminisced about the old days, before our parents knew we hated them, before we painted our lives black, and took sandpaper and hacksaws to our jeans and stitched them back together with resin tipped safety pins.

I told Sav how Benji and I met in junior kindergarten, he turned to me and asked if we could be best friends. Done deal. She called us nerds and said she met him at the skatepark, hitting on her best friend, Jocelyn, after he dislocated his shoulder dropping into a halfpipe.

"Just because he's gone," Sav said, spreading the bud evenly on the pape, "doesn't mean we should end our Monster Madness tradition."

"Duh," I said, keeping an ear out for grievers before they busted us. "If anything, we'll have to step up our game. Find obscurer films to get wasted to."

"As long as we can keep microdosing thrillers."

"Not everyone enjoys Dr. Phibes sifting through Brussels, you derphole."

The tension of horror films coupled with hallucinogens made me anxious. Like cat people were licking my brain. I hated those nights, preferred downers.

"But Benji loved doing that," she said.

"No. He loved broken-down golf carts and rampages."

Sav scoffed.

"His legacy will stay intact," she said, sprinkling crushed T3s into the joint and sealing it. She lit, took a drag, and passed. Exhaling as she spoke, the smell reminded me of a Timmy's drive through before the coffee rush. "Maybe I'd feel less like a sellout with more gore in my life."

"Probably," I said, fussing with my funeral collar. "I feel like that chud from that skater boy video." I loosened my skull tie as I choked on the dry burn.

"It's chode."

"Nuh uh."

"It's chode."

"Cannibal Humanoid Underground Dweller."

She told me she hated me, then squinted at me through the haze. "I see it now. You got that googly-eyed thing going on."

I stole the joint.

"Well I'm glad I got to reuse this dress." She smoothed the furl that accentuated the adorable blip under her navel. A triumph of how many beers she could crush. "Jocelyn helped me pick it out last Easter to piss off my fascist uncle."

Her black dress was littered with patterns of dinosaur and unicorn skeletons. I'm sure she looked ridiculous to normals. That's what she called them. Everyone who wasn't us.

I told her she looked groovy.

I would have done anything to impress the older kids in our clique.

As the buzz kicked in, my half-shaven head began to itch from the fresh dye. Colours popped like a snare drum. The normals were disgusted when we showed up with the other punks. Murmured at the anarchy symbol and cuss words on my cast.

I loved it. Benji would have approved of their curled lips and snub-nosed leers. It showed how little they knew him. We were his friends. The people he chilled with on the daily. The normals knew Benjamin Alfred Nunes. Not Benji.

Crazy Dev had caught whispers of having us thrown out before the service started, which was no surprise, but Benji's mom was in our corner.

My dad said I would be 'taken to the curb' for dressing like a 'tranny clown' when he saw my skinny pinstripe bondage pants and skull tie.

My mother said I looked decent for once. Showered. Shaved. Properly scented. Not my usual street kid stench of cancer smoke, sidewalk dust, and stale pizza sauce.

All I cared about was that Alex said I looked sharp.

Sav killed the joint and flushed it. To my surprise she called me a dapper chud as the joint spiraled, even though I was a poser.

"Why thank you, ma'am," I said, bowing to hide my blush at the older girl's backhanded compliment.

My busted arm racked the TP dispenser and I stifled a whimper. I forced out a falsetto sonofabitch to distract from the weakness leaving my body.

"Classy bastard," she said through a sly smile, tongue pressed against her teeth to hide the crooked ones underneath. The stainless stud in her tongue was heart-shaped with a bubble of saliva glistening in the crook. She curtsied.

I asked her if she was ready, as we checked ourselves in the mirror for bloodshot eyes. I looked like I had been bawling.

"You're not going in like that." Her laugh echoed in the undersized poo closet.

"Like what? You just said I looked dapper."

Sav stepped in close. She was tiny compared to my lanky frame. Neatly packaged like a kintsugi vase with wildflowers nestled inside. Gothic hairband sold separately. I looked like a cracked mason jar duct taped to a gym sock. Bad breath included.

Sav made a face. I made one back, but tried to discreetly square my shoulders.

She wet her hands in the sink and pushed into me, began mussing and fussing with my hair, kneading the gel.

As my high increased, I became aware of her cheap scent. Fake. Like purple freezies with cherry soda on her lips. She was a discount cornucopia of faux fruit.

I told her the local worm babies would love her because she had green hair and smelled of candy. She punched my good arm. Stood back.

"Thanks, mum."

"I'm not done with you," she said, sticking out her tongue. "Settle down, sailor."

"Does this make me Captain Classy Bastard?"

"Of the S.S. Screw You." She stood back, analysing me like normals do modern art.

Her eyes lit up, but I was gone. Full space cadet, talking too fast for her, or my mind, to keep up, ranting about concerts on cruise ships in the Galapagos, switching to horses and wondering aloud if they could tread water, asking if she had seen the photos of high diving horses, and if she knew dead sea scrolls were salt stained when J.P. stole Magdalene's gospel, or did she think they were worked leather like a Norwegian skin suit, corpse britches, corpse britches, corpse britches, one size fits all, bury me in my corpse britches. If you were nude, did you have to insert your-

Sav placed her soft finger on my lips. "Slow down, nitwit," she said, eyes glazed. She pulled away when I tried to tongue her finger like a hamster at a water bottle. "We can't get busted. Benji would love this, but Jocelyn will shit if we're this baked. I told you to get indica."

I nodded once and tensed because I became aware of my hair growing, then apologized for the stupid grin melting over my face.

She pulled my suspenders off my shoulders. They were neon green. Same as her hair. She untucked my shirt and slid a cancer behind my ear. Reserves. Hand-rolled.

"You done, Picasso?"

"Trust those who are violent with their art," she said in a speakeasy accent.

She stepped back. My hair was a rat king's nest.

"Up the punx."

I extended my elbow. She took it.

We sauntered through the foyer in an overexaggerated and pompous manner, scanning for Dev's red mohawk or Ryan's blue curly mop. When we couldn't find them, we went to the foyer where Benji's parents had his guitar on display. It was ragged and chipped. The varnish around the pickguard had been stripped from the endless strums of anarchy. His family and friends had signed the body with a silver paint marker. Alex had signed the head.

Sav took a moment to scrawl a heart on the 7th fret, peeled apart the untuned strings with a discordant twang. When she handed me the marker, I didn't know what to write. I read the names and well wishes and found myself unsure how to say goodbye. I couldn't write 'See you in heaven,' like his cousin Katie; 'Life's a ride,' from Dev; 'See you in the pit,' in Ryan's bubbly caps. Or the 'I have always loved you,' in thin lowercase and signed with an x.

And so, I was stuck with a memory, of last winter when we went on a bender and binged Jackson's *The Lord of the Rings* films before seeing *Return of the King* on release. Nine hours of our lives. Three years of arguing who was the bigger BAMF, Sam or Strider. Benji insisted Strider.

I wrote on my dead friend's guitar 'Not all those who wander are lost,' and for us, at least, wasn't that the truth?

Sav led us to the sparkling French doors guarding the reception where mourners moaned behind frosted glass. By then I had recomposed myself, adorned with my jaded punk rock side sneer.

"After you, ma'am," I said, taking an overinflated bow. My cast accentuated the pose.

"Thank you kindly, *dar*ling."

Sav planted the bottom of her mucky boot against the centre of the doors. They burst open.

The normals in the parlour gasped. The organist missed a beat, trying not to pay us the attention we desperately desired. Ryan stifled a giggle. Pops McGregor was so appalled he dropped his bible into Benji's casket. I was surprised the holy relic didn't turn to ash when it opened on Benji's chest.

"Don't look now, captain," Sav said, "but I do think some poor chap's just died."

Later we swore we heard Benji laughing along with us.

Carnival of Souls.

Crazy Dev used his molars to gnaw his nubby fingernails, ignoring the grit and blood spotting. He spat hangnails onto the grease-soaked pizza plate.

Ryan asked him at a party once why he couldn't 'bite them like a normal person.' He stared gravely and flipped her off.

We sat in Enrico's Pizza, fueling up before the after party—the real party—to celebrate Benji's life. Dev, disinterested and bored with the crusts, messaged Alex, asking when the others would get here.

His mood surprised me. I expected to be eating with Crazy Dev. The crowd killer. Mr. White Riot. But he was just Dev. Benji's and Alex's drummer from the band I came to adore. Sick Sad World.

Before Benji passed, they had built a following. Two EPs, DIY shirts, pins, stickers, patches. I watched them play backyards, basements, D.D. Crust's Laundromat, even The Cellar.

It was a big deal back then. The Cellar was our only official punk bar before gentrification molested it into a hipster joint blasting that droning noise. 'Shoegaze revival.' Wink. Nod. Laugh. Not.

Andrew Cho entered Enrico's, swaggering in with his boys, the jockstraps, in tow. Paige Everett, and Holly Gaspard hung off his every word as he relived another play from the basketball court.

I turned to my phone, pretended to read texts from Sav, hoping Cho would be foolish enough to pull his usual shit in front of Dev.

He didn't. He glared at us as he passed. The freaks. The Halloween kids. Paige gave me the up and down as if to say 'Crusty. Creep.'

Cho told his jockstraps I probably busted my wrist jerking off my boyfriend.

Dev hoarked a wad of grey phlegm onto his plate. Wet thwack. Paige gagged.

I counted her lucky.

Dev motioned for us to roll. Said we'd meet the others at the grave. I did as I was told, thankful to leave Cho behind.

Dev would never admit it, but thrashing on drums was the only thing he had going for him. If he didn't get to smash the skins out of his kit once a week, he would actively search for someone to knock out. When he heard Benji died, he almost killed Duck. Duck was a headbanger who wore thick glasses and had webbed feet. He misstepped in a moshpit. Bumped Dev. His drink didn't spill. It was a bottle. Unopened. Dev threw a haymaker into the back of Duck's skull. He dropped. Alex and Philip had to pull Crazy Dev off the kid. They took their share of blows for saving the headbanger.

Needless to say, I kept my opinions short with Dev. Especially when alone.

Which is why, as we walked down Erie Ave. to Darnley Grove, I watched my words when Dev professed his desire to keep Sick Sad World alive. Before Benji passed, they were in the works of writing new material for an LP. They scored a recording time from an anarcho studio, Six of Wires.

"Alex won't want to stop either," Dev said, as he helped me fashion a pipe from a juice box with his pocket knife. "Don't blame him. No one could rage like Benji, man. For a kid, he knew how to shred. Had feeling. Your generation forgets that punk has soul."

"That's what *Go Fast/Get Pissed* was about, right?"

"Hell yeah, little dude. You gotta have heart. Benji was all heart."

Music was math, I knew, Benji and I had talked about it at 4 am still high from a Cancer Bats show. And just like math, if you repeat the same sequence over and over and over it gets predictable. Redundant. Superfluous. That's why we like the Bats. Punk was about pushing the limits of music, subject matter, not some bullshit about counterculture to make mommy cry and trick daddy into giving you a shiner. Any guitar monkey can slam three chords together, but seldom can convey an alternative ideology to the 'post-modern,' or whatever BS fine art snobs deem meta. Teen angst? Sure. Revolution, in its purest form, is more than plagued teens surfing buzzes while raging to a backbeat.

"What if—" I started but Dev cut me off.

"If you say 'replace Benji' I will punch your goddamned neck off."

I kept quiet. Listened to him rave as we walked up the cemetery hill.

We found Jocelyn at Benji's grave.

Dev resumed chewing his nails, mohawk flipped over his eyes, as he played Closet Monster through his Razor's speaker until his phone died.

I tried not to watch Jocelyn trace the engraved letters on Benji's headstone. She was stuck on the 'J.' Refusing to continue. As if stopping short made him less gone.

She and Sav had grown up in the same building until Jocelyn's parents split. Around that time Jocelyn distanced herself from the local scene. Because she occupied Benji's life outside of our existence, I knew little about her. Only that she and Benji went from being friends to intimate. No titles. She thought they were demeaning. Said they did little but inspire creepers to gush over.

I felt apprehensive about initiating a conversation while she cried. Instead I uncomfortably waited for the sun to drown itself behind the cemetery hill in Darnley Grove, listening to crickets and cicadas sing summer songs in the distance.

The loose soil over Benji's grave enforced the totality of his death. During the eulogy I held a sense of hope he would repel from the rafters, or jerk upright in his casket and pass me a bottle of something with a shit-eating grin over his formaldehyde painted face, or a call from him asking who showed up. These didn't happen. I had buried my oldest friend.

An hour after sunset Dev spotted hagridden silhouettes climbing over the hill towards us. I prepared to be chased off by Officer Friendly, or worse, witness Crazy Dev's switch flip and fistfight another cop.

A blue light of a flip phone illuminated the gravel trail, guiding the silhouettes.

The light flickered as it passed behind gravestones like Gatsby's lighthouse. I imagined a world where he didn't foolishly wait. A world where Daisy searched for him. Where passion won.

We settled down. Resumed our burnout silence anchoring our souls. Dev seemed disappointed there was no one to brawl.

I needed a bowl to relax.

I packed a nug into the juice box toker, asked for Dev's lighter.

Sav's unmistakable laugh betrayed her. She exited the shadows with Philip, Katie, Zoe and Ryan. Ryan wore her signature black hoodie with the words 'Kick Me' sewn in white block letters on her back. Her curly blue hair tucked between her dark skin and hood.

The last to leave the shadows was Alex. His rugged raven features cut through the darkness. He nodded at Dev. Dev pumped his brow before returning to admiring the shortness of his gnarled fingernails.

Alex still didn't recognize me. I wasn't worth a nod.

I had met him for the first time three times. Thrice. And each time he was smashed. Totally dickered. When he did remember my face, he forgot my name. Called me hash kid, because Benji and I picked up weekly oil. Our last encounter had been when Sick Sad World had played at Church—the punk squat under the off ramp of the Queen Elizabeth Way.

I scootched over, stone-faced, as Sav sat next to me. Alex sat between her and Ryan, keeping himself a noticeable distance from Jocelyn and Katie, Benji's emo cousin, while Philip busied himself rolling joints on a grimy textbook. *Sedgeland and Northland: Rising of Sea Peoples.*

Katie tried to pull the whimpering young woman from the gravestone, but Jocelyn pulled away, crying softly to herself.

Sav rummaged through her backpack, producing a 40 of rum and a two-litre bottle of RC Cola. The thick syrup smelled of caffeine.

She sent the bottles rolling into the centre of our circle and we followed her lead. Unloaded our spirits, baggies of pot, hash nugs, three pills of E, a single mushroom Alex had been saving, and four packs of cancers.

The communal pile had one rule: no one leaves until all is consumed.

Katie grabbed the mickey of whiskey, chugged it straight with Ryan, who favoured the E, while she waited for Philip to roll a primo blunt. Sav cracked a can of Alex's PBR, sucked the foam. She passed me the can with a wink, before mixing her rum and cola in a Tim's cup.

Jocelyn abstained.

Her eyes were puffy and redder than her roots from crying all day. I assumed she isolated herself because of her sorry state. Not wanting to turn into a total blubbering mess.

The crew traded vices in silence, reflecting inwards at our loss. The moon towered high above our heads and light traffic vanished from the streets as normals slept. The communal pile was half gone before Jocelyn broke our soundlessness.

"Does anyone have ..." She paused at the soft sound of her voice. Stared at the loose soil littered with empties as she found the appropriate words. "His songbook?

She could never bring herself to utter Benji's name. He was forever 'him.' Holier than Jehovah, more sacred than Elohim. Him.

Alex reached into a backpack and pulled out a weathered notepad. On the cover, in undiscernable overlapping patterns, were lyrics from Benji's favourite bands. Career Suicide. ETID. Weakerthans. Millencolin. NOFX. Sharks Exist. Strike Anywhere. Sick Sad World.

Behind the smudges of makeup, Jocelyn's eyes lit up.

"We need to make a copy," Alex said, dangling the book away from her. "It has our riffs in it. Some song ideas. You can have it. After I make a copy."

"How'd the tickled tits did you get it?" Dev shouted, pulling his limp mohawk from his face. "I watched his mom put it in his coffin for cremation."

Sav smiled meekly, raised her hand like an elementary school kid owning up to a fart. The booze showed in her full cheeks.

"Sav the grave robber." Alex slapped her back.

"To Sav then," Ryan stammered, popping another pill to ride.

We raised our drinks in response. Cheers. Drowned.

"What about Sick Sad World?" Philip asked, starting another sesh, and ending our celebrations.

Sav's eyes met mine in the darkness. She reminded me of a calm lake. In my haze I pictured us, alone, in a boat off Lake Louise, smelling the gelidity of a virgin spring morning in the mountains before it could be adulterated by stale summer heat and tourists. Instead of being imprisoned here, in Southern Ontario, chained to Skunktown, Green River.

Sav's nudge brought me out of the trip. I hadn't noticed Jocelyn leave.

I shook my head. Sav ignored me.

"This nitwit right here," she said, grabbing my good arm and raised it.

"Really?" Alex made a face as he swallowed the tart neon potion from Katie's water bottle. "Gimpy plays?"

"That's why you were keen earlier," Dev said.

"How long have you played?" Alex asked, chucking the empty bottle. It donked off a Victorian cherub.

Since Sav raved during Monster Madness how hot it is when guys play guitar. At the time, she was trying to convince Benji and I that her horror crush, Vincent Price, should start a goth band.

"Not long," I said, lying, hoping their attention on me would wane.

These were guys with a real band, who influenced the local scene, who carried the black flag, went to protests, fought cops, lived in an anarcho squat, gave each other tattoos with Indian ink, and smashed up the Walmart when clerk monkeys gave them attitude for shoplifting.

I was too lame for them.

"What songs do you know?" Alex leaned in, desperate for my answer. I should have told the truth, but in his raven face I found myself desperate to please the older guy in his studded battle jacket.

"A few Clash ones. Rancid. DOA. Black Flag. Early Misfits. Blink's Enema."

Sweet Home Alabama.

"Stellar, dude," Alex said, offering me his pipe. "What you doing this weekend?"

"Jamming with us," Dev said.

I raised my busted arm.

"You can learn the set." Alex reached for a cancer. "Listen to the rhythms for timing and cues. Just make the chords on the frets until we cut you out of the cast."

Sav told them to go easy on me. I was a gimp.

That was the ice breaker for comfortable familiarity to set in. To forget Benji was gone. The rest of the night was how it used to be, filled with movie quotes, battle stories of shows, and plans for the next high to chase. They all signed my cast, doodling dicks and cuss words and band logos. We drank until dawn, toasting and roasting our dead friend.

The others slowly departed until only Sav, and me, and Alex, remained.

Alex cracked the cap of the 40 of Colt 45 he had saved and stumbled to his feet. He poured the contents onto the loose soil, flooding Darnley Grove with the stench of barrel bottom yeast. He watched the beer absorb into the grave, lost in himself.

If I had to describe their relationship, Benji had been like Alex's little brother. I could only imagine what memories flashed through Alex's mind. Some Benji had shared. Like the time they found a dead homeless man and poked him with a rake, or of their party antics when I had to bail early because of threats of expulsion from school. I decided, when I wrote this from inside the bug house, Alex must have thought about the times Benji didn't share. The ones kept secret.

When he finished his goodbye, and returned from the distant place in his mind, Alex pitched the empty bottle. Glass shattered over a red oak sheltering an adjacent grave. Streetlights twinkled on jagged ends, casting rainbows in my wasted gaze.

He hugged Sav, clasping her hand in his between their chests. When he pulled away, she tucked a folded piece of tinfoil into her bra.

She waited until he disappeared over the cemetery hill, listening to birds sing their highs and lows to the rising sun. She screamed.

I used to tell myself it was chemical punishment mixed with sorrow. A different kind of hatred. Loss.

I let her scream until she was out of breath. Red-faced. I placed a hand on her back, rubbing circles. She screamed again. Then wiped away tears with the bottom of her shirt, exposing her pierced navel and nautical stars on her hips. She wept. I held her until my shirt grew moist. Cried with her.

Her voice cracked when she whispered.

“Don’t let me end up like this.”

I hugged her tighter, felt the folded tinfoil scratch my chest.

The Toxic Avenger.

I suppose here is a good point to talk about the three years I spent in prison. I never had any friends at Schwenger High School. All the humans I considered friends—Sav, and Benji, and the other blackhole kids—were either older than me like Dev and Sav and Alex, or attended Green River High like Benji, Ryan, and Philip.

Nothing says healthy competition like forcing impressionable children to fight turf wars in a small town to exploit the failed dreams of unfulfilled parents. Cheers soccer mom.

Cynicism aside, Schwenger excelled in the arts whereas G.R.H. surpassed them in athletics leaving 'friendly' matches staggeringly one-sided. The rivalry reigned in the nightlife. For the normals at least. Party crashers and random acts of vandalism were paramount in the lives of zealot student bodies. Gaggles of gangs fought over everchanging territories throughout the city marked by graffiti tags. Boundaries Peanut, our local Banksy, constantly defied.

I mean it when I said I never had real friends. High school was just middle school but with more drugs, less time alone. I used to have a friend, I guess, but puberty ended it pretty quick. Mine and Benji's neighbour, Arielle.

She was never a real friend. Just another kid on the street. Sometimes she had us over for tea and movies. But when we showed up painted in black, that was the end of that.

My existence since our disconnect summed up to be someone to blather at while we waited for the morning bus. After my balls dropped, I noticed she was just like everyone else at Schwenger. Conceited. Bourgeois. Normal.

To put it into perspective, her mother constantly wore pastel sweater vests on her shoulders. Malls. Mass. Cutting grass. Fetching the mail. Who does that? Cartoon characters. Cartoon characters dress like that. Her father excelled at consumerism. Bought countless DVDs, never watching them as they stacked on the gas fireplace until Arielle's mom dumped them on a shelf. Unalphabetized.

I guess what I mean to say is, as Arielle and I drifted apart, it was only fitting that she sat closer to the chalkboard while I stumbled to the back of Mrs. Tomassi's English class. I kept to the fringe. Back to corner.

I loved people watching. Despite hating my classmates. Hell, hating them probably encouraged me.

For instance, I learned that Miss Queen Bee Kelly Silinsky chewed her pencils, even borrowed ones. In freshman year Jessy Reilly picked his nose and ate it while sharing chips with Aimee Logan. Aimee didn't notice. Luke Livingstone poops naked. Donnie Clarke used his fingers to follow Mrs. Tomassi line by line when she read handouts, like it anchored him. He'd drown without it. My favourite was how much sweat rolled off Dave Henry's neck. Apparently when you're physically and mentally built like a snowman, sitting and breathing at the same time causes unbearable strain.

I personally hated reading. I detested it. I'd stare at the words until my mind abandoned my body. Float in my own thoughts absorbing nothing. Dreaming about the next show or party. My parents blamed T.V. Mrs. Fink, my guidance counsellor, blamed drugs. Even before I tried them. I blamed the books forcibly ingested. Out of all the crap I was told to read, *A Clockwork Orange* was the only thing I connected with. That and *My Wife the Butcher*. I reread *Butcher* every year and handed in the same book report. Word for word. The best part was no teachers cared. They were just happy I handed something in.

I guess what I'm getting at is, the Monday after Benji's funeral I thought about ditching. Probably should have.

Each class bell rang and all the kiddies ittied off to their next prison cell while I deafened myself with blast beats. I was out the door before the bell finished its sharp digital pinging. I mouthed along to screams of anarchy assaulting my earballs as I wandered the halls, forgetting where my classes were, as rebellion stirred my brain into goo. Damaged. I loved turning off the world.

At lunch it was much of the same. Except while everyone expressed groupthink, I had nothing to do but be alone.

I always tried to sit at the back of the cafegymitorium —that is to say, the cafeteria, gym, and auditorium were the same room which stank of deep fryers and gym socks—and I watched the normals feast.

Tables defined unspoken status. Plastic fiefdoms with prison seating rules. If you sat at the wrong table belonging to a tight nit clique, they'd go bonkers. Demand a blood sacrifice for infecting their table. This was just before the zoomers and millennials executed cliques. When art kids got high, band geeks were swingers, and jockstraps wailed on the satanic D&D kids to impress cheer whores. The heavy kids, like me, were blackholes.

Do not misunderstand, I enjoyed being alone. I think that's why Andrew Cho hated me so much. I was comfortable not giving a shit about all this noise.

He sat near the lunch line next to the windows with all the other sportos with their purple and cream letterman jackets even though all our teams were shit. I hated him the most. Proud, tan chest, a jaw so sharp Pythagoras would found a new cult.

I giggled to myself, remembering when the mathletes tried to calculate the angle during a fieldtrip to the waterpark. When Cho found them hunched over an old copy of the yearbook, he tried to drown Thomas Vandervolk. No suspension for superior breeding stock with a steady diet of roids and blow.

I hid my snickers in my leather jacket, pretending I was laughing at something on my phone. I had strategically situated myself as far as possible from Cho that day. I knew after Benji's passing, I couldn't deal with another beating. The whopping from my dad for breaking curfew, and busted arm had been enough for me.

I sent Alex a text, asking him to confirm a time to jam and stuffed limp, oversalted fries into my gourd.

He gave me a rundown of bass tabs and how to fumble through Benji's trashy solo in *Harper Diddles W.*

Sav texted me, asking if I was skipping last period. She had just woken up and Ryan scored shrooms and wanted to play grounders with 'the children of the sun.' Don't judge. When the ground ruptures and sand turns into dancing cricket legs, you know you're playing right.

Ryan was still the reigning champ and Sav planned to dethrone her.

I told Sav it was impossible to beat Ryan. She didn't play to win the game. She played so she could quietly trip out.

I texted Sav an image from the last time we all did salvia. Ryan was curled up into a fetus and stuffed into a bubble window to watch robot ballet.

She told me I was just jealous Ryan mastered the art of making snow angels on top of the plastic tower roof of the jungle gym. In July.

I checked my secret pocket that Benji had cut out for me in my leather jacket for my stash of weed. It felt like a gram or so. Enough to get me going until the others made their way to the park on Mortimer.

Feeling the hole cut along the seam made me miss Benji more. He had shown me how to hide dope on me and it came in handy more than once. Clumps of cotton, officer. Pockets empty, check 'em. Even at shows and Warped Tour the security only ever groped pockets. Cops checked shoes and underwear. Not the lower back of a biker jacket with studs and painted on anarchy symbols. Plus the secret pocket came in handy when I didn't have drugs to buy. Too many times I had forgotten I had squirrelled away a nug or a pill only to be stoked at the reunion.

An animal instinct overtook me in the cafegymitorium. The kind bred into bloodlines for survival. Self-preservation of my ancestors, guide me, homie. I looked up.

An orange exploded on my head. Stinging my eye as my ear went hot from the impact.

I blinked tears as normals laughed at the loner.

Cho scowled across the cafegymitorium, savouring his pitch. His broad chest expanded to assert his dominance. Through his freshly shaven mouth, he reminded me I was a faggot. I forgot. Silly me. My solitude dictated sexual status and Cho's responsibility as basketball alpha was to remind me, for my benefit. Lest I forget.

Like I said. Jail house. Less stabby, more emotional scarry.

He asked if my boyfriend signed my cast. Jockstraps laughed. Props.

Unfazed by the absolute fact that his dick was far larger and thicker than mine, I politely asked Cho if he'd let me gobble his cock.

Bad idea.

Cho deadpanned. He murdered me with his eyes, jockstraps didn't hold him back. I winked.

Super bad idea.

"You're dead, cripqueer." Cho snapped. He and his lackeys swarmed me before I could grab my backpack and run.

"Where are you going, spazz?"

I stopped, turned back to my phone, and held up a finger for Cho to wait until I was done.

"I'll beat your candy-ass so bad—"

And here is where I should have stopped. Walked away. But my 'candy-ass' insisted I stay. I sent Sav a text saying I'd meet her at the park across town and slipped my phone into my secret pocket. I asked myself what Benji would do.

I told Cho he was cute when he screamed.

Worst idea.

Cho grabbed my cast and pain shot through my arm. I tried to turn but lost my footing on the empty chair next to me. His knuckles cracked on my eye, splitting my brow. I wish I could say we fought. My eye puffed shut instantly, tears blurred my vision as he beat me into the ground while I tried to claw away.

When they pulled him off me, Mr. Braun, social studies, held my scruff. My dog collar bit into my neck, leaving a red welt. The teacher dragged me out of the cafegymitorium.

Cho followed us out. Taunting and talking smack as I was hauled through the halls.

I held an ice pack and damp towel over my face while Principal Cooke listened to Braun, Cho's lawyer, as he saved the hometown hero.

Cooke looked more like a parrot thanks to the lamp on her desk. Her short, cockatoo inspired hair and purple veiny beak for a nose cast oblong shadows over her hooded eyes which were the same stained colour as cancers soaking in bourbon. Both of which she reeked of.

"They were going at it again in the Caff," Braun said, standing at Cho's side. "I stopped them before it got out of hand."

Congrats. You earn a banana sticker.

"He called me a candy-ass," Cho said, with his student-of-the-year-voice. "He said he was going to stab me and my friends after class. He has a kill list on Myspace. Everyone has seen it. Freak is ready to go full Columbine."

"Dude! What the actual fuck?"

"Enough," Cooke said, as if she never heard that obscene and lovely word. "I will have none of this in my school."

She rambled off for five minutes about character, discipline, and all those meaningless 'you're good kids,' and the 'we are so disappointed in you' ridiculous trigger phrases.

I wanted to tell her to shove it, but remembered that the others would be waiting for me with shrooms. If I put myself in a mood, I was sure to have a rotten trip. I shut up as best as I could, nodding thoughtfully, searching for a better headspace.

By the end of the speech, they decided I was the problem.

"Suspension," Cooke said. "In school. Two weeks."

Better than my parents coming to pick me up again.

"And panty-sniffer here?" I thumbed at Cho, testing my luck.

"Four weeks," Braun said.

I told him he didn't have the authority, but Cooke raised her hand.

"Andrew will receive one week of lunchtime detention."

And there it was. Cho Untouchable. I didn't expect them to hold back the school's basketball star. We, as a collective hive mind of urban fury, needed to redeem our loss at the upcoming G.R.H. game.

Cho began to tear up with rage. Braun protested, stammering that that's when the team practised.

"I will not hear it Andrew," Cooke said, ignoring Braun.

"He's right," I said, wanting to smash them all with my icepack. "It's not fair. I get four weeks vacation and Cho gets fingerbanged—"

Braun started yelling at me, inches away so I could smell the onions he ate. I called him a fascist.

"School isn't a communist state, mister," he said, furious.

"You done tossing limp noodles in my face?"

Cooke gave me another two weeks for that, though she was holding back a smile.

The Lost Boys.

We jammed in Church's basement. Home, squat home. It belonged to Dev's father, who abandoned Green River when the factories closed. It became a junk house for wayward punks. Wanderers. When Dev learned his father bailed on him, he ditched the youth shelter and moved back in, uncaring that his father dropped the keys off at his bank before buggering off to New Brunswick.

What started as a Canada Day celebration, quickly turned into a week-long event. Eventually no one left. A lot of people passed through Church. A few of us took up permanent residence. Myself included, though that was later. It wasn't much, but it was enough for us.

The house itself was in decent shape for being built before the war. Incandescent lighting buzzed with golden irritation at the skunk stenches of street kids sleeping on stained carpets and couch cushions. They flickered when we turned on our amps.

The cardboard walls were hardly thick enough to fend off the wind, and the eternal battle with weeds and black mold wasn't well fought. My only gripe was the plumbing. The toilet on the main floor suffered from weak flow and was always clogged. Being too expensive to fix, I came up with a solution when I joined Sick Sad World. I spray painted 'No pooping assholes' above the porcelain throne.

Alex had furnished Church thanks to dumpster diving, looting the junkyard off Greenwich, and bulk item garbage days. It didn't take long for the couches, beds, and lawn chairs to earn films of sweat, booze, puke, and bong water.

We knew better than to have electronics in Skunktown. "If we had a TV," Alex said, once when I asked him, "we might as well have Philip standing outside flipping a neon sign that says free stuff."

Church did have electricity. Ryan's brother tapped off a powerline and mounted a baby disconnect to the side of a utility pole. It was sketch, but the thick cable bypassed the metre. He did it for a half-quarter of hash. I know. Fractions are difficult for Southern Ontario.

Dev's new girlfriend watched us jam for the first time after she helped cut off my cast. I felt naked and exposed while she witnessed me fumble through songs, barely able to hold my pick. Between raging, she begged us to play her favourite songs. Flaunting indifference at our desire to jam our own tunes. She felt entitled to a single perfect moment of her own. Share it—past tense—in chat rooms to people equally disconnected from the founding artist's original vision.

I thought Dev was gonna cave when we finished our first run through the set. Swallow pride, and play her a damn song instead of tolerating my heavy hands tripping over discordant notes.

Alex told us to go through the setlist again and Clair heckled over the distortion, calling for Theory of a Dead Nickle Creed, Los Lonely Boys, Hedley Hoggard the Sex Offender.

Alex snapped when she begged us to cover Stefani, not No Doubt. Told her he'd shave off her eyebrows if she didn't clam it. Dev chuckled.

I'll be honest. When I joined Sick Sad World, we sounded awful. Beached whales screwing on shore awful. Yes. A pasty thwack awful. My joy at joining the band was ephemeral.

Alex showed patience with me. I was thankful he didn't wail on me for sucking. I used my busted arm as a crutch. Cheap excuse. It felt thin and weak, and made gripping my pick near impossible. My rhythm lagged. I think he regretted cutting my cast off early as much as I had.

We let the last chord ring out. Clair clapped, indifferent to Alex's threat from a literal minute ago. I tried to stretch my neck, aware of guitar-hunch, as we played under the low ceiling.

Posters and flyers and zine covers littered the walls like milestones through waves of punk. In sparse patches, unadulterated by tags, stickers clotted sections of floral print wallpaper dainty enough for grandma's living room.

Benji had written *Cover the Ugly* about Church. It was the first song he had written with Sick Sad World. Alex kept in the set.

He called for a break so I could ice my wrist with a tallboy. I leaned my flea market guitar against my amp.

"You know that's a jazz guitar," Alex said, lighting a cancer.

I didn't. I just liked the sound. The matte black body and maple head.

Dev joined in teasing me, told me to join Naked City. I didn't get the joke, but laughed anyway.

I'll admit it. I was worried the older guys would think I was lame. More importantly, I was intimidated by them. They dealt drugs. Smoked pot on buses and once hotwired a car and crashed it, on purpose, in the woods near the gristmill. Moshpits. Fist fights. Walls of death. Hardened nails.

Benji had told me stories of how Dev picked fights with boneheads for fun. No warning sounds. Full feral. And how after a brawl, where Benji lost a tooth and Alex hospitalized Nazi Ross, a truce was called with the boneheads. No brawls at shows. No police. No trespassing. I joined the scene after they instilled diplomatic solutions. The punks had to give up Next in Line. It wasn't advertised, because racism is, well, for garbage humans, but Next in Line was Hamilton's last 'white's only' bar. Everyone knew. Even the cops knew! It was why their undercover got pwned by a plug in '13.

I digress, but you get my need for wanting their respect. Right?

When we finished our attempts at cancer, Alex assumed his position at the microphone, bass strapped as Dev raised his drumsticks. My guitar hung near my knees, rested on my thigh like Lars Frederiksen. Halfway through *Free Mars*, I could barely strum, keep time, let alone form the chords Alex needed me to play. Blisters threatened to pop and bleed over my fretboard.

I was the reason why we sounded so awful. We all

knew. Even Clair, who winced as feedback cretched through my amp.

I was the beached whale molesting its blowhole.

The last note of *Cover the Ugly* rang out. Clair clapped and cheered before returning to her phone, fingerbanging away her paycheck by the word. Trying to prove she was savage by association for slamming uglies with Dev.

"Good job, kid," Alex said, sweat dripping from his hooked nose. "But you need to relax. You're too rigid."

"Sorry," I said, out of breath. I pulled sour neon hair from my eyes and the sweat stung my wounds. I chewed a blister from my finger tip.

"Cut that word from your vocabulary. I don't need your pity. And you sure as hell don't want mine. Right?"

"Right."

He dug through his pockets for a fresh bass pick as Dev snickered, reaching for a brew in a bucket of melted ice. He was a different person. Chill. Crazy Dev no longer existed. All that remained was a panting, shirtless dude in his early 20s.

"No regrets," Alex said. "Live by that motto while you're in Sick Sad World."

"Alright."

"Don't scare the poor dude," Dev said as he lobbed me a beer sheen with condensation. It slipped in my blistered hands, almost cracked open on my foot.

"Chug it," Alex said. The beer was cool and sharp in my dehydrated throat. He watched me with dark eyes, making certain I gulped every drop. When I ditched it on the coffee table, he told us to play from the top.

"Which song?"

"All of them."

Dev spun his sticks like Marky-mom-hair Ramone. Counted us in.

We played. And played.

I lost the ability to play quarter notes, then halves.

We finished at sunset. Drenched in sweat. Napalm hands. My fretboard and pickups were crusted with blood.

The basement window had fogged behind Clair and a faded smiley face looked down on me like the man in the moon. I wondered who drew it and when. Would Benji have known?

Dev used his shirt to wipe his face, threw it on the hi-hat, before slumping on the stained couch, wrapping his bicep around Clair's neck. She took a selfie before complaining about the smells of his armpit.

"Who you sending it to?" he asked.

"Ryan," she mumbled.

I finished another beer, belched, dropped it into the milkcrate of empties.

"Looks like Sav was right about you," Alex said, slapping my back. I tried not to flinch. "You're not total trash. And you're too dumb to quit, huh?"

"Thanks."

"We're thinking about booking a show sometime later in the year at The Cellar. You down?"

I refrained from crutching on my excuse of weak wrists. From saying no. Can't. Sorry. I nodded an affirmation, feeling the booze slosh in my head. I wished I had money to eat something instead of spending it on a six-pack.

Alex leaned in close. Close enough that Dev and Clair wouldn't hear over her complaints of armpit juice.

"Did you bang her?"

I knew what Alex meant. Who he meant.

"She's like a sister."

"Some people get off to their sister. It's the next big fet, you know?"

"Some people are nutters," I said, uncomfortable.

"Don't kink shame," he said aware of my unconscious shirking as he invaded my personal space. "That's how their Holy Liar built them."

Alex reached past me for the beer, his chest pushing into my side, as if he owned that segment of air.

He handed me the warmer one, opened the other with his teeth. My hands were too worn to open the warm bottle. I held it limply in my scabbed hand, aware that he wanted to watch me struggle. Sweat seeped into the pink wounds. Burned.

"You don't mind then?" he said after I shifted away, submitting the empty territory between us. His raven scowl had changed to a warm smile. "You'd let me know if there was an issue, no?"

I knew what he was going to say, but I wished I was wrong. Paranoid.

"About what?"

"That I'm hooking up with Sav."

Return of the Killer Tomatoes!

There are three things to do in Green River: get high, get laid, get laid while high. Lonely me? I got high.

I spent my days cheesed out of my brains during my mandatory vacation courtesy of Cho. After school I wandered the city or chilled at Church, strumming my guitar. Building calluses.

I wrote my first song while microdosing 2C-I. I had strayed from chemicals in the past and adopted Philip's 'natural' philosophy after a bad trip during Monster Madness where Lugosi inflated and Sav turned into a lamppost.

'If it doesn't come from the ground, put that shit down.'

But when Alex offered me the chino for artistic inspiration, he suggested not to ingest too much or the bright colours of Terra would smelt my guts into knots.

He wasn't totally wrong.

As I strummed my guitar I beheld music reverberate from glistening strings as notes drained from my knuckles with sonic booms thundering from my blisters. At times I slipped into a blind trance, head inflating the closer I sat to my amp while dirigible bound for the otherworld, humming songs on nihilistic winds breezily drifting through fjords, scabs off, raining perfumed noise from transistors, awestruck as lilac tracerlines behold the citizens of flesh residing in temples of oogonia erected from the hollow hairs snaking from my hobgoblin face.

I continued this way, playing and tripping, until I became aware of my testies. How heavy they felt as they sunk into my pants, grounding me while my butt exposed itself with a cheeky grin. My solution was to use a patch cord as a belt, lest my guitar float away on tracerlines.

When Crazy Dev showed up he was fuming about Clair, ranting and kicking things over in malignant crashes as he spiraled. Her father had said something about age.

Ages.

Aeons?

Aegon long one.

I couldn't focus past my nose. It was too to two tooooo big. When I saw my blue Cramps shirt I began howling. Stripped naked.

When I sobered up at sunset, I was sketching in a coffee shop across from The Cellar, rubbing ice cubes on my chin, faintly aware someone had levelled me. I sat alone, but knew I was supposed to be waiting. Was it about a show? Did I order food? Couldn't remember.

My mind drifted into a lucid trip, lost in the blur of heads lined up for a hipster show. I wondered absently if I had money to pitch for a bowl to quell the sketching.

Crazy Dev bolted around the corner like a feral chupacabra, juggling six burritos in his gorilla arms as he weaved between the crowd. A cop sprinted in tow, wielding his club as he ploughed over the hipsters. Officer Friendly. The same turd who smashed up my Discman and busted Benji's arm.

I wanted to yell for Crazy Dev to lose the pig in the alley we used to get trashed at shows. Where the cop wouldn't be able to tell one anarchist from another. To my amusement Dev did. He darted down the alley, out of view.

I learned later, as we sped back to Church that this happened:

Alex was waiting in the crusty alley, slinging hash to the hipsters as Dev led Officer Friendly deeper within. Dev ducked behind a dumpster, and the cop, with his trusty nightstick in hand, thought he had Dev beat, but Alex hid in the dark of a doorway and bottled Officer Friendly. Alex and Dev said they stole Officer Friendly's taser and pumped him with 50 000 volts. It sent the poor bastard into early retirement, gifted him with a free hospital trip and a commemorative J scar on his crown.

True or not. No love lost. Officer Friendly never bothered us again.

During my second week of suspension, we were out of money, and had eaten all those soggy burritos Crazy Dev had stolen. Alex and Dev heard about the train kids rolling through Hamilton and decided to trade them vices for cash or food.

We walked the tracks from Green River to Bayfront, stoned off our asses on BC bud, searching for buyers. We wandered until we reached the trainyard.

Factory stacks broke the treeline, coughing plumes of toxins into the air before polluting the lakefront. Sorrow overtook me. They called it a clean burn. Water exhaust from cooling systems. The propaganda papers rarely mentioned the poisoned fish, acidic levels of Lake Ontario, or the pale gelatinous runoff along Burlington Street, or the layer of brown dust forming on parked cars and gardens. Best intentions don't give a damn about reality.

The three of us screamed our outrage at the dying planet until we reached the train kids.

They traded us food they had grown in their boxcars, some cans of jam, and nutted butter. A few played us songs with their washboards, grandpa's guitars, and fiddles. Alex sold them hash, traded mostly for narcotics.

It was here I met Peanut, the tagger, who was picking up a nug from Alex. He introduced himself as Bry.

"Is your brother Helmet from Rusty Tampons?" I asked, sizing up the Viking horse farmer. His beard was as thick as his arms.

"Something like that," he said, laughing and clapping my shoulder.

"A big man can't be called Peanut?" Alex's dark eyes dared me to defend an assumption I wasn't attached to.

"Took the tag from Hessman," Peanut said, oblivious to the tension. "Smallest kid on the polo team."

I said I didn't know who that was.

"Probably missed him because he was so friggin short. Took the name when he went off to college."

"Is it true that you hit the Green River Review several times over five years?"

"Mostly bull," he said, counting out bills for Alex, who was already working another deal on a Serb with dreads and razor-burned knuckles. "I hit them four times, which is close enough to several, I guess. Haven't got busted yet, though. Just a warning when I was a minor niner."

"You don't care if the pigs catch you?"

"Still 17. What are they gonna do? Make me clean up the tags?"

I was baffled he was my age.

I smoked bots to pass time with Peanut, who was chill, but was more into country, and not at all punk like his brother.

Bots, you should know, are the pride of Southern Ontario's stoner scene. Bots, or bottle tokes, are how we smoke hash to inflate the high. Burn a hole in the bottom of a plastic bottle, put a nug of hash on the tip of a lit cancer, let the smoke fill the bottle. Unscrew the cap and inhale when ready. Don't tell your parents.

I wished Peanut well with a fist bump as Alex yelled at me and Dev to fall in. We made enough to get right good and wasted when we returned to Church.

Of course, we didn't wait. Got as far as the train bridge along the Green River escarpment with bellies full of popcorn chicken. We watched the sunset, chucking stones at the city below, popping Molly to ease our bunions, and waited for a train to split the darkness of the cityscape.

When the train came, I was in love with the world. It trilled and grinded towards us on worn tracks, hunting with searchlights.

I wrapped my body around a guardrail, squeezed myself away from the bridge as anxiety purged my glee.

Dev crouched on the slope, ear pressed to gravel. Alex ran to the tracks, splaying himself between the rails, face to the stars. The train bored through the fatal blackness, horn blaring, ordering evacuation. It consumed him as my hair scattered over my face, lashing my eyes. In the spaces between the wheels Alex lay still as a gravestone. Unblinking. He screamed. Chuggas drowned his thrill of chaos. A single movement, a penny on the rail, an involuntary twitch, could kill him.

Alex was addicted to chaos. Violence. To being literal millimetres from death. He was a goddamned madman. A void-caller.

Ju-On.

I never understood mandatory vacations. Exile kids who don't want to be in prison. It's only a punishment if you live with your parents, or care for marks and banana stickers. It serves to punish the kid by making them fall farther behind in their classes. They get frustrated. Ditch again. Get punished again. Then again.

The in-school is worse. You sit in an empty office room with nothing to do but schoolwork, which, let's be honest, you're too bored to do. Plus if you are able to stay on top of your classwork, you're rewarded with hanging out beside the photocopier, watching blue lights swipe you with cancer.

When my vacation ended I was ordered to read that play with that nymphet Abigail Williams. I never opened the book. I had learned all about it from going to punk shows. So instead of participating in Tomassi's lectures, I doodled Sick Sad World logos on grid paper, dreaming of shows, riffs, getting high, wishing the fallout from my parents would blow over.

I chewed a whole pack of gum to ease my desire to chainsmoke through class. Barely tasted the peppermint.

I dragged my feet to my next class. Law with that chub gut. I never learned his name and he never bothered to learn mine. His blonde hair was pulled back so tight his roots were ripping out. I swore his forehead grew larger each minute.

I slouched in a stiff chair, breaking my hunched posture, legs stretched in the aisle because of how cramped they felt under the pathetic desk.

When Mr. Chubgut left to make extra copies about consent to fight legislature, I heard tapping at the window behind me. I averted my eyes. Thought it was Cho with his jockstraps coming to ream me out. They had taken to calling me Poop-eye, supposedly a play on Popeye, on account of my shiner. Witty guy.

The tapping grew louder the longer I ignored it. Dave Henry poked my thigh with his sausage finger and nodded his melting snowman brow at the window. I chucked my pencil at the glass.

Silence.

Two slow well-placed raps. I turned.

Sav wore a mock frown. Behind her, Philip and Ryan mimicked her like gogo dancers. Ryan broke character first, snickering at something Dev said. He was stoic, and visibly uncomfortable being back on school grounds after dropping out years prior.

I mouthed 'I can't leave.'

They rubbed pretend tears. Sav's moans muffled through the glass. The classroom erupted in murmurs, I felt self-conscious, knowing it was expected of me to ditch, but I felt lame, like a sellout, trying to do the right thing.

I made a crude gesture and Philip dry humped the window. The class collectively laughed at the stocky stranger and his studded belt rapping the glass beside my head.

Dev pushed Philip aside, slammed a baggy of weed against the window. Sunlight cast a rainbow through the plastic.

From the front of the room Arielle gave me a concerned warning. Irresponsible worm baby.

Sav and Ryan displayed the pot like showgirls, Sav stepping into her role as Vanna White while Ryan, eyes glazed, giggled uncontrollably. They pranced in pinup poses while Dev stashed the devil's lettuce in Philip's backpack.

The class watched me pack up my binder. Horrified at the sight of the illegal gateway into chemical happiness their parents warned them about. I slid open the window. Arielle stifled a cough as the stench of weed wafted into the room. She gave me a look that reminded me rules mattered. I had no doubt she would snitch when Mr. Chubgut returned.

I pulled out my lighter from my secret pocket and lit a cancer inside the classroom before climbing out the window. I racked my knee on the sill, much to my friend's delight.

The warm sun played cat and mouse with the scattered cloud cover, causing our hike to be within the uncomfortable manic range of irritably hot to unwelcomingly cold. The escarpment trails behind Schwenger High smelled of nature, dirt, and thick pollen which caused Ryan to slip into sneezing fits.

Dev led us on winding trails that followed the bends of Shallow Creek and away from the city. We cut through the bush past an overgrown and forgotten vein, cutting our shins on brambles.

Above us, casting shadows over treetops, loomed concrete supports of the abandoned railway bridge. Old Bridge, the locals called it. The support columns were dull and cracked where concrete crumbled away exposing rusted rebar. On the centremost support, painted in red black and gold, lay a beautifully detailed heart. Scrawled across dribbling parchment was 'Chloe.'

As we panted past, I wondered who Chloe was. What she meant to the artist and why he decided to immortalize her here, within this hidden scrip sheltered from alien eyes. Did this spot hold significance, or was it merely to avoid city cleaners and give longevity?

I decided that the artist adored her the only way they could, in secret.

Sav caught me staring at Chloe's heart. I was confused by a tag, almost a signature. It was our boy Peanut.

"What's the deal with this bridge?" I asked, no one in particular, pretending I hadn't noticed Sav watching me.

She filled me in as we trudged up the next tier of the escarpment to reach the Devil's Punch Bowl.

She said the local news legends insisted that during the Great War two trains collided headfirst on the single track. One was full of ammunition going to Halifax, the other was packed with passengers going to Berlin—the city later changed its name to Kitchener for obvious reasons.

The bridge exploded. Hundreds were taken to Schwenger High. Turned the school into an infirmary.

"They say you can still hear their keening wails when the halls are empty," Sav said, with forced mysticism.

"That's just the sound of swirly victims," Dev said from the front.

I told Sav she was watching too many horror films again.

We crossed the creek on a galvanized footbridge with jagged spikes for grip. I told Philip I thought they looked like the mouths of sea lampreys. Ryan said she, once at a G.R.H. bush party, had tripped over the bridge and gouged her knee. She said it probably needed stitches. When she got home she dumped superglue on the wound from her brother's space marine model kit. Dev called bull. Ryan sat in the dirt, rolled up her pant leg. Dev owed her a gram.

We came to a steep ridge. Dev's shortcut. We scrambled up it, crawling and climbing over deadfall. I helped Sav, used the trees for support. I crouched, changed my centre of gravity, took her hand, and kicked-off, hoisting her up with me. We did this several times until we collapsed at the top, breaking for cancers. It left me exhausted, my face tingled as I replaced oxygen for cancer.

Ryan was last up. She had fallen down twice before 'conquering the summit.' Her 'Kick Me' sweater was filmed with soil and burs and twigs and crushed leaves. As we continued, Dev picked off the seedlings and brushed away the dirt.

The shortcut shaved three kilometres from the hike. We continued along a gully and met back up with the stream. It took us another hour of banter about films and music and trashing our parents and normals and war stories of moshpits until we reached our destination.

The stream opened into the valley under the Devil's Punch Bowl. Cliffs reached skyward from either side, holding us within the overgrown trail and thick deadfall which birthed boulders that tumbled from erosion centuries ago. Dense moss nestled on their weather-worked surfaces. The moss matched Sav's hair. I called her a fairy queen again and she pushed into my shoulder and called me a taint-tickler. Her perfume smelled like free samples from the mail. Sharp like cleaning products or cough medicine rather than womanhood.

"About time," Dev said, who smelled like a skunk's butt.

The pounding of the waterfall pouring over the Devil's Punch Bowl grew from murmur to ruckus as we approached.

They call it the Devil's Punch Bowl, though I don't know who 'they' are. There is no sign or plaque. Just a crescent of eroded and calved rock from the escarpment next to an eerie, illuminated cross tens of feet high and dedicated to the jumpers. Thoughts and prayers.

To be fair, the lamenting waterfall billowing over the ridge, the hum and drum of it pouring into the deep jagged bowl as hawks circled above for rabbits and fieldmice shaded under poison oak as flowers wilted under the steel cross, is, and will always be, my favourite feature of Green River.

"How much longer?" Ryan said, lagging behind as she squinted up at the cartoonishly white cross above us.

"Five," Philip said.

Ryan spat.

When we reached the natural pool at the bottom of the waterfall cascading over the Devil's Punch Bowl, we rested our weary legs and put our hands to work. Assembly line of rolling joints and spreading out food. Sav popped a bag of all dressed chips—off brand, sweeter, less vinegar—passed it around then helped Ryan distribute juice boxes. Philip rolled joints on my law binder, as Dev distributed papes. I spun the grinder.

I wanted to roll, but the others threatened to drown me in the pool. I was too slow. Which was why I wanted practise. I said if they were all in such a rush to just use the juice box, or one of the cans of Arizona. Philip was offended, like I had just accosted the gods.

I kept quiet after that. I knew Philip was the kush connoisseur. Undoubtably he rolled the best, could do any shape or size. Crosses. Blunts. Diamonds. Pinners. At Benji's last birthday, he designed a cone with a reusable filter.

Looking back, I realize a part of me envied him. He never had to fight for respect. Always sure of himself. Never needed others to validate him. He was a 'high functioning' addict. Could keep pace with us when we pumped only god knows what into our bodies, but never allowed it to control his life. He graduated at the top of his class. Rode a scholarship to Toronto. I found out after my daughter was born, he became a history professor at a prestigious university in Freedumbland. He ditched his 'natural' philosophy. He was content to rock fentanyl on government grants and was still able to pump out major studies and papers. His wife and kids were damn proud of him. Though I doubt they know the extent of his recreational habits.

The girls and Dev were restless when Philip finished rolling. Five in total.

"One for each dick holster," he said. "Two now. Two for the walk back."

Dev snatched the largest out of Philip's hand. Lucky he didn't get hit for giving Dev orders.

"What's the fifth for?" Ryan asked, as she unlaced her shoes.

"Me," Philip said, striking a match. He believed butane ruined the bud, said the taste polluted it.

Ryan stuffed her socks in her shoes and chased after Dev for a drag. They both undressed at the pool's edge. Dev kept his ripped jean shorts on while Ryan stripped to her black bra and little boy's boxershorts. Dev looked pasty next to her dark skin. His hairy chest and arms made him appear more apish without his drum kit to hide his skinny legs.

Ryan caught Dev ogling her and teased him. Said with confidence that she'd be more comfortable naked, but didn't want him to get a nervous boner. Dev snorted. Made fun of her boy's underwear. She said the girl's panties sucked too far into her butt. Sav cheered in agreement, swearing by seamless.

I was about to light my joint when Sav mussed my hair and stole it.

I felt embarrassed at the caustic gelatin stripping the dye from my hair. It was the last time I took advice online about cheap hair gel alternatives. I decided to go back to wood glue.

Sav clambered the grassy side of the waterfall thundering overhead, and snuck around the rocks along the falls. I chased after her, slipped, and gripped for the long grass. Clumps ripped out as I slid and I thought I'd smash into the rocks below. I found my footing, thankful I stayed mostly dry.

We hid beside the falls on a boulder above the pool, out of sight of the cross with the roar of the torrents fending off the outside world on the borderland where the rocks started, but the mist ended.

We watched Dev and Ryan talking between puffs at the water's edge. Philip wandered off, as usual, inspecting the intricacies of the expansiveness of his surroundings. He tried to cross parts of a stream without touching anything wet. It reminded me of being a kid with Arielle and Benji, making believe the floor was lava.

"Focus, nitwit," Sav said, poking me with an orange graffiti marker. She tapped on our boulder, at the S + between us. I initialed. Feeling the marker squeaked as I dragged the tip over the rough stone. I handed it back.

"Why Alex?" I shouted, competing with the waterfall, hoping Dev wouldn't hear.

Her eyes traced the curve of the Devil's Punch Bowl far above us. "I don't know. I mean, why not? No one else seemed interested in me since Hardcore John dumped me." She drew an equal's sign. "How's your eye?"

I told her my wrist was worse.

Ryan's scream startled me. Dev had pushed her into the pool. He paraded around the edge with the joint between his lips, flexing to the sun.

"She likes him, eh?" Sav said, lighting our joint.

"Too bad Clair is in the equation."

"I know right? She's been crushing on him since they were kids." Sav passed me the joint.

"I thought Clair met him like a month ago at D.D. Crust's Laundromat."

Sav punched my arm. "No, nitwit. Ryan. You'd think they'd get it over with and just make a move."

"Dead horses and the company they keep." I blew smoke rings into the mist.

"Look at you go."

We watched Dev and Ryan in silence, the joint burned slowly between us since Philip baptized it. Ryan splashed at Dev, who cringed from the frigid water. She called him names. 'Limp dick,' brought him closer to the edge of the pool, fury growing on his brow.

"I've killed cows with this," he belted, taking a handful of himself.

"Cuz the only ones that'll put out are heifers," Ryan screamed.

Sav laughed so hard I thought she was going to slide off our rock. I motioned to catch her, but she steadied herself, unaware of the risk.

Dev heard the outburst and mooned us. Then his shorts were around his knees. Ryan yanked them down so fast I thought he was wearing a pair of black briefs underneath. It was hair. Thick and twirled. Dev lost his footing and fell in the pool, tumbling headfirst onto Ryan. She tried to swim away, but he was too quick. They wrestled in a torrent of thrashing limbs and froth.

We laughed at the ridiculousness. Puffed and passed the joint.

"You ever gonna tell me who hurt your eye?" Sav said, checking if the equal sign between us had dried.

"Circle pit," I said, lying, not wanting to relive the embarrassment.

"Was Andrew Cho headlining that show?"

"Where'd you hear that?"

"Small town, nitwit." She took a long drag, held the joint between her fingers and turned my head with her free hand. She kissed her forefinger and rested it on my cheek, it was warm and damp against my bruised skin.

"Alex told you he asked me out? He literally just asked me to go official yesterday."

"Told me at practise."

"Right. You're in Sick Sad World now."

"Thanks again for that awkwardness. Jerk." I nudged her. She took another puff and passed.

"Anytime. Now you'll get all of them punk bitties."

"I'd make a rancid Casanova. Who could resist?"

"Don't fret. I got you. We'll get you some tig ole bitties."

I coughed from inhaling too sharply. Sav rubbed my back until I could hold air, telling me to breathe deep. I thanked her.

"In the meantime," she said, peeling off her shirt, shoes, shorts, and piling them on our rock. She wore men's swim trunks and a pinstripe bra. I tried not to look at her chest piece. How the chrome heart and eagle wings soared under her clavicle, or the Japanese squid stretching up her thigh at the nautical stars on her hips. I tried to give her space.

"Stay golden, pony boy." She winked, then climbed down to the pool, telling Dev she's seen labia longer than his dick.

I killed the remainder of the joint. A swift breeze peeled apart the trees obscuring the cross at the top of the Devil's Punch Bowl. Peering over the edge, a lonely woman stared at her phone as she looked down on us. I gave her the finger as I snuffed the roach on my rock. Under Sav's equal sign was a sideways eight.

I quickly followed after her. Left my shirt on. Bruises hidden.

Videodrome.

We were studying self-fellating poets in Mrs. Tomassi's English class when she split us into groups to overanalyze the 'great' 'modern' works. Ginsberg to Frost. Whitman to Poe. No mention of Marley or Guthrie or Kharms. She had each group read a piece, discuss it, then present about how 'it spoke to us' and how relevant the words were in contemporary times.

I told my group I had a theory that 'the greats' were only great because they were in the public domain. Cheaper to reprint. Tricking the masses into thinking the mundane—and royalty free—wordsmiths are timeless, relevant. It was more profitable compared to the intricacies of Saint Kavan or Zoo Station. Kimya. Aesop. Pat the Bunny.

My peers ignored me. I wasn't even worth telling to shut up.

Although this exercise interested me, getting shot down encouraged me to further withhold my opinion. I lay my head on my desk, feeling my jaw flex as I chewed a wad of intense gum, counting down the minutes until lunch so I could day drink and survive the afternoon.

The weight of tallboys in my lap, hidden in my backpack, brought me comfort.

When Tomassi came to sit in on my group's discussion, she stood above my shoulder, birddogging my blank page. My hand froze in my secret pocket around my lighter. I tried not to draw attention to my backpack of beer.

She asked how we felt about our poem, *The Raven*. Paige droned on about rhythm and speed, and trailing the reader on, and on through the slow burn of madness. The bare minimum and expected. Which is why, as expected, when Paige finished rambling in her irritating bubbly voice, Tomassi asked the group if anyone had anything else to add. Obviously directed at me, the non-participant. I did have a lot to say, about Poe, and backbeats, and hebephiliac incest, spiraling rivalries, substance abuse, and the corruption of Freedumbland's electoral system.

Mrs. Tomassi's stubby sausage hands clasped her pudge, waiting for an answer that never came.

When the groups presented, I refused to get in front of the class, said I was good. Tomassi didn't argue.

When the bell rang, Tomassi told me to hang back, I pretended not to hear her, feigning focus on the prospect of lunch, but she stopped me at the door. I shifted my backpack to my other shoulder, tried not to shake the tallboys. She waited until the room emptied.

Here we go again.

I wasn't in the mood for another 'I'm worried about your future,' or 'untapped potential' speech. It was poser.

She told me to remove my headphones, I turned down the volume, but kept them on. She waited a moment before her voice sliced through the bridge in The Distiller's *Hall of Mirrors*.

"Do you know what this is about?"

I'll take Reasons Why I Hate School for one hundred.

"Yeah."

"Why do you do it? Do you think you were being funny?" Tomassi asked, going to her cluttered desk and handing me back my report on Abigail Williams from The Crucible.

I did think I was being funny. In my report I referred to the accused witch as a commie harlot. Jailbait. Tease. I even went as far to call the whole play Marxist propaganda and blamed it for the sole reason why, I myself, was a baby-punching heathen.

Truth? I never read the whole thing. I tapped out. Pg. 99. My closing paragraph concluded with a list of reasons why national-socialism was irrefutable proof that work sets you free.

I said nothing to Tomassi, tried to find faces in the woodgrain of the classroom door. Hoped she'd finish her bit and allow me to return to my state of callused dead boy.

"You need to start taking yourself seriously. You'll be stuck here forever if you don't."

Fact: Once a person turns twenty-one they are no longer allowed in high school. Fact: At eighteen a human can leave school of their own volition. Only a few weeks left.

"I don't care, Tomassi."

"You should." She sighed, and leaned against her cluttered desk. "From the few things you do actually hand in, you're able to grasp more than your peers. You picked up on the political undertones where the others your age can only see the surface level story."

"Isn't that the whole point of art? Hide a bunch of crap for others to find while you jackoff to a mirror. Besides"—I shook my busted Discman in my hand causing the CD to skip—"I listen to noise all day."

"You need to start trying."

So I can fail? I'd rather get high.

"Stop being a smartass and pull your shit together."

It was the first time I heard a teacher swear.

"What do you know about my sh—"

"I know more about it than you do." She unbuttoned her cardigan.

I thought she was going to come on to me. I couldn't remember if I had taken shrooms, or had smoked laced weed at break. I thought I was tripping. Hallucinating the interaction in Church like some sex pervert with abused genitals. I hoped I wouldn't cream my pants.

She showed me her arms. From her chubby wrists to lumpy shoulders she was covered in black and grey tattoos. Staring back at me on Tomassi's bicep was the unmistakable, but faded, face of Debbie Harry.

"Wow."

"Wow is right. Those were fast times. What you're doing right now I've done before you. I do get it. So stop this nihilistic nonsense. We both know you don't want to be here. Get in gear. And get the hell out of here with a diploma. You'll regret it if you don't."

"I'll think about it."

"You better." She buttoned her cardigan. "I gave you a C on that essay. It's well written, and funny and self-aware, and you can convey a cohesive thought. However due to the amount of derogatory words used, and calling Abigail a commie skank, which is misogynistic, I was forced to burn you. And you cannot use obscure black metal bands as source material. It was about the contents of the book. Not the events around the real Salem Witch Trials. You need to follow instructions. I understand you dislike being told what you can and cannot do, but I want to help you get out of here as quickly and as painlessly possible."

"Thanks," I said, not coldly.

"Don't do it again. I'll talk to your other teachers and we'll see if we can get you along. You only need a 50 to graduate. I think we can all work something out. Deal?"

"Deal."

"Good. Now, since you have difficulties—" Principal Cooke squawked over the PA reminding everyone of the upcoming coffee house. Standing next to the speaker stung my ears, crushed my head like a potato in a vice grip. Tomassi waited until Cooke finished. "Difficulties with others. I am giving you a make up assignment. Since you're passionate about music, I want you to listen to the Deftones, pick two songs, and write two pages about what their lyrics mean to you. Get as political as you want. You pick the songs. I don't mind if you dislike them. I want you to write about how the music makes you feel. Understand?"

I nodded. She told me to get to lunch, but I turned to her as she sat down at her desk to mark the other student's assignments.

"Tomassi?"

"Yes?"

"Ever meet her?"

She smiled a warm smile. "If you ever see me outside of school, I'll happily tell you about the wild times before I smartened up."

Metropolis.

I spent more time wandering Green River than in class. Rain. Sun. Hail. I couldn't help myself. It was always walking weather. I became notorious for it. Before I could chug my tallboys, Principal Cooke ambushed me in the smoker's pit. She ordered me to follow her back to her office. I ditched my bag in a bush, afraid someone had snitched and spotted my tallboys.

Her emu haircut bobbed as she closed the door. She asked why I kept missing classes, why my grades had slipped since I was a minor niner. Low teens.

I shrugged.

She asked if it was to do with the fact she, and other faculty members had seen me wandering the streets alone. Headphones keeping me company.

I told her not to be so impolite. She should wave and we could do lunch together in a less formal environment.

She said this would be my last warning about cutting class. That another suspension would be required.

When she ran out of words, I exited through the locker room, hoping no one pilfered my backpack.

I skipped my next class, math with Mr. Arthur. I

spent the afternoon wandering around Bayfront Pier as an act of defiance.

I still have problems explaining my wandering to normals, to my wife. I've only ever met one person who understood it. A young architect, a Quebecer with a love for pit bulls. She called it *Dérive*. The Drift. I was glad I wasn't the only one.

I guess what I mean to say is that my best days were the ones spent walking around urban jungles. Alone. Feet burning. Legs screaming. I wondered what it would take for them to give out. Now that I'm older I still do this, but in my car, circling streets, counting stoplights.

At seventeen I got high and read after a long wandering. Nothing heavy. Light novels. Anarchist zines. Inserts of CDs I stole from Sam's. Other times I would write my thoughts as they bled from my mind once the high subsided, then set the pages on fire and burn another bowl. I enjoyed the idea of impermanence, that the next high would differ from the last and my written thoughts represented a moment in time. Nothing more. A distant representation of the human I once was.

My favourite pastime after wandering is people watching. Observing others imperfect lives, dropping eaves on passing conversations, and creating stories for normals came all too naturally. They talk about their most sensitive topics on busy streets. Open therapy. Approach or confront them with dissertations and feedback and they lose their minds. Keep quiet and trail downwind, you don't exist.

On that frigid day in spring after Cooke scolded me for ditching, that's what I did. I pretended to watch the sun settle behind smoky clouds until it drank from the lake. Headphones in to avoid suspicion, while I listened to normals circling the pier's looping trail. One couple doing laps debated if they should tell the woman's husband about their affair. The woman, forties, sounded worried. The man, late twenties, sounded like a college freshman bro. With the gusto of a cult leader he gloriously talked about if Hank found out, he would 'take him to the curb.' 'In the name of our love, babe.' 'My boys will set Hank straight.' The woman protested.

I never learned the resolution. Jocelyn walked past the bench I sat on. Her red hair was wild in the wind and her petite body swam inside an oversized man's sweater made from canvas. She reached into her back pocket, held a metal charm in her hands for a moment, whispered thoughtfully to herself, before casting it into the lake. She blocked my view of the splash, but the golden ripples ebbed from her still body. She unburied her ears from her thick hair, exposing them to the twilight. One had an industrial piercing and the other had a single freckle on the tip. I wondered if she knew.

The wind kicked dirt and pebbles into the air and the lakefront grew dark and chilled. I wiped a raindrop from my knuckle. Jocelyn hugged herself, turned around.

"You," she said, holding her hips with one hand and pulling away windswept hair with the other.

I was unsure how to respond. If I should. I hadn't seen her since we buried Benji and I probably smelled like it. My mouth went dry and I swallowed back the taste of stale cancers. I did what I normally do when I lose confidence. I talked through my ass.

"I'm hungry."

"Eat," she replied.

Groundbreaking.

I knew this was not how humans converse. I tried again, but she cut through my awkward stutter.

"No," she said, screwing up her face. "Sorry. It was a question. Wanna grab food with me?"

Enrico's Pizza sat dead nuts centre in Green River. It was owned by two brothers, Dizzy and Justin Alonzo. Enrico was Dizzy's infant son. The flickering neon sign in the shop window advertised the 'Best Deal in Green River.' For under thirty bones you too could be the devourer of two large two topping pizzas, wings—Mild, Spicy, Effing Hawt—three drinks, a roll of garlic bread, and celery sticks with choice of dip.

It was the closest I had been to sober at Enrico's since the days I stole quarters from my dad's change jar. It was odd seeing the yellow paint of the steel-framed seats peeling, revealing umber metal underneath as the overwhelming stench of vinegar stung my eyes. The walls resembled deep blue waves of open sea and flaking in places to show the white undercoat. Cheap battered frames lined the walls like viewports in a ship's hull looking out on distant shores. Sunshine. Families. Laughter.

Jocelyn was glued to her phone, content with the awkward silence growing between us. Looking up occasionally at the normals braving the buffeting rain, failing to dodge the droplets.

Dizzy never cared when we made a mess. We ate a meal a day here and practically put his son through college.

I picked at the calluses on my fingertips, unsurprised to find my prints flat and scarred. I forced myself to stop, and noticed Jocelyn's hair had remnants of purple fading to her tips in her sopping ponytail. It had a sheen to it, not the straw like Sav's, or the grime and tats like mine from pumping in anything I could to spike it. If I had to guess, the last time she dyed it was when Benji was alive. We had that in common, at least.

We scarcely spoke a word since we entered and were greeted by Dizzy, who knew we had come for the Best Deal. Meat. Veggie with fire. Effing Hawt wings and spicey dip.

As I said, I didn't really know Jocelyn, but from the handful of times we interacted, she seemed chill. Though I could tell, she was deeply depressed. I think she asked me to get food so she wouldn't feel so alone.

The misery girl who sat with me was far from the girl Benji had introduced me to when he asked her to join us to people watch. When Sav asked her about it the following weekend at Benji's birthday bash, she had laughed and said he and I were tittering like two old dolls about strangers. She said it was better than cable. Benji told her to eat a dick.

I found it mindblowing how people could change. I wondered if I had.

Normals walked single file along the sidewalk, wary of speeding cars threatening them with puddles, as torrents rolled over flooded drains and clogged gutters. There was a waterfall across the street. Each person on the conveyor belt did the same thing upon approach. They stopped, judged the litres blocking their path, then passed as quickly as they could. A select few with umbrellas and raincoats risked the dash between buildings, shrinking themselves before racing through.

Others braved the gutter puddle, opting for soaked shoes over shirts.

None checked across the street. Where there was no urban waterfall and had ample overhead coverage to keep dry.

I smiled, thinking back to the pool under the escarpment at the Devil's Punch Bowl. We had wanted to get into the frigid water. But now, when forced against my will, I wanted to stay dry. Everything happens on your own terms. If you're stubborn enough.

Jocelyn had lost interest in the normals, she returned to her flip phone. Again. She wasn't texting, or looking for music. She was captivated by a photo. A leak from the past.

I didn't have to see it to know what it depicted. I had seen it many times. Looked at it frequently before sleep. Still do. Sometimes for hours. It was of her and Benji. Her purple hair bleeding on her lifejacket, Benji's shag matted to his laughing face, holding her as she snapped the photo of them canoeing with her mom's hippy boyfriend in Algonquin. Benji's caption on Myspace said it was the 'best day ever.'

It was the last photo taken of him. I always wondered if he knew what was going to happen to him.

Jocelyn forced a smile. She didn't seem ashamed, or worried, that I caught her in a vulnerable state. She looked exhausted. Worn. A paint drop spread over an entire canvas.

She returned to the picture. I resumed picking calluses.

She missed him. We all missed him. But at that point in my life I couldn't imagine what she was going through. Benji was my best friend, sure, but she was his lover. And without Benji, her main confidante who listened to her frustrations, insecurities, and dreams, she had no one. According to Sav, Jocelyn had cut everyone out of her life since the funeral. No one knew why, and everyone was willing to bury the hatchet, but Jocelyn insisted there was blood on it.

I decided that was why I was so anxious. I didn't know where I stood with Jocelyn.

I went out on a limb, felt dumb for thinking about it, felt dumb executing it, and felt uncomfortable and alien as I placed my hand on her shoulder. I expected her to tell me off, snap a preloaded jab for trying, but she pursed her lips and sadly nodded to herself.

"Best Deal ready up," Dizzy said, raising the fresh pies above his head.

I was eternally grateful for the interruption.

I carried our food to the table, motioned for Jocelyn to stay seated when she tried to help with the dual pizza box cooking my hands with scorching grease.

I sat next to her, starved from burnout, and salivated at the smell of melted cheese and crisp dough.

As we reached for those first steaming slices of za, our tongues uncoiled.

Food creates normalcy.

"About time." Jocelyn blew on her slice. Cheese, double hot pepper, sriracha instead of marinara. It smelled like napalm.

"Best deal, best meal," I said, immediately feeling lame for my word choice. I folded two slices of meat lovers and stuffed my face to save myself from my lack of, well, everything.

"So." She held the vowel, content with her za and unaware how stupid I felt. "What did you need a Deftones album for anyway? I think I still have his copy of White Pony, if the library doesn't have it."

"Some school thing. If it's a problem I can just bootleg it. I'm sure someone has thrown up a torrent on the Pirate Bay or Kazaa."

"No. No. I'm happy to help," she said, overeager. "If you want heavier stuff I can give you stuff from my Swedish doom metal phase."

The joke caught me by surprise.

"That stuff's too digital," I said, following her lead. I stuffed an Effing-Hawt wing into my mouth, sucked the bones clean. My lips numbed. Hiccups to follow.

"If you want, I could teach you how to record on clay pots. It would make any true archaeoacousticologist cream their pants."

I stopped eating. "Is that really a thing?"

Jocelyn was halfway through her slice when she grabbed a celery stick and dipped it into the Effing-Hawt sauce pooled at the bottom of the chicken wing box. Vegetarians are broken.

"It works like a record player," she said. "They did it 'in ancient times.' No idea how to play it. I fell asleep before the doc ended."

"Well find one so Sick Sad World can be the first punk band recorded on clay."

"Dev would love that. Mad clay skills—"

A moment of harsh silence lapsed between us. I replaced Benji. She looked like she was slapped with the force to dislodge a tooth.

"How've you been holding up?" I asked, staring at a glob of marinara between fallen bacon bits and New York pepperoni.

"Holding. Just holding." Jocelyn's hand reached for her bracelet, absently twiddling the beads on hemp twine circling her pale, freckled wrist. "I'm going to leave Green River."

I didn't need to ask questions. She was like a deer trying to outrun a train. If she talked faster, she could out speed her pursuer.

"I need to leave, I mean. The town. Province. The 'world.' We were supposed to get out together. He couldn't ... I can't stand the scene. It's just. I feel like I'm beating a dead horse by staying here, reliving moments, dragging the carcass along with me only to beat it again and again for the sake of beating it. And I'm like why? I'm sick of dead things. Of betting on wrong horses. I'm sick of being beaten."

She sighed. Cleared her throat.

"Newfoundland maybe. This place, Renews, looked wonderful online. Or Banff. Live in the forest. Or a hole. A place where I can make art. Alone. Now. He told me to quit my job at Cool Clay Café and practise my own art. He promised we would get lost with each other. But he was wrong. We were lost here. I just want to find myself, you know? I can't do that here. I want out."

Her words stayed with me. They made me think of the man on my back, the one that tries to hold you down. Eventually, if you let him, he wins. Pins you down. Lethargic until your soul dies. Your failures become you.

"Do it."

"You're the first to say that," she said, returning to her napalm pizza. "My mom and dad flipped. Said I was being reactionary. 'Don't be rash, Joce,' 'think it through after you're finished grieving.' Like I can control my sorrow."

"Screw that. You can't control the blues. And leaving was always your plan."

"Right?"

It was hard to see her like this. I remembered how positive and witty she had been at shows. She always laughed at our group of misfits, was the first to smile at Benji's lame jokes. I think that's why she and him had been so good for each other. They were glue holding the crew together as we chaotically spiraled out of control.

I've never been able to express myself properly—ask my parents, my wife, daughter—but Jocelyn needed to know it was alright, that her life would get better. I wanted to tell her, felt the need to tell her, but my tongue ties when I'm not being an asshole. I awkwardly hugged her from the side, thinking that was a thing humans did.

For an art hippy, she smelled nice. Rain. Sweat. Mangos. I was certain I smelled like a trash panda. She didn't say anything, just squeezed me back and held on longer than I was comfortable with, but she seemed like she needed it, so I didn't complain.

When the moment was over, I could see a faint light in her eyes. She thumbed her necklace of black rope with two silver beads on either side of a jade stone. I continued eating, as if nothing had happened.

With our bellies bloated, she indicated outside at two normals rushing under the waterfall between buildings. They debated crossing under the downfall of gutter water and after a moment between them, the boy took the girl's hand, and led her across the street towards us. It was Andrew Cho and Paige Everett. Cho held an umbrella while Paige cowered under his letterman jacket.

They made the sprint to our side just as a car screamed past. The jacket and umbrella did little to stop the tsunami. It engulphed them, leaving only their shocked faces exposed from the wall of water.

I howled. Jocelyn laughed. Weak, but a laugh.

I swear I could see steam rising from Cho's ears.

Things were looking up.

House on Haunted Hill.

"Punk is supposed to be haphazard," Alex said, before he ripped a line. His battered bass slung over his shoulder. "An ultraviolent boogaloo. It can quickly transcend into routine. Three chords. Four bars. Four riffs. A clone of a clone with a mimicked melody. You get it. It's supposed to be about progression and pushing music to the extreme, then push it farther until forever crashes down. Dig?"

"He means," Dev said, scratching himself with his drumstick, "next time you bring something to workshop, kill the generica."

I nodded stupidly. Hurt they wouldn't even consider my suggestion. I reminded myself this was their band.

Alex spun his finger. "*Never Say Die* from the top," he said. He used his forearm to wipe sweat from his brow. A crust of grey wood glue, which he used to hold his spiked hair, outlined his jet hairline. He had freshly dyed a quarter of it—from forehead to ear—bright red.

We spent the better half of the day raging. I graduated from beached whale to cunnilingus orca. I was making progress, learning to break keys, defying rhythms oppressed by time signatures. I had listened to Korn and System and Megadeth to learn how to incorporate grooves over Alex's violent bass and Dev's trashing beats. Benji had me beat. He had mastered grungy solos whereas my picking sounded mechanical. Technically correct but lacking soul.

When we workshopped Alex's two new songs, which we recorded and tossed online, my pride stung. I could expand on an idea, but had yet to come up with my own without being dumped on.

After a few shots of rum, shoplifted courtesy of Sav and Clair, I loosened up. Even found myself giggling as we played *Prom Night.* The totally true and not fabricated story of short king Jimmy who was rejected by the tall queen of his dreams. Depressed, Jimmy wound up at the zoo, looking to feed himself to the bears, where he met the love of his life. Deko. A giraffe. During the fadeout Alex changed the refrain, swearing he could still hear Jimmy on cold nights making love to his zoo bride.

Like I said, one hundred percent true.

The song ended and I was laughing like an asshole as Clair and Sav clapped and cheered. They asked for an encore, cancers between painted nails. Alex and Dev exchanged glances. Sav booed. Clair hissed.

Dev threw a splintered drumstick at Clair. She curled in a ball, crying that he popped her tit. Dev shrugged and Alex gave him props. Sav looked unimpressed.

Alex hung his bass on a stand and took a seat between Sav and Clair, wrapping his sweaty arm around Sav as he kissed her forehead. She reluctantly leaned in.

I fidgeted with my pedals, ignoring the couples as I turned dials. Scanned for new balances, before powering down my mangey amp. I lit a cancer and sagged on the stained carpet, peeling stickers I stole from Hot Topic and Value Village and carefully placed them over my guitar.

"The Cellar show is too far away," Clair said.

"Need time to get the noob solid," Dev said. I ignored him.

"He's still too sloppy," Alex said, disinterested. I could hear him counting pills. Dividing them into stacks as he counted out how many he could sell until he could use for free.

Clair stuck out her arms like a child, beckoned to Dev. "I wanna see my babe play live."

Dev rolled his eyes and joined her on the couch.

"Unless you forgot to mention," he said, "that you own a club with a PA, what you want doesn't amount to jack."

Clair wrapped her legs around Dev. Begged. Whined like a purse puppy choking on a tampon.

I shifted nervously. Out of place and unwanted like a feral mutt snarling Dillinger Escape Plan while a church choir swelled to Bach's *Cantata No.147*. Maim the overture.

I wanted another shot. Smoke a bowl to fade my apprehension, but was too dry and embarrassed to bum off the others. I turned to my guitar, hunched over the body, and began strumming chords at random. A solid F always calmed me. I hid inside the Am, back to Fma7, then the obvious C and cliché G. Masked my discomfort, a lagging fifth wheel, in becalmed stillness, and pretended I didn't register my loneliness.

"Nitwit. Listen."

"Yeah?" I refused to look while I diddled D7.

"What do you think about it?" Sav asked.

"About what?

"You got the world up your ass or something?" Alex sat forward, obviously furious at my feigned disinterest.

Sav whispered something curt. She stood up, fixed her yellow tartan skirt. Her hoodie was hewn in wide stripes.

"Church hasn't had a basement show in a while," Alex said, eyeing Sav's body within the hoodie, faint bruises from moshpits spotted below her laced—

"Could turn it into a potluck," Dev said, untangling himself from Clair to unlace his crusty knee high boots. "We're low on food again. There'd be a bigger turn out than just charging cover."

"Let's get a party going!" Clair clapped her hands together, bracelets jangling as she bounced like a child.

Sav grabbed Alex's worn acoustic guitar from the corner of the basement and knelt next to me, donning it despite the size. Birch showed under the chipped paint where Alex had tried to spray paint it a glossy red.

"We think you should play," she said, buzzing discordance.

"Only if you can clean up," Alex said, leaning back, resting his soulless Cons on the coffee table between grimy empties and pail set. He popped one of his pills like a mint. "Tighten your riffs and I'll grant you my blessing."

"Think of it as a trial run," Dev said. He quickly snorted something, and wriggled his nose, eyes tearing. "If they boo us out of our own house, then we know if you suck or not."

Sav made a face at him. "No one will boo," she said, turning to me.

"You literally just booed," Clair shouted, like it was scandalous.

Sav shushed her.

"You did boo," I said.

"Shut it," she said, poking my side with the head of Alex's guitar and I told her to quit it. "Don't be a little bitch. I've got leftover paint to make a banner. I just need canvas or board. I'll see what Osler's has for supplies."

Clair became giddy and got handsy with Dev who nudged her off so he could polish his boots. She paid him no mind, held him hostage as she raved about arts and crafts and sleepovers.

Alex waited for my answer. His dark eyes regarded me with indifference as he ripped the bong, coating the basement in a dull skunk fog. My throat became a desert. My head perspired like a booze bottle tortured by a summer sun. I knew I had to agree. Prove to Alex my worth. Sav was the reason for getting me into this. I couldn't let her down.

"Cool," I said.

Sav burst with joy and the others continued planning about who they would call, what playlists to make, who and if there would be openers, what substances to abuse. You know, that game.

Sav leaned on the acoustic guitar, holding her face to the neck.

"Thanks, nitwit."

"You owe me."

"That so?" She teased, exposing her tongue ring.

"But," I said, raising my brow, "I'll only play if you sing a song. Right now."

"She can't play." Alex cut in, like a disinterested father as he picked a scab under his new Operation Ivy tattoo.

Sav turned to him, rightened the guitar. "My lumpy butt I can't!" She strummed erratically with her thumb. Strings open.

"You're holding it wrong," I said. "You look like a nipple rider."

"Stop slouching."

"Your fingers are too small."

"Wike wittle baby nubs."

"I'll show you nubs!" Sav said, jumping to her feet.

She danced around the room, playing improvised discordance. Screamed obscenities and ordered us to shove various objects uncomfortably into all orifices. She was out of tune and time as she ittied around us, legs kicking wildly. As she shot her mouth off, she pointed the guitar like a rifle. Blasted her friends. When she aimed at me, she winked.

Mad Monster Party?

When I arrived in Skunktown for my first live set, I was late and uncomfortably sober. Darkness had taken over Green River by the time I escaped a lecture and a beating from my father. It left me with a desire to pulverize something too small to fight back. But this isn't about any of that noise, or how they found my stash. What's important is that I cleaned myself up enough to hide the bruises and welts and snuck out once they went to bed.

The punk house looked cramped and dingy in the twilight under the highway onramp. Along one side was a phalanx of bicycles. Tangled handlebars poking through spokes, braced for one last assault. Stenches of stale piss and soiled rodents buoyed in the humidity. Weeds sprung unfettered from the sidewalk cracks like pathetic soldiers warbling with shellshock.

The door to Church was locked, which I found odd, I didn't even know it had a lock. I knocked. Mosquitos convulsed on the incandescent glow of the porch light. My knuckles echoed off the peeling door, inaudible over shouts and cheers and deep bass thumping boom bap.

Across the street, a hefty man in a high-vis work vest sat on a lawn chair like he was the king of Skunktown. He crushed a beer and threw it into the street. As if daring me to tell him to recycle.

I tried to pay him no mind, kept my face glued to the door as another beer can skittered. I pulled out my phone to text the others, worried they were too wasted to read, and I'd be stuck outside with the brute judging my loner ass.

I felt claustrophobic. Exposed. Like the King of Skunktown read my fortune with the bruises along my backside. I sucked another cancer, nervous about being late, popping my cherry with a real audience. Etc.

"If you came on time, you wouldn't be locked out," I grumbled to my shoes.

If I hadn't trusted a stranger with $50 to buy my underaged ass booze, they wouldn't have ripped me off. If my dad would beat me less when Mrs. Fink, my guidance counsellor, snitched about how much class I cut, I could have met up with Alex and he could have bought me booze. If Benji were still here-

I blamed Cooke. Cursed her name as I killed my last cancer. I flicked it at the road before shambling to the side of the house and hopped the fence for the backdoor. Behind me the King of Skunktown tossed another empty into the street. It clattered. Mocked my misfortune.

Church was barren. Well, barren of furniture. In the places of pilfered tables and chairs were bodies. Tall bodies, short bodies, boy bodies, girl bodies. Fat. Skinny. Stout. Starved. All hands held bottles of somethings.

I walked room to room for familiar faces. Found strangers. Consumed. A group of skaters were reminiscing

about the last time they got high and attacked a drive through with mops. In the kitchen a group with shags and emo mullets did shots. A normal, babyfaced and misty-eyed, puked into a solo cup. A Jersey Girl balked at his weak stomach, challenging his manhood.

I pushed my way to the basement, the door had been removed from its hinges, stuffed into the adjacent bathroom. The one with weak water flow. A musk of booze and kush and cancers assaulted my nose as the putrid cloud wafted from the basement. It wasn't a bad smell, but there were too many bodies to push past the bottom riser. I swear I saw Cho, chatting up a white-haired heroin chick. Palms sweaty, knees weak, I turned away and went upstairs to where Dev slept. Convinced myself to work top to bottom for the others. Besides, I could hide in the bathroom until Sav rescued me.

The upstairs was full of the hipster crowd, smoking skinnies like Audrey, and lounging ironically in a room haphazardly stacked with all Chuch's furniture, surrounding a hookah, talking shit about goth kids blocking the foyer.

I tried the bathroom. The knob resisted. Go figure.

"Gonna be a while, brah," someone behind me said.

It was a hardcore kid. Stretched ears. Snakebites. He slouched against the wall with two forties of Colt 45 duct taped to his tattooed hands. A malignant shag hung over his face like a funeral veil.

"Tony's getting laid," he said.

"Real?"

"I wouldn't lie, brah. I'm all learned and stuff about this stuff. Stufffff."

It wasn't even ten and this guy was KOed. Dickered. Shittered and slizzed.

"You see Dev around?" I asked, thumbing at my phone in my pocket.

"What's a Dev?"

"The guy who owns this house."

"I own this house." He hit himself in the neck with his beer. His well-worn Refused shirt soaked up the discharge. He didn't notice. "I won this place."

"How's that?"

"I named it, brah. I came in here and was all—Dibs! But that jerk Donnie said."

He never finished his sentence. I tried to coax it out of him.

"Nuh, it's secret."

I told him thanks, tried to dip.

"You don't walk away from me." He attempted to stand, but more or less slumped farther on his side. "I'm the Beer Walrus! I demand respect." He brought both bottles to his mouth and started barking.

"You're drunk 40 hands."

"And don't you forget it!"

The bathroom door swung open and the scent of spray paint and bile levelled me as Philip shambled past. His mouth was a smear of crimson. He was too far into the bag to recognize me, and I assumed he had forgotten which planet he was on.

The Beer Walrus shuffled to his feet, and bowed to Philip, calling him Tony. He tried to swim through the air to reach the bathroom. It was pathetic and I felt secondhand embarrassment. I held him steady and led him to the porcelain throne, thinking he'd let me cut out one of the bottles taped to his hands. I tried to hold my breath as he sunk onto the bowl, worried about the residual spray paint giving me a headache. Ruining my buzz, if I ever got one.

"Thanks, brah," he slurred with a wide, senseless grin. "You're alright. Have a beer."

"Maybe not while your dick is out. But I'll get scissors to cut one out."

"My sacred tusks!" He recoiled, offended, disgusted. "My stash is in the fridge." He whispered. "It says Steve from Accounting."

"Thanks Steve."

"I'm not Steve, you pylon. I'm the fuggin—"

"Beer Walrus."

"You're goddamned right I am. Now stop watching me poop. It's a little gay, brah."

He sacked me with his sacred tusk. I stumbled out, cradling my nuts, coughing from the pain.

I was surprised that the Beer Walrus hadn't lied. There was a two-four case labelled with black sharpie: Steve from Accounting—No TOUCHY. I had a mind to drink them all. Chug it all down as payback. I cracked one open and stuffed another in my back pocket.

"Stealing beers are we?" Jocelyn wagged her finger in my face. Her chewed nails were freshly painted black. To my surprise, she had coloured out her purple tips, embracing her natural rusted copper tones which accentuated the dauntless freckles dusting her nose.

"Steve said to take one," I said, looking between the beer in my pocket and the cold one clenched in my fist. "Counting isn't my strong suit."

"Who's Steve?" Jocelyn toed the fridge door shut.

"The Beer Walrus," I said, aware the air became stale and oppressive. I used my keys to pop the cap, threw it into the sink.

"Is he not the greatest?"

"Friend of yours?"

"I just met him tonight. He called me his 'brother in Nubia' after I told him about the new place I'm renting. Turns out his boy lives on the same street."

I asked where the others were hiding.

"Basement," she said, pulling a cancer from a vinyl case, closing it with a harsh snap. I asked to bum one and she handed me her lit one, got her own. I sucked the pink outline where her lips kissed the filter. I didn't mind the waxy feel. I traded her my pocketed beer, fighting with the damp fabric to dislodge the bottle.

"They were in the backroom," she said.

"Didn't know they had one."

"The posters on the walls make it blend in. Kinda weird, don't you think?"

"Little bit."

She gave me back the unopened beer. I held it in my cancer hand, unsure if I should fight with my pocket again or chug my opened one.

"Philip says it's where the boogans lives," Jocelyn said, nodding at him as he jabbered to himself about sea people while filling a new bag with paint. Blue.

"What's a boogans?"

She shrugged, and left me alone to ponder it. I chugged my beer.

I followed her to the basement. Despite the heat inside, she wore a knitted sweater that hung just below her booty shorts. Her dark tights were the same tone as her

Docs. On anyone else it would have clashed, but on her it looked alright. A trend the next generation would assimilate. Master. I felt unfashionable in my roadkill jeans and stained Guttermouth shirt.

The last of the furniture was stuffed into the basement. Bodies filled the three chewed couches pushed to the side, a gang used the foldout table for a beer pong tournament, and a mattress was folded against the far wall into a seat for bodies to passout in. Clair was ahead of the game. Out cold in a lump of skaters.

Above our band equipment was Sav's banner. Sick Sad World with a mystic spiral from the Twilight Zone behind it. A blackhole to nowhere.

We walked through the partiers, pushing past a skank pit raging to the crack rock steady beat. It reminded me of wading through the swamp near the abandoned gristmill. Benji and I would hike there to blaze on the weekends, surefooted to avoid leeches on our shins. I moved the same in the basement, trading earthy bog water for BO, mosquitos swarms for upstrokes. I stepped carefully as Jocelyn led me past the improvised stage in calculated paths so as to not disturb the unexplored ecosystems of strangers chanting 'Super Orgy Porno Party' when the track changed.

The backroom's door was hidden beside the faded smiley face drawn on the basement window. The concealment was almost calculated. Posters obscured the seams and were stapled over the doorframe. Randos left their tags. Some read 'eat ass' or 'aliens exist' and 'All my life I've lived in a cage.' Even Peanut had left his mark.

Before I could try the knob, the door eeked open. A dim light bathed the room. Bodies on the floor. Bodies eating air burgers. Bodies heaped in a pile on mattresses. Alex and two men with hunched spines and thinning hair and ash skin stood in our way.

Jocelyn backed up.

"You're late," Alex said, looking through me.

Jocelyn turned away and Alex averted his gaze. He brushed ash off his bare chest, smudging it over his Operation Ivy tattoo.

"Long story," I said, making sure not to apologize. I had gotten good at removing 'sorry' from my vocabulary. "Where's Sav? I sent her a text."

He pointed at the stage area. She was talking with her girlfriends, laughing over an old zine she had tried to start. She had dyed and cut her hair. Blue. Pixie like a boy's. It suited her face. Went well with her sailor's tank. Our band logo was screen printed over her chest. The design with Horus's eye that Benji dreamed up when he first joined the band.

"Patched Up already finished their set," Alex said, hacking up a wad of grey phlegm. "Get your shit on. We're going live."

He stalked the stage like an apex predator. Shouldering his way to his bass. His mic.

As we unloaded our gear, the bodies in Church began to congregate around the coarse carpet we used as a stage.

There was no sound check, no tuning, no 'Hello, how ya'll doing tonight.' It was just us and them.

Alex cranked his bass amp. Feedback split the casual conversations. I followed his lead, but wasn't fast enough at setting up.

"Louder," he barked into the mic. "I said louder."

Elevens.

He started the bass intro to *Doom Squad* and Dev tumbled down the stairs, crosschecking some hipster in flannel, to get to his drums. His sticks cracked together and for the next hour we were animals.

Individuals ceased to exist. There was only a seething ocean of flesh hammering on itself like cells comprising the muscles of your middle finger flipping off the world.

Strangers put their arms around me as I played Benji's chords, and they belted Alex's words at me. With me. The circle pit was our gospel. Preaching unity to spewing heathens. I found peace amongst chaos.

Alex screamed for a wall of death while jumping into the pit during *Mockingbird*, letting others rage through the mic, his amp spitting feedback and disdain, while the room experienced interstellar freedom. It's what guys like him are made for. They have an indefinable quality inside them that gets people moving, hanging on to every violent whim. Alex was king.

In the end I was sweaty, sore, and had broken some kid's nose while headbanging to our cover of *White Riot*. I found the dude I hit after the set, bleeding in the kitchen sink. He said it wasn't his first time getting leveled, that he 'popped it back into place and kept raging until some prude' told him to stop bleeding on her.

Up the punx.

I can still hear that last note ring out during *At the Bottom of a Pit*, as Dev kicked over his kit, stabbed his stick into the wall, Alex's raven eyes wide and vengeful as he slouched over the mic, wailing 'I'm not me' until I faded from the stage, blissful as bodies patted my back like a goddamned hero of war. Sav found me in the kitchen, sucking a cancer with a wide dumb grin on my face while the Beer Walrus poured me a shot. She wrapped her arms around my sweaty neck and congratulated me.

I felt so alive.

Drunken haze.

Bloated like a pizza hog with more booze than my body had room for.

I have no memories after the set.

Sobriety returned as I fell over the Beer Walrus's stolen bottles in the backyard. The ground bit me and I kicked over Steve from Accounting's box. Puke dribbled out.

I recoiled from the smell, dry heaved, and crawled through the unruly grass, apologising to everyone, before I realized I was alone.

I lifted myself from the coarse weeds and onto a cinderblock overgrown with tussocks. My ankles itched from fleas. I lost my left shoe.

Time blipped and I was hunched over trying to pick up a cancer from the dirt and return it to my dry lips. I needed to mask the vile taste filming my teeth.

A ringfort of sticks at my feet stabbed into the uneven ground and surrounded a clay ashtray like a burial mound. Blue and chunky. Carved in the centre was a misshapen heart buried under nicotine stubs. 'For daddy, love Devin.'

I dry heaved in my lap. Thankful my guts were emptied.

"So this is where you ran off to."

Jocelyn's silhouette leaned against the door, loosely holding a two-six of schnapps in her left hand. She drank straight, her face flush like-

"Shove your bum," she said. I did, giving her most of the cinderblock. She smelled of a nameless flower. It was pleasant, but too strong. I fought back a gag. It reminded me of the time I had drank too much vodka during Monster Madness and I ralfed from the smell of Doritos.

"Ugh you stink!" Jocelyn held her nose. She lit herself a cancer and exhaled through her nostrils, sneezing like a cat from the burn.

"Thanks, tips." I curled on myself, in part for warmth, another to stop the world's rotation.

"You did good."

"Think so?"

"For sure." She took a swig of her schnapps. "I didn't think you had it in you."

"Probably."

She nudged my shoulder and I felt as if I had detached from Earth's orbit and spiraled toward Mars.

"Argonauts in towww!"

"You're super weird." She let it hang in the air. "A loner, but you're alright with it. Confident in solitude. But unabashed. I don't know. What I mean is, I guess it was nice seeing you out of your shell."

I wanted to tell her about how the Ninja Turtles had shells, but I was more interested in relieving my fleabites. Jocelyn thumbed the collar of her bottle.

"Do you remember puking on that girl Lisa's shoes?" she said after a time.

"I can confidently say no."

I apologized to Lisa, even though I had no clue who she was or where she was or what that meant.

Jocelyn asked if I was feeling better, and I was, albeit cold and chewed. I reaffirmed, more to convince myself, that I was practically sober. Just haggard. She laughed.

"Haggard will do it," she said, and I asked her how she was doing. "I've been out of sorts lately. Been kind of secluding myself, as I'm sure you've seen. But I just needed some time, you know? I thought 'it's time to go out and allow yourself to have fun.' Get back to living, I guess. Thanks for egging me on to come out. I know it's not my scene anymore, but I do appreciate it. I feel like I now know where I belong. Sorry. I don't want to complain. Not to you. I haven't been drunk since- Look I'll shut up before I start sounding lame. We both don't need that."

"Impossible."

"Think so?"

"Benji only kept groovy people around. You of all people should know—"

She withdrew. I felt the shift in the air change as she buried back inside herself. I placed my hand on her wrist and was about to apologise when she stood up.

"Don't, asshole."

"What?" I asked, snuffing my cancer on Dev's heart. "I thought people need hugs and shit. Sor—I'm not great at being human."

"All night all I've heard from everyone else was 'sorry Jocelyn,' 'it'll be alright, Joce,' 'you're sooo brave for coming,' 'he's always with you, never forget that.' I just wanted one night away from that. One night without guilt where I could be myself and not this bitch named misery."

I didn't know what to say. I said nothing.

"I thought you of all people could sympathize with that. It's why I came tonight. I thought you understood what I'm going through. You were the only one—"

"How about I roll us a joint. We can get stoned and we don't have to talk. Just hang."

She thought for a moment, asked if it was indica. It was hybrid. She pulled up the recycling bin and sat next to my ringfort while I fumbled with a weed bag which I had hidden in my jacket's secret pocket. I couldn't place who I bought the gram off of.

We lit up. Listened to muffled bursts of lukewarm laughter. Low bass beats from industrial vampire freaks who assumed control of the speakers. Bitter laughter of souls stomping for the last bus home.

I don't know how long we sat, smoking my damp weed, only that the crickets sang us a symphony far more surreal than the one happening inside. My guts ended their rioting as the buzz took over. We giggled at nothing, trying to keep quiet, resisting our promise of silence.

"They strum such sad songs with such small hands," said Jocelyn. Her eyes were red. I couldn't tell if she was tearing up or just stoned.

"What?"

"I'm sorry for snapping. I didn't want to ruin your big night."

"It's all good."

"That was your first time playing live?"

"I never knew how exhausting it was."

"It's from all those acrobatics you were pulling. What was that? A triple axel salchow? Don't worry, you'll get used to it."

I killed the joint, flicked it at the lichen growing under the hose nozzle, and asked her what she meant.

"Your body learns how to deal with it," she said, pulling at her sweater sleeves. "The abuse you put it through, I mean. Pain fades like a memory. Then, when you're at your peak, you'll need it to function."

"I am too stoned to climb a peak."

"Duh. What I mean is: look at Alex, at Devin. This is how they cope." She pointed at Church. "They don't care about anyone. They don't care who listens or won't, so long as they can scream and bang away and fuck up their lives." She tried to stifle a laugh. "Sick Sad World is a coping mechanism. They're in there, able to function since they released their frustrations. I think that's what humans need most: a way to deal with life. Everyone has their own vices, sure, some work better than others, some don't work at all. At the end of the day all we can do to carry on and overcome is to bang and scream our pain away. If we don't, we kill ourselves."

"I too am a fan of banging the pain away," I said, giggling with her. "What about you?"

"What about me?" She rubbed her sole in the soil, her glee faded.

"How does the sage Jocelyn cope?"

"Paint, draw, sculpt. All that artsy crap. I used to brag how one day I'd master the doodle. I'd tell everyone I'd get by as an artist selling scribbles I made on bus schedules and coffee shop napkins."

"And now?"

"Everything is mirrors." She frowned.

I didn't understand.

The sound of Sav sliding open the door pulled Jocelyn out of herself.

"Hey, nitwit. You out here?"

Jocelyn stood up, took the cancer from my hand. "Catch you around, 'nitwit,'" she said, before staggering through the side gate with my cancer.

"Quit being a psycho. Come party," Sav said, reaching her hand out to mine. I took it.

She led me to the basement, past the straggling party creeps with no roads leading home. She leaned on the door to the backroom, playing with her tongue ring between her teeth as she squinted at me through her blue bangs, withholding something she was both anxious and excited to reveal.

She asked if I wanted to feel alive. I told her I did.

She opened the door. Around the room were things wearing human suits that resembled my friends, eerily quiet and laying like spoons on a king-sized mattress, limbs tangled and entwined, careless of who touched where as the bodies knotted together en masse like cultists worshiping an eldritch god and fused into a single seething form. The only ones incapable of mutation were Alex and Dev.

They were arguing about whether I was ready or not, while Alex slapped Dev's forearm, just below a shoestring.

"Be cool," Alex said, coiling the string around his fist.

"If you don't want to," Sav said, holding my hand.

Alex's gaze looked down on me. Told me he thought I didn't have what it takes to party this hard.

"I'm cool. It's alright."

Please tell me everything will be alright.

Sav pulled me in for a hug. "It's amazing. It's only my third time, but I've never experienced anything like—"

"It's better than sex," Dev said, cringing away from what Alex was doing to his arm.

"That's because Clair is a shit lay," Alex said, feeding Dev through the syringe.

Dev went limp. Alex lay him back on the mattress between Philip's body and Ryan's.

Alex nodded at me to come. A gesture which reminded me of my father on Christmas. I complained about Santa forgetting my new bike and got a thumping. When our extended family came for dinner and we had to take photos he told me to sit on his lap. 'Happy families smile in their photos.'

I obeyed Alex, dismissing my anxiety. I wanted to prove myself.

He worked away at my body with mechanical finesse, before my instincts overrode my rational mind.

"It'll take seven seconds," he said, his voice a world away, "and feel hot as hell, but that's normal. Look at me. Normal. You'll need to relax for a better trip. Understand? This is normal.

"We're right here the whole time. Ryan should climb out soon. You won't be able to move until after the peak. Whatever you feel like doing after that, just do it. If you're too far down, I've got Narcan upstairs, or we can use some of the Devil's dandruff to bring you back up. Dev recommends a teenth. Breathe. Remember. You wanted this."

"Good luck, nitwit," Sav said, leaning back as she fell into the sky.

No.

I fell . . .

Felt it crawling through my arm. Each beat of my heart pulled the napalm farther into my chest until it hit my heart, exploded through my body until everything went warm, soft, perfect. I basked in its endlessness.

Sav caressed my neck. Honest hearts beat in time. Alex fed her next and soon she fell beside me.

We became spoons.

I awoke in a pile of sour smelling strangers. There was a girl with white hair, whose face and name I couldn't place. Her hand was in my pants, gently wrapped around my limp cock.

My head became a swarm of bees building a hive out of my neurons. I was mortified. I couldn't remember the last time I had showered. All I could think about was smegma. A wave of nausea rose as I debated checking my dick for cheese. Did she even consent? Did I?

Stop this.

I went to the bathroom to fix myself as my brain itched. I puked in the sink. I rinsed, puked again. In the broken mirror, Clair slept peacefully in the bathtub.

On my way out, I passed Dev and the Beer Walrus in the kitchen. They hoovered rails off Ryan's stomach. She pushed her pelvic bump into their faces when they crushed a line. She giggled, told them their stubble tickled as they dragged their chins past her hips towards her vertical smile.

"Cheers," was all I could manage.

As I slipped on my missing shoe, I thanked Steve, the Beer Walrus for his beer. He asked what beer? All he had were 40s taped to his hands. Dev asked who the hell Steve was. I still don't know.

They Live.

The second last time I stepped foot in Schwenger High was for the end of the year Coffee House, janked together by Arielle's student council for the socially prepared. 'Cafegymitorium Expo.' Politically speaking it was well planned, however it was poorly run, executed, advertised, and functionally unpleasant unless you're of the student body's upper crust.

Rumours were that Green River's Red Hat Association decided the primo time to allow students to express themselves was before reading week to 'assist student relaxation before the gruesome examinations to follow. Encourage them to form fresh long-lasting friendships' before the disassociation of past lives stagnates with the glorious heatstroke of a boiling planet. Put bluntly? It 'lowered' the suicide rate. Balanced it like the fucking GDP.

After the Sick Sad World show at Church, I found myself addicted to playing live. I fantasized about it. Wake. Dream. Pass out. Repeat. I'd run through interviews and antics and stunts to do while I raged. Had the audacity to wish about playing an arena.

The inevitability concluded when Arielle asked if I would purchase a ticket. I was tanked at lunch, numbly watching her carry around a gallon jug of cash and a roll of tickets. I was thinking about stealing the cash and blowing it all on junk when she asked me. I told her I wanted to play a solo set. She dictated I had seven minutes and could play whatever I wanted, but warned me about how recklessness and curses were the leading cause of detention. The other performers got ten.

I think she was afraid I would infect hopeful alumni with my rot, play pornogrind, or masturbate on stage with SpaghettiOs in my butt. Call it high art.

I kept the others in the dark about the gig. I didn't have a reason, I just wanted to do it alone. Test my waters.

The doors opened at five and the cafegymitorium cleared out at ten to adhere to the Red Hat Association's by-law. I went on just after six. I prepped for the show in the parking lot, watching normals and their parentals take photos of darling little Johnny's big night. I choked on their inexpensive body spray, popped collars. Cherries. Rad.

I realized how detached from humanity I had become without Benji as I chainsmoked cancers chased with screwdrivers. I had no one to snicker with about suburban rappers spitting how hardcore and real they were, or the cheerleaders starting their egirl careers early as they learned the art of grifting incels, or poser 'hard rocker'—pop music—play Floyd and Beatles. I hated Jimmy Page. Still do.

In my buzzed solitude I decided art existed to get into people's heads and hearts. Make them feel. Think. Believe in something. Narcissists collecting digital counters like Pokémon cards to fuel dopamine highs infuriated me. Clout exchanged for killcounts was not what art should be about.

That's why I did this alone. I felt like a sellout for convincing myself people would like me if I strummed a guitar. I wanted to deprive myself of validation. Be authentic.

When I walked into the cafegymitorium I feared the crowd. That Cho would wedgie me in front of the school. Jockstraps holding back the mob as he beat the spit out of me.

I sat on the piano bench to the side of the stage, cradling my guitar with soggy hands. Hiding my panic sweats while I waited for my set. Ignore the crowd gossiping about the loner preparing to crucify himself for their pleasure.

When Arielle introduced me, no one clapped, no one silenced. No one cared. They turned away from me and nattered amongst themselves.

I played, in this order: *Jaw Knee Music*, *Love Will Tear Us Apart*, *One Great City!*

No fadeout. No encore. No cheers. I walked out.

From the bathroom, I heard laughter. Mike Reilly's stand-up routine. Roasting the teachers. I took a dump, chewed T3s I scored off Ryan, and chased the chalky film from my gums with my leftover orange juice.

As I washed my hands a minor niner approached me. He wore a Straight Reads The Line shirt, stuttered out words I was too dickered to follow. He began with some elaborate tale about some kid, Collin, caught cheating somewhere. I stopped him and asked what he wanted.

"I don't spot."

"It's not that," he stuttered out. He blushed. "Our guitarist bailed on our set."

He continued his story about Collin, his guitarist, being caught by daddy with a gram in his stash sock.

"Wrap it in dryer sheets," I said. As the T3s kicked in, I found myself unable and unwilling to focus. I asked him about the cheating so I could zone out. When I grew bored, head pleasantly numb, I asked him what he wanted.

They were going to play a Blink song. He asked me to fill in.

Normally I would have told the minor niner to suck the lead out of a battery, but T3s make me docile. I would be glad to help. He thanked me and then I asked him if he's Scott Green. He said he never heard of him. I was bummed.

I spent all of ten minutes searching for guitar tabs on my phone, practised the song once in the foyer, before stumbling back to the cafegymitorium, ignoring Cho's taunts about how hard he was going to 'pound my ass.' I was too high to care.

Arielle stepped in, giving Cho harsh Christian words as my world spun.

We played. I bungled the second verse, but quickly regained myself. Stutters and his friends were thrilled with my performance. High fives. Remember those? One dude, who smelled like cabbage, hugged me. I told them if they ever need hooks to holler.

I texted Jocelyn from the foyer, my guitar case slung over my back as I meandered towards the teacher's parking lot.

I lied to her. Said I was at Church and suggested she come hang with us. I wanted to thank her in person for suggesting art as therapy, but she never responded back.

I was fine with it. Decided to celebrate after I picked up junk from Alex if he was holding. Alex was always holding.

Above me Cho shouted my name and chucked a cup of piss at me. It fell short, splattered at my feet, misting under the parking lot lights. I waved at him, numb and pleasant. He called me queerbait and told me not to move.

I bent over and mooned him. My pale ass glistened in the starlight as he shouted death threats into my cornhole.

"Put that thing away, mister!" Tomassi shouted, her fat hand gripped Cho's polo. Her chubby face careened out the cafegymitorium window. "I said now!"

I waved at her, smiled wide and stupid.

She shook her head, fought and failed to hold back a grin as she pulled Cho inside.

Mrs. Tomassi was good people. She was the only adult I respected. I never told her. Never thanked her for trying to save me from the blackhole I was spiralling into.

No. She never marked my assignment. However, I did write it. Promise. I chose *Knife Party* and *Change in the House of Flies*, wrote about how they meant more to me than *Howl*. To this day, when I see flies, I think of how she tried to stop me from plucking off my own wings. Alive and numb. Misguided control. Blah blah blame. Thanks for trying, Teach.

The following Monday I dropped out.

The Thing.

The next few weeks were uneventful. In freedom everything blossoms. It was pretty to some, horrid to some.

It was a Sunday when Sav called me. I was burrowed under a mountain of sour smelling blankets to extinguish the sunlight assaulting my hangover. Alex was chewed up and sketching in the bathroom, curled in the shower, from shooting with me last night. I checked the clock before I opened my cell. 14:15. Still early. I reminded myself I needed to panhandle tonight to pay my phone bill.

I grunted into the receiver.

No response.

"What?" I snapped.

Through the white noise, Sav's voice was distant. Empty.

"Can you come over?"

I was dressed before I hung up.

Her apartment was on the outskirts of downtown at the end of Blackwood Drive and looked like a beaver's butthole. That is to say, a hollowed russet cube with courtyard tiles snared in the centre, stained like burnt coffee, and the focal point was a lonely bench under a dying maple. Benji, after a night of Monster Madness, said the building looked like a beaver defecating a frothy woodchip.

The landlord, a blockhouse of a man who wore a shower curtain muumuu like a super's cape, refused to remove the dead tree. It was planted in memory of his great-grandmother. The last time I was in Green River it was a rotted stump. Dedication plaque still embedded in the dirt beside the bench. My daughter was too young to understand irony.

Sav buzzed me in. The inside of the building was just as unkempt as the outside. Yellow and brown pinstripe wallpaper peeled loose and cobwebs clotted the crooks where walls met. The whole place stank of stale coffee and cat piss, hot dogs and grandma's plum perfume.

A hunched 'out of order' sign duct taped to the elevator hung cocked as it had that night Sav and I first met.

The elevator that did work looked like a four-year-old's colouring book. The graffiti blotting the door was illegible and unskilled save for a single line that read 'i nailed tina' and the sloppy response, 'tinas an slut!' When I punched Sav's floor I noticed Peanut had scratched his tag in the E-stop.

Sav's apartment door was ajar so I let myself in. Her mom kept it in slightly better condition than the lobby. Not bad for a single mother who worked two jobs. She did her best cleaning floors twelve, sometimes sixteen, hours a day in banks and grocers and offices all to give her daughter a semblance of stability. Her only day off was every third Tuesday. Which is why when Sav hit puberty, she became a night-owl so she could see her mother for a short time after work. The two rarely interacted. I could count on one hand how many times I have been in the same vicinity as Missus Moore. Sav never knew her father. Swore to keep it that way. I learned from Missus Moore that Sav's father was a dockworker, who ditched for the US to dodge child support and because 'Canada was becoming a Chinese communist puppet state.' Bore.

Wait, shut up. I need this: The day Sav and I met was nothing spectacular. I had lied to my parents, said I was crashing at Benji's place for the night. He told his that he was staying at mine. Suckers bought it. What they didn't know was we snuck out to my first punk show.

The venue was underneath a 24-hour laundromat on Dewitt, believe it or don't. The owner, D.D. Crust, secretly held shows in the leaky and limy basement of his elegant establishment. Lead pipes. Knob and tube. Fuse box. Asbestos blocks.

We didn't call Derek Dorian 'D.D. Crust' as an honorific punk title because he allowed us dirty punk kids to rage and get head over ass in his dingy basement. It was because even though the laundromat upstairs was cleaner than an operation table, he himself was filthy. He looked like stale farts wrapped in burnt bacon.

Sav first caught my eye while she sat on a full amp stack next to the stage. By 'stage' I mean the green painter's tape designating where the furnace was to keep us from busting open the gas line. Pink fishnets tattered and frayed. Liberty spikes. Bleach-stained booty shorts with band patches sewn into them. Nausea. AFI. Orchid. Against Me! Jack Off Jill. Bosstones. Jayne County.

I felt foolish in my pristine Black Flag tee I got from Hot Topic as she and Abby, and Zoe, and a girl I'd later learn was Lisa, and Jocelyn with her gothic makeup raged to Nip Discharge and The Rusty Tampons. The older girls smoked cancers and traded swigs of warm beer they got with their fakes. She fed off the ritual's energy. Knew the chants. Belted lyrics. Scarred her lungs.

Sav watched Benji from the booming amp as he tore up the moshpit with Crazy Dev, who was dating Abby at the time. Sav resembled a Roman aristocrat absorbed by colosseum culture, laughing at the gladiators moshing under her. All barbarian tribes repped their set. Punks. Crusts. Skaters. Sharps. Skramz. Rude Boys and Hardcore kids. A lone bonehead, Nazi Ross, brought a keg as a piece offering so he could see RT. Simpler times before lines carved in stone divided the scene. Before 'screamo' knocked us aside.

After the show, Sav was hoarse, hair slick with sweat. She hugged Benji from behind while he and I tried to flag down a cab for Blake Bulimia—a name the nervous boy received because after every show he spent the night ralfing. Sav helped stuff the waster into a blue cab, after which Benji introduced us. I, 'the hobgoblin nitwit' and she 'the weirdest dude he knew.'

She asked us what we were up to, she was looking to keep the party going despite her friend's need for sleep. Benji and I exchanged glances, not wanting to tell her about our lie that left us without a place to sleep. That we were just kids.

Sav explained her mother was doing nightshifts as a cleaner, and asked us to spend the night at her apartment if we were willing to let her bum some pot. It was a no brainer.

The apartment was neither sparse nor cluttered and modest enough for a single mother and her only child. We drained Missus Moore's liquor cabinet and ignorantly refilled it with water and RC Cola thinking the two liquids would mix while we watched black and white horror movies until sunrise.

I burntout with Sav's bruised legs on my lap, Benji on my shoulder. Both had drifted to sleep with me in the middle, neither trapped nor uncomfortable.

I learned in therapy that the lack of human contact common with western men was called emotional starvation. It explained why, later in life, being in close proximity to normals filled me with disdain. But back then, before my brain broke, it was dope being cuddled in a heap with my best friends.

I twiddled a loose thread on Sav's fishnets, watching Vincent Price waltz with clockwork wizards, as a dead girl swung a golden axe, until I passed out.

I woke at noon. Hungover. Starved. The three of us promised as we took turns puking and chugging Sunny D that we needed to hold waster horror nights on the regular. Once a month, when Missus Moore's shifts changed. For four years we crammed on Sav's single mattress surrounded by discarded chip bags and $5 cakes, pony bottles made ashtrays, assorted pipes and bongs, mushroom bags, and pills of anything, watching the classics. We called it Monster Madness.

Eventually we started to theme Monster Madness. Benji's idea. Zombies and car bombs. Jack and cola slashers. Deer blood and vampires. My favourite was broken-down golf cart and rampage. Which was Benji's favourite drink: almond amaretto, midori melon liqueur, and a dash of lime. Sav preferred cranberry over the lime.

The goal was to out-obscure the others with any films we could get our snotty hands on. Benji always won. Banned. Red listed. Over-the-top gore porn. Rape revenge. Things that would kill Dirlewanger's boner.

The month before Benji died, we hopped a train to Toronto for better picks, pillaging back-alley smut shops. You will never believe the things people get off on. It made the internet's digital footprints look like a tame herd of wild horses galloping through a field.

After Benji's death, Sav and I intended to continue the tradition. Unfortunately, you cannot bring the dead back with good intentions. We tried Monster Madness once as a duo—as I was about to tell you before this ramble—but the luster was lost. The missing pieces within us drowned in the big sad. We got high instead and listened to powerviolence, tweaking and sketching until her mother came home. But I'm skipping time again.

I waited in Sav's room while she finished in the cramped bathroom. Steam blew under the door as I contended myself to thumb through her burnt CD collection splayed across her desk. Fall River. Sam Lawrence 5. Planet Smashers. Crass. This Bike Is A Pipe Bomb. Non Passive Resistance. I was surprised to see My Chemical Romance cozied between Fifth Column and Excuse 17.

I wanted to call out and ask if she wanted to get high, but knew I had no money or drugs to offer.

She came in while I flipped through *My Wife the Butcher*. Her eyes puffy and her blow-dried hair was a rippled mop of blue waves, not the pointed and pampered ironed job I had come to expect. It was the first time I had seen her without makeup. It was strange. Dark rings sunk under her eyes and I never suspected the lonely freckle under her eyebrow.

She exhaled bitterly and flopped onto her bed. I joined her, leaving the odd book. She pressed play on her boombox and the Horrorpops' groovy stomp filled the apartment. We lay there, deciphering band posters and lyric inserts and magazine clippings from the anarchist zine, *Heretic Hands*. She had used sticky tack to mount them on her walls and ceiling. Oblong stains seeping through their corners.

Sav sank to the ground at the foot of her bed and went through her collection for a new mix.

"You alright?" I said rolling on my side.

"Fan-fricking-tastic." She pulled her sleeves into tight balls, quit her search.

"What happened?"

"Didn't want to be alone."

She forced her boney arm under her mattress, when she pulled out, she held a stainless beauty case. Inside she hid her cancers, pills, and a bag of pot. We cracked the window and sucked in filtered cancer.

She asked if I enjoyed the house show the other week, smoke drifting from her throat.

"It was alright."

"No. I mean, did you enjoy ... it?"

I'd be a liar if I said I didn't. I'd be a liar if I said I never planned to do it again. The dots I had acquired on my arm was proof I enjoyed it. A tally of medals, proving I partied hard.

"Sure," I said, pretending to think it over. "Don't remember much."

She nodded to herself, as if weighing options on how to proceed. I asked if she wanted to do it again, and she harshly told me she 'was done with that noise.' Her response made me feel gross, like I didn't want to be with her sober if she was going to trash me for something she convinced me to do. I became nervous and itchy, feeling avoidant and apprehensive at starting an argument. The same irritation when interacting with my mom.

I spaced out while Sav ranted about disliking drugs, wishing I hadn't come.

"You remember Lisa, right?" All bitterness gone.

I nodded thinking back to the party. Alex had told me she was the girl who slept on me.

"You could *not* keep your hands off each other," Sav said, teasing.

"I thought she was cute."

I couldn't summon her face in my mind. She was a tatter of platinum hair.

"She likes you, nitwit. If you can believe that." She reached into her garbage for a cola can to use as an ashtray.

What was there to like? Strung-out, blacked out, lonely. As long as the body is warm, right, Alex?

"You want her number? She needs a decent guy."

This is a bad idea.

"I don't know, it was one night, and a long time ago at that, a fling or a wasted accident, like a game normals play with their boy toys for validation, no substance all hormones."

"You're right, it was a dare."

"Really?"

"Shit no. You're that scared of girls?" Her words drifted like cancer smoke. Each whisp propelled past the lonely freckle under her brow and coiled into a single word: Coward.

"No." Liar. "I'm burned out."

She grabbed my phone, and punched in Lisa's number. I shamefully picked at a concert ticket stuck to her wall.

We killed the remainder of the day watching dated horror films from the 70s. *Straw Dogs*, *Body Snatchers*, *Blacula*, and Sav's favourite, *The Abominable Dr. Phibes*. Just like old times.

We both had difficulties focusing, kept talking about getting high, while at the same time not wanting to call up Alex to score so we could use. Sav pendulumed the hardest. One moment she was cursing drugs, the next she toyed with the idea of running down to Barton in Hamilton to pick up. She didn't want to use Alex's stash, said it'd be cheaper to use his dealer. Then the next moment she'd be back on team sobriety. I asked her what was going on and she confessed she had just finished detoxing. She survived her first ringer.

During a dubbed version of *Mecedora de Lucifer*, we deviated from the plot, invented our own names for characters, yelled at the television who the killer was and why. General Cigaro and his desire to punch babies for hound overlords. It was the only way we could survive the sterile dialogue until the gore.

We breaked during *Blacula's* second act. I was sketching. Cold sweats and gagging. Sav crunched up pills that she told me would help with the shakes. It did for a while, but I caved and asked her if we could smoke a bowl, so I could get too stoned to care about sketching.

Her bud was mostly stems she was saving for tea. Her baggy looked more like decaying pressed leaves than the crystal bud I was used to smoking. We blazed the sticks, smoked bots to accentuate the high. I had wanted to do pails in the shower like we used to with Benji, but she was afraid I'd slip and crack my head open.

Harsh smoke blackened my lungs. It felt good, but didn't last long. I ended up scratching burnt resin from her pipe and smoking it too.

When Missus Moore came home from her first shift with spaetzle and goulash, my brain had faded and fogged, and I was trembling, shaking, sweating, in Sav's bed. She explained to her mom that I had contracted the same virus she had just gotten over, that my mom was diabetic—which was true—and afraid of catching the sick for fear of death. Missus Moore delightfully allowed me to sketch while they ate, caught up on each other's lives while I died in agony, as Donnie Sutherland confronted a dog with a human head.

She stayed long enough to refuel and then was immediately out the door to wash floors for the G. Tian building down on Saint Mark.

After eating and hydrating, I felt better. We listened to the Explicits in the living room on Sav's alien head ghetto blaster. Black. Oval. Pug-mouthed tape deck in the centre. My gut still rioted, but the sweating had stopped.

In the middle of *Over It*, Sav broke down. I put my shaking arms around her. Her breasts shuddered against my chest as she wept. I shifted to hide my nervous boner—though I know my body didn't have the energy for it. Cried with her.

"I was doing so well," she said.

It sneaks up on you. The big sad. When you disentangle yourself from the chaos, you lose control. A single song lyric. The thrum of a chord. They throw you overboard. You drown.

She waited until the cloudburst ceased to speak.

"It's Alex." Her voice was thin between the bassline.

Do not misunderstand, I cared. Truly. But the selfishness of us both was killing me as I tried to regain lucidity. The unholy triforce of adolescence forcing us to play this game of threes, and triangles are cliché. Overused. No matter who the characters are. But I was sketching with nowhere to wander off. I didn't want to be involved in the drama with a bandmate I respected and, since Benji was gone, my closest friend.

"We went to a party," she said, starting her story, "a bush party at the gristmill. You know the one above the escarpment across town? Everything was fine until it started to die down. It was cold and the trees and ruined walls didn't block the wind. They created a weird tunnel where it was so windy and loud and I was shaking, wishing I had brought a sweater. I wanted to dip. Head back to Church and get high and warm. Only party creeps drag out.

"Ryan made a comment about how skinny I've gotten and that if I had more meat on me, I wouldn't be as cold. We argued about it.

"I like getting loaded. There I said it. And yes. I like how I look, it's not my fault that stuff is slimming. Sure. I hate my wide boney hips, but it's just. It hurt when Alex laughed. It was cruel. And I know he was probably just being a dumb man, laughing because he was wasted, but I started to blame him. I got in his face about how all he wants to do is shoot. His words hurt so much. Like he enjoyed calling me all those things.

"Sometimes I think I'm just there to please him. Keep him distracted, or grounded, or whatever. Let him use my body when he is sober enough to get it up. I exist so he doesn't become a blackhole kid."

"Blackhole kid?" It was the first time I heard the phrase.

"Punks past their prime. The ones that don't grow out of this lifestyle. They refuse to grow up. Sellout. Die. I don't plan on doing this all my life. I want things. I need things. Alex wants one thing. The high.

"Just past one a.m., I asked him if we could leave soon. He grabbed me by my wrist. Hard. Like he wanted to snap it. 'I'm not done yet,' he shouted. Shouted! 'You leave when I say.' Who does that? I knew he was loaded, I was too, but he had this awful expression, like a child relishing ripping off a bug's wings and immolating it under a magnifying glass. He enjoyed making me afraid of him. It was the second time I'd seen him like this. I pulled myself free, but his fingers bit deeper as he twisted. I struggled and he pulled me in. He decked me."

My heart stopped beating.

"It wasn't that hard, I've been hit worse at shows, it was the shock that fucked me up, I counted myself lucky since it was openhanded and I think it was the momentum that made it sound so crisp, but he told me how sorry he was immediately. He gathered his stuff and we walked back to town. When we came back here, I had a long shower and then we …

"Don't say it. I know I'm stupid. But I haven't used for a few days now, and he is doing the same. We agreed to time apart. Take a moment to calm down and think things over before we decide what's best for us.

"The morning after the fight, Alex told me he didn't remember much, just that I had pushed him, that I hadn't pulled away. I 'slipped.' I can't fully remember. God. My brain feels like melted cheese. He said he reacted 'on impulse' and he didn't mean to swing. I believe him. But after detoxing, and listening to that stupid song, I just thought what if? What if this is the rest of my life, and I become a blackhole kid, that I'm in too deep, but worst of all, what if I was so loaded that I have no idea that I hit him. What if I'm violent? Like my piece of shit father."

"I don't think you're violent," I said, unsure about my own past few weeks.

At this stage in my life, I never regretted a single moment I lived. True, difficulties recalling past nights and days are common when you're blasted on junk, or overboard on a bender, but I was certain Alex had been with me and Dev jamming new songs and shooting together last night. Didn't we crash a house party at that Serb's place? Had I assumed Alex was sketching in the shower, like he did every morning? I didn't actually see him. I assumed I was misremembering that Alex was suffering from post-party depression and nothing more.

I kept my disjointed thoughts to myself.

"How do I know I'm not violent?" She poked her chest. "I've been thinking I should quit for a while. Sellout. I tried cutting back, made rubber-elbowed rules about when and where and how much to use, but it was too difficult. Philip says when it stops being fun, that's the sign to move on. I refuse to be—"

"A junkie."

She pulled away. I didn't know what to say. I didn't consider either of us junkies. Reckless and wild, sure. But recreation doesn't equate habit. And habit is impartial to dependency. Right?

I wish I had said something to her in that overheated apartment, told her her worth, showed the value of our friendship, how she inspired me to play guitar, write songs, learn how to sing. I looked up to her. I was more than some loner kid along for the ride into adolescence. But as she poked her finger through the holes in her ankle sock, fishing for the spaces between her toes, I realized she was more than the impact she left on my life. I adored how she treated stray cats. She'd greet them, gain their trust though most were feral. She called them Lumpy Kitties, and told stories about the previous Lumpy Kitties to the current one who was unsure if she was trustworthy. She always asked if they knew each other. They would brush up on her, accept her kindness with the stories of other strays. I pretended all the Lumpy Kitties purred legends of the fairy punk girl who showed them kindness.

"Please don't tell the others." She ran her fingers through her faded blue hair. "It's been a rough week and

I don't want to put myself above them. It's just one of those days."

"Right. One of those days."

Sav lay back in her bed, settled into her dye-stained pillow. Her chest calmly rose and fell. The CD ended. I popped in a mix labelled with gold Sharpe 'dun b sad, lets dance' and Atom and His Package sneezed through the speaker.

"When was the last time?" I asked as electropunk redefined music.

"What?"

"You said you saw Alex mad like that another time. When was it?"

"Before Benji died."

I fell silent for a moment.

"It was his last day and we were in the basement back room, decaying on Alex's mattress. It was my first time, you know, shooting. Alex invited a few of us over to party after Sick Sad World jammed new songs. Benji was late.

"He stormed into the basement, began tearing shit apart and trembling. He could barely walk. He must have dropped his smoke a dozen times. Alex thought he'd burn Church down. He pulled Benji aside, ignored everyone else, and dragged Benji upstairs where they just started screaming. We sat in the backroom, listening to the disjointed argument, for several minutes. We didn't know if we should intervene, or break it up, until they came back down. Alex's face looked like he would crush a puppy with stilettos and Benji was wiping tears on his sleeve, hiding his sorrow from us. I wish he would have told us what was wrong. I wanted to ask, hug him, but was in shock. I had never seen a boy cry before. The alien-ness of boy tears freaked me out.

"Alex climbed on his nightstand and pulled down a ceiling tile, and sat on the edge of the mattress with his stash. The veins on his forehead threatened to explode. I swear I saw blood seething as his heart furiously pumped.

"He told me and Clair we 'don't want to be here for this.'

"I told him not to tell me what to do.

"He dumped the kit into his lap. I froze. Just like you did the other night at your first time. I had heard Alex and Dev talk about getting clean, tut me like a child and say to never start using that shit, that it wasn't worth it, how much they regretted using, but at the same time held it above my head as if it gave them status. 'Look how cool I am for suffering.' Bullshit. But when I saw the delicate needle and puny glass tube, it all looked so harmless. The powder. The spoon. What difference was it compared to all the other shit I had tried?

"Alex started weighing the powder and before he gave Benji a cut, he asked if he was going to get paid this time.

"Benji threw his wallet at his feet. Not as a joke. There was a seriousness to it. Like he knew he would never need it again.

"Alex swung at Benji, screaming shit like 'do you know how much this cost?' but Benji dug in his heels and swung back without a word. They just stood there, whaling on each other, standing in place until they were out of breath and too tired to go on.

"When Alex was done, Benji's face was cut up pretty good. Alex loaded shots. Dev first. Then Ryan and Clair. He let me dip and dab since it was virgin. During my trip, I remember Alex and Benji were yelling again. Indistinguishable, obviously, but one sentence stood out. 'Was it contagious?' I think it was Alex who asked.

"When Alex and I hooked up for the first time I asked him if he had bugs, and he said no. I was relieved, but I remembered that question. Contagious. I asked the others if they remembered anything from Benji's last day, but they didn't. Lisa thinks it's part of the grieving process, but I don't know. What if Benji had something that passed on? That it infected Alex. Me."

"Did you get tested?"

"Duh! I'm not new. My results came back negative for everything. You have no idea how much it hurts having a Q-Tip shoved in your pee hole."

"Don't tell me Benji got a blood bug."

"I asked Joce about it. She thinks it was bad junk and Benji overdosed. Blames Alex. And me by association. I'm 'protecting him' because I don't remember where Benji went after I shot. When I came to, he was gone. Honest. Three days later I got the letter in the mail and Jocelyn refuses to talk to me. Any of us. Except you, nitwit. I was surprised to find you together in the backyard. She cuts us all out of her life, shows up to the party unannounced, then just leaves when I confront her! What was she even doing?"

"Grieving."

"Grieving?"

"I can talk to Alex for you, if you're alright with it. About Benji's last day and what happened between you at the gristmill."

"I don't know." She started arranging her CD collection in an order I couldn't discern. "I don't want to create a rift between you guys, or the band."

"Probably won't."

She thought it over once everything was ordered to her liking. "Alright. Promise not to argue over it, though."

I agreed.

We spent the rest of the night exploring forums for new music, smoking cancers until moonlight crawled across the stained carpet and reflected off Sav's VCR TV and illuminated the room. She wormed under the covers, me over them to combat the heat and the remnants of sketch sweats. She passed out as *Shape of Punk to Come* finished. I started it over, let it end once more before I decided it was time to leave.

I thought about kissing her forehead goodbye. It felt like the correct thing to do. But I didn't. I snuck out silently instead and made for Church, knowing I was going to use.

Night of the Living Dead.

I rode a rundown bus with shredded pleather seats slit with pocketknives. The bus company had patched and crudely sewn them back together like Frankenstein's dearest. Dusty air pushed around the commuters until an elderly man with puss-swollen ankles, which smelled sickly of infection, joined us. We were overcrowded when we hit the core. Enraged commuters waiting for pickup shook their fists in the summer heat, unaware of the cesspool stank trap barreling down Cannon.

I found solace in solitude. Learned to enjoy my own company while lost in 160 BPM. Presto in hand, I appreciated conversations and daydreams I shared with broken sidewalks, coffee cups, and cancers, thankful for each wad of gum willing to listen to my thoughts. My only worry was getting high. Where when how. I could have called others to join me, as I begged, and wandered, but never did. I enjoyed being a loner. A faded ghost. It was in those moments, tripping along Queen or

Loch where I could hear my own voice over submerged noises of human screams. I miss it.

The bus stopped at the Four Corners—the intersection where the four major banks stood in Green River. I listened to an old cellphone recording of *Traumatize Thy Neighbour* to better learn Dev's drum cues. Distorted static. Alex wailed bedlam. Benji: delirium overdrive.

The bus lurched to a halt. Refused to continue its route imprisoning us in the rancid stench of puss-ankles. The bus monkey honked at the taxi idling in the bus lane. The taxi monkey refused to oblige the painted words on asphalt. A spiderweb of tar intersected the bus lane.

"How are we supposed to pick up clients?" the taxi monkey yelled, leaving his car. He spat at the bus. "Buses steal our business!"

The bus monkey grumbled to himself. "Maudit Anglais."

"Why do you get special treatment?" the taxi monkey said at the driver's window.

I tuned it out. I could fill in the rest of the argument without listening. Insert an excuse about tax payer money as income. Ripping off fuckboys on Hess. End with a rant about rich folk mingling with lower-class populace to promote unity, humble capitalist goats. Get it?

I exited the bus, bored with waiting. The interaction continued without me.

Without being told where to find the others, I headed to Enrico's. Like I possessed a keen sense of sniffing out deplorables. I found them inside, half-stoned sharing a Best Deal. A riot of punks crammed into the modest storefront, dressed to kill and ready to celebrate Benji's would-be birthday. They needed nourishment before our bender. I knew most of them from parties and chatrooms, but I pushed about searching for my pack of vagabonds.

Alex and Dev were talking shit about D.D. Crust closing the laundromat while Ryan ignored Clair natter on about the upcoming Rock Against Racism show at The Cellar. I could tell that Ryan, fed up with hearing another caker's perspective on civil rights, preferred to paint with the swamp of pizza oiled acrylics than pandering to white guilt.

I offered a trade to the tables. A joint for a slice of pie. Alex deemed it acceptable. Told Ryan to pass me one of hers. Hawaiian.

When Sav exited the bathroom, she ran to me for a hug which knocked me off balance and into Ryan who pushed us upright as Dev teased her for getting in the way.

Sav whispered into the small space between our cheeks. "It's worked out. You don't need to do the thing, alright?" I nodded. "Thanks, nitwit." When she pulled away, her eyes were glazed and distant. She adjusted the bandanna tied to her arm to cover the track mark bruise in the crook of her elbow.

"Sit," Alex said, taking his feet off an adjacent chair. He looked thinner, nose larger, and hooked under the chattering lights.

"Slim chance of bumming a drink, huh?" I said joking, avoiding eye contact, and uneasy about taking the seat across from him after learning what Sav told me.

Alex pursed his lips, ignored the question.

Did Benji ever feel this way? Was that why he never told me about this world, and kept me on the fringe?

I didn't want to be his filler. I wanted to be me. What would Benji do in this situation, crack jokes and wear the awkward interactions on his sleeve?

I doubted Sav would have told Alex that she spilled what happened at the gristmill, but I couldn't help but sense the growing tension between Alex and me. I felt insecure about the possibility and guilt of knowing secrets. Personal drama aside, I needed to know what happened to Benji during his last night alive. I had known him the longest, he was my best friend, and I deserved to know. Entitled to it.

I decided to order a drink with electrolytes. Anticipated a burnout after the bender. Dizzy thanked me for paying in dimes and nickels and I tossed a few pennies into his tip jar.

When I had returned, Clair had gone for a piss, so I took her spot to keep my distance from Alex, knowing Dev and Ryan wouldn't mind.

"Uh. Hey," Lisa said, when Sav dragged her to our table.

"Hey stranger," I said with my mouth full.

She was taller than me, pure heroin chic with sharp cheekbones and a tall feisty nose. Her white hair stood out amongst the sea of black everythings. The sun shimmered in the reflection with a high intensity discharge that would halt a charging moose. Despite meeting her again, I had no recollection of her from that night we spent together.

I fuddled through small talk, unable to crack my drink lid with my greasy fingers. I wiped my hands on my shirt, relieved Alex was talking rhythms with Dev as Sav fidgeted in his lap, unaware of my inability to master basic survival skills. Lisa found it precious. Teased me for being too clumsy to function. Sav gave me the thumbs up as Lisa opened my drink for me, then hung off Alex's neck, absorbing his attention so Dev could focus on Ryan.

Our riot of punks shrunk as we headed to Darnley Grove to visit Benji's grave. He would have been nineteen.

We all joked about his life, how Alex dared him to sneak onto a soccer pitch during the house league season and steal him the game ball. The time he and I attacked kids playing street hockey with supersoakers, got caught, and received atomic wedgies. I kept a memory to myself: The time he ran away from home. I found him living in a bush along the forest beside Schwenger High, starving to death because he couldn't catch fish in the puny stream. He'd been trying for two days. I took him to the library to learn how to catch and skin fish, but as I hunted down books, he spent the day on the computer, searching for a youth shelter.

The walk to the cemetery was a special kind of hell. I had Ryan tittering on about nothing in one ear, Lisa hanging off my arm explaining industrial, all while Sav glanced my way with a look that said to take the damn girl's hand.

I know I should have been grateful to garner attention from a girl as decent as Lisa, what with my hobgoblin face and all. But oxytocin deficiency and steady withdrawal have a way of ruining a mood. Sav was with Alex, I reminded myself. Complicated or not. I did feel protective of her but I didn't want to. I refused to be that guy. The 'nice guy' gushing over a girl who wants nothing to do with him, who watches her ogle another dude, and cries while he spite-masturbates his feelings into oblivion. I tried to convince myself I was feeling resentment for not knowing what happened to Benji, that I wasn't obsessing over Sav like a pervy brother.

At the graveyard entrance I gave in. Took Lisa's hand. Surprised to find it warm and soft like early summer sun. She squeezed my hand with satisfaction. I was just happy she shut up. Ryan's words became less and less, until we carved a slice of social setting for ourselves. Sav smiled back at me as she locked arms with Alex, who skulled a mickey of rum before we reached Benji's headstone.

Over the graveyard's hill a decrepit man with a bowler hat sat on his walker, content to read his paper under the orange glow of dusk while a gang of young boys fought with sticks, wielding branches like short swords and shouting commands to storm the forts and unleash hoards.

We halted under the carcass of a maple when we noticed Jocelyn at Benji's grave. She wore her Tim's uniform which was a size too large for her boyish body and had placed her visor on her knee as she ate. Squinted in the sun.

Pad Thai coiled around her reusable chopsticks as she conversed with his headstone. She spoke more than ate, as if the green takeout box existed as a means to keep her hands busy. She laughed suddenly. Leaned back with each titter, covering her mouth with her chopsticks as if to excuse herself.

Then the moment was ruined. She stiffened at us skulking in the shade, waiting for her to leave. She placed a bouquet of wildflowers beside his headstone, gathered her things, and walked the long way around.

"What is with that bitch?" Dev asked, pulling a six-pack from Ryan's backpack.

Sav, red-faced and tight-lipped, stared at the leather peeling from her boots. She was about to call out to Jocelyn, when Alex placed his hand on her back and whispered in ear. She nodded.

Jocelyn deserved better than to be othered by those who used to be her friends. She was good people, kind to me, and Benji adored her. We should have invited her out with us. Benji would have wanted it.

I tried to relax. Told myself to make space. Everyone grieves differently? Right? I promised myself to confront Alex tonight when the party died down, or if he dipped for a piss out of earshot.

Evening crept into night and I lost my confidence. Lisa encouraged me to consume and I obliged, knowing it was easier to melt my brain than expose my feelings. Rationalized to confront Alex when there was less pressure. I felt like a traitor so I consumed more. When the stars broke the clouds, I ran out of vices.

Alex cracked his last 40, slurred a toast. We whooped as he drowned Benji's grave, soaking Jocelyn's flowers. Runoff smothered bruised pedals.

When he finished his speech, we sang Happy Birthday to our dead friend. Dev convulsed on his back, squirming in the grass and tearing at his crotch like a rabid badger goring a finch. He pulled out a baggy and thrust it into the air. Triumph.

"Vi-o-la," Sav said, laughing.

Inside Dev's bag jiggled white beans. He passed one to Ryan, then to Clair as if in afterthought, before taking two for himself and handing Alex the bag. Alex slipped two on his tongue, French kissed Sav hers. Lisa grabbed the bag and did the same to me.

"Here's your ticket to the show," she said, pulling in my neck. "Admit one."

The beans were thimble-sized eggs, flattened and stamped with an eerie smile. As she kissed me, they felt like baby teeth. I dry swallowed, feeling it catch in my throat. I knew better than to cough, and forced it down with a wad of her spit.

Half an hour later the transformation was underway.

The windows of time opened, shattering the otherworld, and I became my best-self and my worst-self at the same moment the same moment the same MOMENT while I conversed with strangers surrounding dead teens and together myselves traversed the cosmos, ever searching, ever screaming and flying and fighting and dying, until the rebirth of my omega-self—my ancient-self—which concluded the download; the inevitable installation required for my broken mass—my broken-self—to rebuild my damaged prison of meat and grief, who in turn ignited my past, present, past-future in an arcane infernal blaze enraptured deep within the recesses of firm ground where the omega-self sowed seeds of revival into the desolate desolate desolate desolate desolate landscape called reality, then, the omega-self lit as a thunderstorm which rained Wotan's wrath as the Dagda wept for my sentience until my omega-self found its place in the universe, a place without hurt where human husks reigned supreme, sanctioned by higher powers who purified in wildernesses of husks until the I and I became the Holy Liar, listening to mortal's prayers seared wroth in my essence and my eldritch omega-self extinguished humankind on this plane of existence before teaching me ancient orisons known only to the trees and sages and whores of long agos, long agos, and it showed me how to solve poverty, puberty, the troubles of the external and the recesses of one's structural and singular mind, where soon after, the omega-self's immran bestowed upon me, you, and yours and pleaded with the chill crawling your spine as these words phased from my past to your future into being then the omega-self showed me the company it kept; a pack of shadow-beings purged from outer darkness and plunged into the divergence of Armageddon, they liberated me from my cage of meat and sinew and sucked my ethereal soul into infinity, where I watched Terra burn as Tannhäuser sealed the gate from the skies, shaped as a one-eyed raven until the Venusian chorus crescendo carried me back to the otherworld. She begged me to bring the Thall, and then:

"Listen."

"He's mashed."

Ride's over, please remember to collect your belongings and enjoy the rest of your stay.

I grunted. Struggled to lift my head.

"You've been drooling on yourself."

"For like an hour."

Alex?

My brain drifted. Blinked like a flipbook. The world adjusted from my incursion.

"Come on, nitwit."
"Everyone's fucked off."
"Want to get left?"
"Help me drag him to the cab."
Lisa.
"Everyone grab a limb."

The room where I regained consciousness was full of alternative stuffed animals. No heart-shaped noses, or clean seams. Bloodied maws. Crude stitching and patchwork skin grafts. Care Bears stuffed through a teeth machine after a cage match. Whoever sold these stuffed abominations was a sick, rich bastard. I tried to ignore my demented surroundings and drifted back into unconsciousness.

The clitch clitch clitch of Hades the rat gnawing her fluid tube stirred me into a rage. I got up.

The bathroom was a cramped red and gold wallpapered closet. Knees wedged between sink and bowl. Head thumping. Forced to watch myself defecate in the mirror. Pants warming ankles until the world stopped spinning.

I wore the same clothes as the night before, my Joe Strummer shirt stretched at the neck and stained. Sweat. Whiskey. Grass. Hair flat and crusty where glue flaked. I looked like I exploded. Claw marks carved along my neck and back and face. Badgers. I lost a fist fight with a gang of rowdy badgers.

I rested my cut chin on the lip of the sink and puked. It trickled out in runny swabs. I cleaned myself as best as I could, used my finger as a toothbrush. Gagged on the off-white, gritty, tasteless, baking powder reacting on my crooked cancer-stained chiclets. I wished I could puke again.

After mustering the courage to shuffle back to the Care Bear hell pit, I found that Lisa had woken. She looked how I felt. Knackered. Deflated. Ghoulish. I bet those badgers got her too. Her hair had reverted to its natural wavy mess during the night, her makeup peeled off her face and onto the pillow.

Relief washed over me when I pulled back the covers. She too wore the same outfit from the night before.

"How was the ride?" she asked, as I curled into a ball.

"This your place?"

"I was worried you'd choke on your puke."

"Romantic."

"You owe me," she said, digging through the gored bodies of stuffed monsters for her glasses. Wireframe. Bent. Too large for her thin nose.

An awkward tension experienced by strangers in an intimate place crept over us and for the next hour or so we stared at her ceiling fan whirling above us in a pleasant, and much desired, spiral. Unlike the others, her bedroom walls were barren of punk aesthetics. Instead she had dance trophies, volleyball medals, and academic certificates with ribbons painted with high math marks and scientific achievement awards.

I built shapes and faces in the popcorn ceiling, indifferent to her double life as hellraiser and cherub, as the sketching settled in.

"Do you remember anything from last night?"

"Some."

She bit her lip. "You told me I was an angel." She curled into my side, her touch smouldering as my body tried to sweat out the toxins from last night's trip. "It was the most precious thing anyone has ever said."

"Oh." I failed to will the memory, but the slices I recalled were like watching a film through wax paper. "It's because of your hair. No one has white hair."

"You always go on about it." She combed through the curls resting on her clavicle piercings. "You're a good kisser. Like you're trying."

She held my hand under the blanket. I accepted it, despite how sweaty it made me. Too fried to resist.

"We didn't come back and, well, you know?" I asked a bit too seriously.

She rolled over top of me, pressed her flat chest into mine. "Nope." She giggled at my relief and her abs grinded into my ribs as she dug through her purse.

I feared that in my wasted state I would have forgotten a rubber.

"I'd rather you remember it. Boys like to brag, right?" She leaned farther, delicately placed her hand on my thigh to steady herself from falling off the twin-sized mattress. My eyes found the dimples on her lower back, as if calling for my fingers to slide over them and use them to pull her into me. She swung back into bed with a pair of cancers. We lit up.

"We could, though. If you wanted." She traced my jawline with a finger.

"I'm still a little fried."

But as we killed our cancers, her petting became more, my sketching dulled enough for blood to venture into my pants and we undressed under the covers. Her nipples were dark and soft, large compared to her breast size and stiffened when I inserted my finger into her vagina. I tongued them. She went down on me, and I on her. My nose rested on the thin strip of hair that led to her clit. She moaned. She pulled me to her, bit my nipple so hard it hurt, she mistook my pain for pleasure and tried to remove chunks of my flesh for her own enjoyment.

We did this for half an hour before I softened and she bit harder so I'd grow harder. But the best my little guy could do was a soggy defrosted bratwurst. In the end I came. I held her hair, and released into her mouth, she leaned into it. Choked herself for my pleasure.

When she came up she kissed me long and deep and I swear she only came because she enjoyed the thought of making me taste my load.

"That's two you owe me," she said, cleaning her mess.

"Gimme a minute," I said, knowing I had nothing to offer, "then we can go for real."

"My parents will be back from the cottage by 6. Will Molly help inspire you?"

My heart skipped a beat, at the prospect of screwing on the love drug. I wanted to prove my unenthusiasm was the burnout's fault.

"Does a bear shit in the woods?"

The Fly.

I waited for the bus at Chegwin Plaza, Green River's modest strip mall, promising myself I wouldn't get high today. Cancers only. My tolerance had grown and I found my taste too expensive for my means. I chainsmoked to cope with the fading shakes and invented tasks to keep me away from Church. Besides, I really did need new strings for my guitar. Right?

I hacked a lung. Spat tar at the ruddy brick wall in the shadow of oxidized copper roofing.

Hundreds of these strip malls littered the Great Ontario Horseshoe for normals to lurk and avoid nobodies like me in wide sweeps as they hunted for discounts to spite the big boxes. The great lie Suburban Joe tells himself: threads imported from Europe to Ma and Pa shops, and the yellow-tag sales of big box stores, and dirt malls for the poors, are not created equal. Fact: they contain the same items—be it books, clothes, dollar mart cheese, local produce, knickknacks, etc. The horrible truth is they all come from the same sweatshops and slave fields. No exceptions. From dirty commies to humble capitalists. Insert your own joke about compliance and gentrification. Inspire change within your life and be proactive, my dude.

I stifled my coughing fit and returned to the book I stole from the library. Ice. Anna Kavan. The pages burned my soapstone retinas, reflected and magnified the sun's fury and disoriented me like an orgy of lesbian lizards from Canada's toilet.

After checking the schedule, and learning the bus was over 40 minutes late, I left the crowd of normals and weekend shoppers for the shade of a forgotten relic next to the bus shelter. The pillaged telephone booth's cracked receiver and shell were bombarded with Peanut's tags. The crusty rings of dirt reeked of failed teenaged dreams.

The sun stretched across the sky and I shifted with the shadow, fighting for cover, until it parted from the curb. I crouched on the sidewalk over my book, wondering if Glass Girl would ever escape the psychotic Warden and the addicted Man. My hobgoblin shadow served to blot out the sun burning my neck. Back cramp. Knees. Pins and needles. I stood. Went back to squinting.

My Discman's batteries shimmied out when I adjusted. I cursed and pushed them back in, wishing Alex had offered duct tape and not painter's tape. Fucking cops. Screwing me over months later.

A Boomer approached me, walked to my side of the telephone booth as if to distance himself from the meth head busking for change between the underground Lasermania and Beer Store. Boomer wore a suit jacket and tie and had the air of the type of normal who earnestly believed giving the impression of 'respectable professional' was of the utmost importance. Not happiness.

The type of dolt who voted to end forests, kill single mothers, usurp working-class, and comfortably drop slurs in casual conversation, because equality meant sharing the ability to use the same vocabulary, but scorned slang for butchering his caker language. I was daydreaming about him snapping pictures of teens at the beach when he mumbled something at me.

I thumbed my volume dial.

He refused the hint. Leaned in. Spoke louder. Gestured to the busker.

The bass of his voice was audible over my static mix. I ignored. He persisted.

When I tried to crank the volume, my batteries popped out. I wrenched off my headphones and was about to cuss him out when he beat my punch.

"Howdy partner," he said.

You hear that. We're partners.

"Eh?"

"Lovely day," he said, looking about the packed parking lot for something 'lovely' to point at.

I think what he meant to say was he enjoyed the blinding death star overhead scorching the earth as the delightful and fleeting weeks of summer delivered nostalgic memories of his youth. What I heard was, 'I'm a cowboy looking to saddle up with a bus buddy to ranch longhorns.'

"Alright," I said, popping in my batteries and returning my headphones.

He spoke again.

"What?" I asked, sounding irater than intended, thinking he'd have the social wherewithal to know when to piss off.

"That's an interesting getup you have on. Whacky, huh?"

Interesting? Getup? Whacky?

I returned to my music, punched shuffle, as Silverstein's melodic sorrow drowned out his noise. Lisa had insisted I give them a shot so I added them to a burnt disc. I wished they were heavier, 'whackier,' and more fitting to sneer at the window licking boomer. A blitzkrieg of distortion. I dressed this way to be unapproachable. Remember it.

I hated how much the boomer reminded me of dinner with my parents. Disinterested silence, prodding soggy carrots, another black eye reflected off a dirty glass.

I shifted to the other side of the telephone booth. Took my storm clouds with me and lit a cancer, blew smog his way. He backed off and I wanted to call out to him, tease him for fearing long-term effects he would never live to see.

When the bus came, I let Boomer enter before me, taking note of where not to sit. The last thing I wanted was a bus buddy—sorry, partner—to torture me, make my twenty-minute ride feel like twenty hours.

I lowered the volume on my Discman, and thanked the bus monkey for a transfer.

Bus etiquette to be followed by all meat sacks are as follows: Never sit beside a stranger if there are empty seats, sit between one person instead of two, allow the handy-capable—mothers count as disabled, Stacey—to sit, fill the vehicle back to front to pack in as many bodies as physically possible, never leave bags on seats when the bus is full. Lastly, always hold on to the holy-shit handles when standing. Bus surfers suck.

I mention this because when Boomer ignored the unwritten codex of public transit, and clogged the side door instead of finding a seat, I panicked. I had to choose between a normal sweating butter, and a street person. A fare hopper, no doubt. A perpetual shell of human living their best life on the road, dodging police and malevolent teens, with nowhere to go, dreaming for a safe place to rest.

I hated my choices, but I couldn't stand next to my partner. Sure as shit I'd be forced into another riveting conversation, lulled into kinship as his perpetual black-hole voice sucked me into meeting him again tomorrow, become on a first name basis, swap life stories, impart knowledge he wish he had at my age, go for coffee, hold deep life chats, get sponsored for the local Quitters Anonymous and discuss woke gays infiltrating the Jews in Hollywood or someshit, meet his darling daughter with her designer dog and pedigree education at his cult's fair day, and come over for national indigenous rape day and nut in her butt because she only spreads for Jesus, damnit!

Jocelyn waved to me from the upper steps. Shifted her shoulder bag on her lap and scooted over. I practically ran to her.

In unison we removed our music and I thanked her.

"Let's be honest," she said, pointing at a sliver of seating beside the heifer and hobo, "you're not that skinny."

I laughed a little too hard and a mother behind us, squirming son in her arms, scolded.

Jocelyn ignored her.

"You know, if we keep meeting like this, people are going to start talking."

"Oh, yeah?"

"You stalked me by the lake, graveyard, and now on a crowded bus. You're getting bolder. I should probably flee. You could be a 'stranger danger.'"

"You could always pull the panic lever, tuck and roll."

"Maybe once we're on the escarpment," she said, "I think I could totally out roll you, lose you in the woods. Who knows, maybe it'll take me where I'm going."

"Where's that?"

She scratched the back of her head, exposing her ear. A pearl stud rested in the crook of her lobe. "Osler's."

I knew the art supply store well. It was where Benji and I bought spray paint to tag trails in Green River with DOOM. We used to laugh at all the wannabe Alex Pardees and Bankseys from the university that cycled through every year before they dropped out.

"They're expensive," she said, clearing her throat, "but worth it compared to the art surplus up the mountain. Where are you headed?"

To be alone.

"Chanson's."

"That's the music store on West Ave, right? Pink and green building that looks like a sex pervert gloryhole with the Quebecer."

"Mr. Roseaux. He gives me a deal."

"Well, his store looks like Disney's opium trip."

Jocelyn uncomfortably rolled the sleeves of her baggy shirt, exposing spotted freckles under her ginger hairs. I caught a quick whiff of mango and flowers. It was my turn to clear my throat.

"So he's got the mad hook ups?" she said awkwardly.

"Fo sho. Homes?" I said, just as awkward.

She forced a smile, and unease overtook me. I replayed the scene in my head, feeling like a mouthbreather. But as the bus shifted gears onto Main, I realized she too must be just as embarrassed. I felt better knowing I wasn't alone. Convinced myself she must be replaying our idiocy in her own mind as she stared out the window at the self-defeating traffic lines. We were strangers after all. Nothing in common but a dead teenager who lived briefly in our hearts.

I found myself nervously purging Lisa's bombardment of texts, before returning my phone to my pocket. Silent mode. And just like that, my anxiety bled away as we crossed Colborne.

We sat in a strange, but comfortable silence for the duration of the trip. Neither of us returned to our headphones to exclude the other from our shared silence. It was as if by doing so we would shun the other, cease our newfound connection. She leaned her head against the window, watched cars speed past. Her eyes fluttering lazily like she was following an invisible man bounding over the sidewalk.

She cleared her throat and pulled the yellow cord. Speakers pinged, but the 'Next Stop' light remained unlit. Apparently bulbs aren't in the city's budget.

I stood to let her pass.

"Chanson's is only a block and a half from Osler's," she said, swinging her bag past me. "Want to get off and head over together? I'll only be a minute."

I almost said no.

Osler's Art Supplies shared a lot with a gas station and was larger than it appeared on the outside. The building was hollowed out, save for cream support beams which fell victim to stock photo madness. The same horrid couple butchering a wedding cake pointed their icing-soaked cleaver at art snobs. Eyes screaming 'Isn't our vocation wonderful?' in wallet, diploma, and poster size.

Jocelyn ittied around the store, zigging and zagging through aisles as I lingered behind, fussing with my shirt, unsure why it felt like fibreglass slivers scratching my skin. I tried not to itch. Busied my hands with looking over premade ceramics, pens, canvases, and felt pads. I convinced myself I was allergic to ragweed. They call this denial.

"Seven types of purple?" I said, trying to itch my eyes with the backs of my hand. "I can barely name three. This is too much passion for one colour."

"Much to learn, you have, young padawan," Jocelyn said in her worst Yoda voice.

She pointed to the rows of white acrylics. I was levelled. Dumbfounded. She found me dumb. As I looked at the 30 shades of white, it finally made sense why they call them art snobs. I'd feel an air of superiority if I knew the differences between snowflake, salt, and old lace.

The dreaded clerk smelled of kush and dandelions and made small talk with Jocelyn who happily talked about the latest addition to her portfolio. I had nothing to offer and found myself wandering, searching for people to watch when I saw a sale on silkscreen kits. DIY graphic tees.

"They work, you know," Jocelyn said, tucking her paint into her satchel. "He had me up all night during the last Rock Against Racism fundraiser making a run for Sick Sad World."

I nodded, unsure what to say.

I remembered when they made them. They were so proud of the crooked white logos on black tees. Off-centre illuminati eyes. Tilted lines. I still have mine.

She smiled sadly at the memory and I held the door for her. We cut through a cramped alley at Hishabishion where Provo joins Razum and reached Chanson's before the traffic lights turned. Jocelyn said Benji had shown her the shortcut. She called him an atlas of the obscure.

It was surprisingly clean compared to the one by The Cellar, where we drank and consumed before shows. The doors here weren't boarded, and it lacked the sheen of broken glass. Instead, eloquent graffiti draped over spalled bricks and sunken mortar. I spied for Peanut's tag. It was faded under murals of skunks with poisoned witch's brews next to pop culture cartoons. Jocelyn pointed at a fire escape where Daphne Blake from Scooby Doo cried off her makeup as she clawed at the jaw trap from Saw, struggling to find the lock. My favourite was Harper in drag.

Mr. Roseaux greeted us with a sad smoky smile when the doorbell chimed. His curt accent chopped Anglophone and Quebecer into a nuanced blend of culture war. A drowning pool of red wine with cigar boogieboards bobbing in ripples.

While I explored the store, Jocelyn followed behind me, peeking at price tags and nodding in time with the swing soundtrack. She mentioned, as casually as she could, how her cousin saw me play at the Schwenger High Coffee House. I told her it must have been someone who looked like me. She made a face and said her cousin recognized me from Benji's profile pic. When she asked how it went, I pretended to pick loose hairs from my shirt and shrugged. She asked if I kept it from the others and when I said that I had, she dropped the topic. Giving me the space and letting me keep the memory for myself. I thanked her. I meant it.

"I felt naked," I said, hoisting up a custom Charvette with toggle switches and LEDs. The guitar felt too small compared to my Goden. "Like everyone watching could see parts of my soul spill into the room."

She laughed. "A little melodramatic."

I told her she was probably right.

I sifted through the racks of strings until I found the thickest gauge, hoping to sound as chunky as possible, and had Mr. Roseaux ring them up.

"Hostie!" the old man said, choking. "He is thick, my heart. Take for help." His shaking hand counted out four dour picks. They were three times thicker than the alien head I had at Church. "The thins have sans balls for these string. Those fingers are soft, like ta petite amante. Take on moi."

I thanked him and tried to hide my blushing face from Jocelyn. Thankfully she was oblivious, busily adoring the line of ukuleles nestled beside the fiddles. I thought about making an excuse to keep hanging out with her, invent a new task to keep me out of Skunktown and fulfil my promise of single day sobriety, but I couldn't think of one in the seven paces it took me to reach her.

I cleared my throat, hoping a solid lie would come to me in the moment.

"It's still early," she said, as if she knew my struggle. "Wanna grab a coffee?"

When I had agreed to drink, I thought she meant something cheap like Tim's where she could score a discount. She chose Saetia. Fucking Saetia. Overpriced craft beers with ethically sourced monkey dung beans and aesthetic finger foods for bloggers. Sorry. It's artisan.

I audibly gulped when we entered. A shockwave of shoegaze droning about love lost but not forgotten hit me, and I thanked the gods of punk that it was at least empty and only the till monkey with spacers and a floral tramp stamp witnessed my disdain as I counted out the last of my panhandling haul, hoping for enough coins to trick her into believing I belonged here. I ordered a 4$ lemon square. The cheapest thing for the brokest kid.

Jocelyn found us a table next to a bricked wall splitting Saetia from the shawarma joint next door. The hardwood furnishings bordered antique and the varnished stage was stabbed in a hovel by the bay windows.

We chatted about music, films, and the bad art collection circling the walls. Jocelyn couldn't decide if it was intentional irony, or if it was hip to have poor taste.

After a smoke on the patio, she ordered me a green tea, despite my protests. I had no way of paying. She insisted, offering to pay because 'It will change your life.' It tasted like pleasant dirt. Very her. She laughed and said I needed to get out more. I agreed.

We talked about the future as tea leaves stained our mugs. The topic was alien to me, a vagrant who lived day to day, never seeing farther than a month at best. She expressed her need to create more art, plans for her portfolio, which schools she had to choose between, unsure where she wanted to run away to. I told her about the upcoming show at The Cellar and she said she would try to get the night off from work. We both knew she wouldn't.

The sun lazed in the window and a top-heavy waitress with fine hair and black glasses opened the bay window doors behind the stage, flooding the interior with the distant hum of traffic. Saetia soon filled with bohemian bodies. An 18-litre water jug circulated for donations, which I aptly ignored.

The mood changed when the bar opened. Jocelyn ordered a round, I did too—after excusing myself for the bathroom and selling my last gram for a tenner to a lanky dude with an emo mullet. When I returned to Jocelyn I realized I didn't have a fake and ordered a virgin blowjob. I played it off as a joke, which she fell for. Howling at the sincerity of my choice. She convinced me to do a shot with her and the top-heavy waitress who chose a Popped Cherry. Har. Har. The waitress got friendlier the more patrons that stuffed inside, flirted with Jocelyn and I every chance she got. Jocelyn, cheeks flushed, became overgenerous with the tips. I wore my nicest smile, pained though it was, and thankful not to be carded.

Our drinks came in chilled mason jars. Jocelyn's beer was a dark pit. She offered me a sip and I found it thick and sweet and far better than the garbage juice scraped from the bottom of the barrel I was used to drinking at Church.

I lapped my dainty cocktail, disgusted with myself, but before I could down it, Jocelyn waved down the flirtatious waitress and ordered us another proper round. Bent my rubber elbow. We picked the same craft lager. When they came, the house lights dimmed and a man introduced himself as a master of ceremonies.

Enter the pseudo-intellectual poser, behold the power of his microphone holding hand. Mighty be thy grip!

Either the brew in my blood, or the way Jocelyn's eyes lit up with enchantment when the first performer entered the stage, held my snarky comments. If it was Sav beside me, we would have heckled him. Torn him asunder for his choice in pants and father's poon-stache.

By the third act, I had loosened up enough to enjoy myself. I do not remember where the nameless poet with a nondescript loose v-cut shirt said he came from, but I adored his refusal to speak into the microphone. Quietly introducing himself and his piece to the sidewalk and not the onlookers in Saetia.

He dove into his poem, shouting carefully chosen words to the hushed room and crowded passersby about raven dreams clawing his insides, devastation on the day he realized his father was not a superhero and simply a man, and passions lived in mental institutions.

I clung to each word. Enthralled by his pain. Conviction. His ethereal cries. Therapy of woven words. Saetia grew dark when he left the stage. Indifferent to the applause, he bowed to the streets and not to us. Then sat at the bar. Alone. He cured himself by wearing his hurt and scrawled in a tattered notebook with taped pictures of a ghostly looking child.

He was beautiful. Rembrandt. London Particular. Wagner on Bits of Paper. Clockwork Orange with an Against Me! tracklist. Punk at the peak of the movement. I needed more.

We stayed until the house lights came up.

"Well," Jocelyn said as we stumbled to the bus terminal, "what'd you think?"

"It was another world," I said, slurring.

"I lied to you. Sort of."

"Wench!"

"I planned on going solo to the slam. My friend, Carmen, the cute waitress with the blonde hair, told me about it. I figured if I asked you after the music store, you would have rejected it. 'It's not punk enough,' or some shit."

"You're right, my dude. There was a noticeable absence of doom."

She made a crude gesture with her hands.

"You should lie to me more often."

She squeezed past me and into the bus shelter. Her breath a warm alcoholic glow.

"I knew it! You're not the arrogant loner you pretend to be. You know a lot of those people in there were survivors."

"Of what, terrible fashion blogs?"

"Last gen punks," she said, lighting her cancer. "Where do you think they end up? They grow out of gutters and bloom into poets, activists, who push the revolution dream."

I sensed it. The ruddy complexion sneaking over her face, the dampness of her eyes. Words failed me. I vomited idiocy.

"I get it. This therapy of yours. 'Everything is mirrors.' Reflections of former lives and we are all hollow marionettes dancing and singing lies through leaks until we believe them." She tried to stop me, but I was too drunk to end my rambling. "Nonono. I get it. Honest. You stick to public places when you feel alone so you don't feel so alone. But you cannot hang on like this. He died, Joce, these things suck ass, but they happen. No one saw it coming. No one could have prevented it."

"What's wrong with you?" She threw her cancer at the ground.

"I'm not Benji."

Those words were my noose.

She raised her hand to slap me. I flinched. Touching my warm cheek, I rubbed her ghost hand, wishing she had struck me. The absence of violence stung like hell. Worse than the beating my father gave me when he found my stash, and kicked me to the curb for dropping out.

She stormed off into the night, alone, leaving me in the dank bus shelter, rain stirring in the blackness above. I pulled out my Discman only to find the batteries had died. I whipped it at my feet, smashing it beside her cancer, and stomped on it with Lisa's music still inside, watching my feral face sneer up at me in the shattered disc. I tried to hold back my tears as the cancer's ember faded out.

Salò.

Condor Tongue and Laughing Man traded positions on stage as we traded pills in the cramped bathroom of The Cellar. Each surface, save for the shit-stained toilets, was littered with band stickers, tags, blood and bile. Punk aesthetic. No dividers for stalls or urinals. Unisex. Progressive because the owners couldn't be bothered to rough in another bathroom for sex segregation.

I knelt to the porcelain throne on the right, thankful for the temperance of futures where I'd forget what a fuck up I had become. Benji's voice. Jocelyn's disappointment. Welts and bruises from parental disgust.

A paste of burnt umber grimed the bowl with a rusty tampon protruding like a perfectly rolled cancer. No. The smell did not bother me.

I unwrapped my offering, aware of the line to use stretching behind me. The blue bill holding the audacious and calcareous kit-kat had dampened from my sweaty palms. Bone dry powder and fine for hoovering. Jubilance filled my lungs and spun my mind as I reeled from the nose burn.

Business completed, I returned to the show, waiting for the kat's full purr, and gazed deep into the red velvet curtains backdropping the stage as they stretched further and further into the black walls with black scars like blackholes. The Cellar's invisible event horizon, stars of dust wished past my outstretched—

Duck pushed past me to avoid Dev, who looked almost unrecognizable now that he had shaved his mohawk. He wore a Baphomet ballcap with studs to hide his insecurity. I shambled past him and Ryan as they laughed about Clair's store-bought outfit. Gatekeeping. Green Day. Sellouts. Traitors. I had no opinion of *American Idiot*. Numb indifference equates bliss.

I tripped over my feet, as Laughing Man raged, ate the floor and felt nothing but the fascination for the woodgrain stage worn past its varnish, studying aeons of pits until I was yanked to my feet, unaware of my busted lip. I smiled at dozens of fist-sized holes punched through the ceiling. During *Break Stuff* Dev drove his heel through the drywall as Philip hoisted me up to crowd surf. Alex set fire to the bathroom. Fire marshal. Police. No witnesses came forward.

I blinked—

and found myself in a circle pit, loose necked and discombobulated. Used a headbanger for support as Punks Clever Punks finished their set. Royal Mount. Two-step during the bridge. Separatist lyrics exploded on foreign ears. Savage, rusty, true. I relished it. The song violently-

Another blink—

and I was outside, failing at lighting a cancer. The thin tube escaped my fingers, rolled to the ground. I saved it from the gutter, marveling at the pink and green banner hung above the scarred door of The Cellar: Rock Against Racism. I couldn't remember how I got here.

"Oi." Alex flipped his thick overgrown shag out of his eyes. Sav on his arm, Dev beside them. He asked if I wanted to get low.

"Halfway there."

I struggled to teach my lighter to spark.

"Ryan's scoring us some. You in?"

"Shoot? Here?"

"We're more discreet than that!" Sav said, sneering.

Her teeth yellow like daisies' anthers. Her hair had faded green and greasy. I wanted to pet it. Feel the texture. I wondered if she smelled like kelp. Kelp. Kay-help.

"It's a pill, nitwit."

I saw my desire in the light reflecting in Sav's oceano hair. Ghost touch of the comet. Climb my arm and into my essence. Contact explosions during breach. The atmosphere of my soul was a glow cloud. I wanted to fill my spirit with—

Time skipped. The kat was doing its job. The rosewood bricks and peeling paint should have been vacant. Prearranged, Alex told us. The boneheads put out a notice to clear out for Rock Against Racism. But inside our alley stood two silhouettes. Three if you counted Ryan's pathetic mass curled into a ball. Her dark skin and curly blue hair glowed under the streetlight like an underwater hydrogen bo–

bruises covered her face and arms darker shades of brown. The man above her folded something into his pocket.

Years later I learned his name was Rexington Windsor. Rex wore a crisp plaid buttondown and spotless jeans. Pant legs rolled to expose steel toes. White laces. Just like him. Beside Rex chuckled his girl, Annabelle. Straw hair curtained her winged eyes. Baggy frilled dress and laced lace laced lacey lace panzer tank. I wanted to flick her sausage neck rolls but Sav—

"Place is ours tonight."

Alex's voice cut the cloud of Jane's breath between the alley walls. "What'd you do to Ryan?"

"Just having a chat, brother," Rex said, thumbs hooked through red suspenders.

That's what it's called. A chat. Brute force and ignorance. It's Ryan's fault she evolved to produce eumelanin. Am I Melony?

"We spoke with Nazi Ross and he cleared it," said Alex, grabbing Dev's shoulder, grimacing about a truce. Truths? My pants felt too large, and I tried to show Sav, but she walked towards Alex. I called my chin rude.

"Rule of Three," Sav slurred.

In my wasted state I remembered the diplomatic discourse created for these situations. It meant if hostilities arose on neutral ground the offending party, in this case Rex and Annabelle, had to answer three questions to justify their trespassing. If any of the answers were deemed suitable the offenders could pass in peace. Waiting for the bus, picking up, dealing, out of towners. Vibe.

Rex spat a brown glob of chew at Sav's feet.

"Don't," I said to both Rex's sneering at me. I blinked until there was only one.

"Fine. I'll play." Rex filled his mouth with more bacon flavoured chew.

"Why'd you come to our show?" Alex asked. "We had a deal."

"If it ain't white, it ain't right."

"Rejected," Dev said, spitting.

"Rejected," Alex said, pacing the alley, separating Rex from the other exit.

A mass of punks congregated. Lisa among them. Her Ice Queen hair flowing like a halo around mohawks, liberty spikes, and rainbow shags. I pet the sparkling locks, rubbing her scalp, as glitter flickerererered in the streetlight. I leaned against the wall opposite of Rex. Here, but not here as Clair bumped past me, sent me reeling into mortar. Dev ignored her tears when she reached out to him. He slapped her away like a rock tingler. Leggy buzzers.

Time skipped.

"A suggestion, boney," Sav said, pointing her finger. "Watch your mouth."

"You're so savage, little bird," Annabelle said.

Sav flushed with rage. I wanted to touch it, wondered how warm it would feel next to my own. I abandoned Lisa. "Keep your hometown ideals to yourself, hick. You get it, boney?"

"Where I'm from fags rule the day and nigs rule the night. If you're straight and white, you're the minority. Outbred by libtards. I get slammed for my skin, so fair is fair. Fuck Ross."

Alex and Dev stalked through the ever-growing mass of bodies that left the show to watch the spectacle unfold. Virus strains circulating masses, restless to infect hosts, crowd killers itching for the wall of death. I felt the need to tell Sav how pretty she looked arguing with white trash pieces of shit. Lisa pulled me away from the mob, tried to make me twiddle her hair again. I became fascinated with my fly.

"This isn't a fucking game, you waste of meat." Sav said calmly. "Get out of our alley."

"Choke on a dick you junkie cunt."

Sav stepped forward to swing, but I grabbed her wrist. Delighted how I could feel the pressure of her muscles resisting, but not the softness of her skin. I wanted to tell everyone to hug it out.

"Brother," Rex said, "you can't allow your woman to disrespect a man like this."

The kat I swallowed dug in her claws. My vision jerked like a rowboat lost in the expanse of an oceanic storm. Capsize in silence.

"Brother? I'm not your brother," I said into my chest as the riot of punks surrounding us chattered and spat and swore, calling for blood. "Fuckin. Your heritage. My dude. Listen. Munge cake. Pride? Bah. We're all human beeaanss. Start acting like. Yup?"

He met my words with silence, but not compliance.

"You don't talk to my man like that," Annabelle shouted, wagging her finger like I was a child. I fought back a laugh, unsure how she misunderstood my monologue of peace and acceptance. Love was so clearly needed.

Sav stepped between us and began to fix her nautical hair while intently looking just above Rex's eye.

"What are you doing?" He stepped back.

"Using your bald head as a mirror so I can look hot while I kick your ass."

Rex threw his fist into Sav's stomach. Knuckles wrapped around a copper band, above each finger hole were studded pyramids. He pulled his fist back to bury another punch in Sav's ribs. Alex soared in like a demon, fist guiding his way. A lighthouse pleading violence ashore. He purged Rex's face. An audible snap. Lisa screamed.

Chaos ensued and I'd be a liar if I said I didn't join in. I'd be a liar if I said I didn't enjoy it. In the end, we took turns holding, punching, kicking, and thrashing Rex. Two girls, Zoe and Ruin, took care of Annabelle while Sav fought for breath. They gave Annabelle matching raccoon eyes and chipped teeth, before they carried Sav and Ryan from the tempest.

I climaxed. K-hole. Peepshow peering through a tube of wrapping paper while playing pirates with Benji and noticing a horny housewife bent over her kitchen sink - world - bundled - red curtain - blood swimming over my eyes. I loved how I felt none of the blows cutting my brow as - fend us off.

Tunnel vision narrowed on Rex's broken nose, shattered cheek, pressing to the crimson brick wall spattered with his skin and teeth as Dev smashed smashed smashed his skull against it.

I let go.

Threw up.

The brawl continued onto the street and Dev and Alex's fists became hate incarnate as they hurled them into Rex's limp and mangled body.

Three dark skinned men with beards and vibrant headwraps tried to pull Alex and Dev off their victim.

A thick accent: "Let him go. Please."

Alex snarled. "He's a bonehead!"

Confused, the man's grip loosened around Alex's studded jacket.

"He hates you because of your skin," I said, trying to right myself on the sidewalk as the world swam through me. Bile seethed between my teeth.

The beards talked to themselves in a magical tongue that reminded me of warm summers at the strawberry farm before my father lost his job.

"We didn't see anything," one said, reluctantly and in poor English. "We will pray for you."

Alex and Dev continued the beating.

As Rex's face melted to pulp I could hear the headliner from The Cellar play in the distance. Their steady do-do-kah pounded my ears, timed perfectly with Alex's fists.

I puked again before time—

The Tingler.

It's getting worse in steady increments, I said to my other self in the mirror. Gutted with a crowbar. Oldboy post-sedation. A rotten pumpkin demolished by a crew of malicious worm babies wriggling from impossibly tiny holes, confounding my flesh as they eeked out towards the flickering vanity bulb. Abroad in an emptied skull, gnawing my eardrums. Scream. Laugh. Relish my pain. Silencing their cries was all I could-

I rummaged through the medicine cabinet. Hoped to find anything to send me away from the premature crash. Morphine, or oxy, or whatever the hell I consumed today.

I chewed a handful of T3s, chased them with a mix of other pills I couldn't pronounce. I popped a morning after pill. Would it even do anything? I didn't care. I needed to stop the hurt. Ride the wave until I forgot my hobgoblin hairlip. Name.

I returned to the party, unable to recognize the apartment. White walls tried to murder me. If heaven is clouded in foam I want nothing to do with it. I closed my eyes, traced floorboards until I found a couch to die on.

Strangers surrounded me with slow, distorted voices from another world. Hel bled into Midgard during Samhain. Torture mortals.

I saw a rat boy snorting blow with a mantis man while a ghost girl flirted with Chloe while a lighthouse burned in the tempest's wroth. Blue butterflies melted into a horned raven as a doe cried. I don't belong here, the doe wept a chorus of sorrowful chords, and I agreed, wishing for another way as we drifted towards ashen skies of Mars, Argonauts rowing through galactic hurricanes, I prayed for peace, asked her for forgiveness because I forsook Arielle before losing consciousness, before she could guide me through the storm. I cried as the horned raven watched Prospera burn.

I was higher than Mars' stratosphere and could hear and feel every individual blood cell pump through my body and taste the sharp tartness of bile and the rubber chicken blend of gut rot pressed into prepackaged McNuggs. Terrified and uncontrolled, I laughed. Manic. Spry.

Mars' population consisted of myself and a Serb with dreads who screamed at a dark eyed Croat. No English, I remember thinking—Not that I was in any condition to comprehend what language was.

The Serb pressed his foot through a stone wall like walking through mist. Thigh deep. Trackpants coated in gypsum. Toe wriggling around the causeway. He tried to wrench himself free but landed on his neck. The Croat guffawed, rammed his face into the wall, splitting the stone and his brow.

They spent the next several minutes leveling ramparts

with chests, elbows, and knees. I begged them to stop before Mars collapsed, but my cries were drowned by a gaggle of Slavs cheering them on until a scrawny wet rat of a kid in a blue do-rag became a human slingshot. They catapulted Rat Boy into the wall. He pulverized it, revealing a mechanical cave in blistering heat. He racked his shoulder against a stud and raised his dislocated arm with his good one. They cheered.

I blinked and lay on an oblong chessboard. The only pawn. Peanut was next to me, guffawing like a Viking horse farmer. His beard shaved to a stubble. He dragged me onto a balcony overlooking a parking lot and asked me to hold his legs while he stood on a railing. I complied, hugging his knees tenderly as he tagged the adjacent brick wall, which stalled our orbit like an asteroid belt, with wide sweeps of his spray can. The mist drifted in pink speckling space clouds as Peanut cursed at the distance between Mars and—

We ran as the Space Force chased us through Mons. We scattered. Docking bays. Mineshafts. Alien farm market, save us from flurries of flashing lights, and stampeding space cadets surrounded us. We were being boarded. Surrender or flee, I didn't know, but then the Croat with a raven beak pulled me from the docking bay. He spoke with Alex's cruel and calm voice, told me jump from our flaming escape with him.

When I asked him about Peanut, he told me he would be fine. Underaged. Wrist slap. I said we needed to go back for him. The Mons! He owed me for the hash. Alex pushed me off the balcony.

I fled Mars. Feared the gods were mad.

I learned two weeks later when reading the Green River Review and begging for beer money that Peanut—real name Brian Schultz—had been arrested at a house party in Hamilton while celebrating his 18th birthday. The police built a case around his vandalism tour. The untouchable youth who tagged Green River was busted and charged. They had waited until he was an adult. Handicapped him for all future jobs. Busted with a gram of hash. Mine.

I returned home, to Church, around four in the morning, without knowing how much of my life I had displaced. At least ten days, according to the photos on Myspace. As I melted in the predawn glare, birds shed their nests, chirping me and my soggy pack of reserve cancers and dehydrated lighter.

The punks inside Church were either passed out or too loaded on junk to stand. I debated crashing on the mattress on the landing but decided I should pop a laxative, in case the trail mix of pills I ate on Mars constipated my guts.

Nothing worse than surviving a bender only to live with clogged bowels. A lie. One thing was worse. Returning from a bender and learning someone put shit in your pants.

I dragged my heavy legs up to the working bathroom, stepping over Philip and Zoe and the Beer Walrus to reach the landing. Clair slept peacefully on the mattress, shirtless and curled in a sleeping bag, using my tartan button up as a pillow.

So much for dying on the landing.

I snuck past her and into the bathroom, desperate for the laxative and water.

Alex lay facedown in the tub.

Alex was facedown in the tub?

Why is Alex unconscious in the tub?

Motionless. Covered in a summoning circle of puke and urine. Skin bleached and damp. He looked so small curled under himself. Like a worm baby unable to survive without a host to leech resources from.

I almost did nothing. I almost left Church entirely. Almost held his head in the orange and pink chunks coated in discharge and asked him how it felt, if he missed Benji, if it was worth it, and as his heart beat faded he told me it was, that the memories burned brightest snuffed out soonest, that Benji, that I, and Sav, along with himself had chosen to live fast, die young and he was simply continuing on to the most logical conclusion as he begged me to hold his hand as soggy pasta chunks clogged his throat, no, he didn't scream as he choked, he laughed at my futile attempt to render him dust as a million waves of rust-water crashed upon his black teeth, and while sucking for air, he looked up with his raven eyes gaped over his crooked beak of a nose and asked me that once I was done with him, to leave the horror here, forget about-

Clair started screaming. High-pitched. Ear-splitting machine cant frequencies.

No one in Church woke.

She pulsated like a howler monkey fucking a football as I peeled myself away from my seat on the toilet, hands at my sides, clean, and not around Alex's throat.

I yanked Clair out of the bathroom, unsure how long I had spent fantasizing—or was this still part of the trip?—about Alex's death.

What is real life?

Clair clawed at the doorframe, called for Dev. Though his body was at the foot of the stairs, his mind was far away dreaming of electric sheep.

I calmed her until she formed human words. Dev had Narcan yesterday.

Yesterday.

There was no telling where it ended up.

We tore apart Church, bounding over the wasted, smashing plates, and upturning beds and sofas. I found the kit between the toilet and Alex's quivering body. He must have tried to jolt himself before his seizure.

His face turned a deep shade of purple by the time I unzipped the case. I had no idea what I was doing, I was too mashed to read the instructions. I ripped loose the needle and stabbed Alex in the chest, felt it scrape a rib. I hammered the plunger, but it wouldn't move. He didn't jerk upright like Uma, gasping for breath and thanking me. I tried again, pulled out the needle, and stabbing wildly, tried to clean the needle tip, thinking I had blunted it on his ribs, and stabbed again. Again. I searched for a visible vein to shoot in, but it was all scar tissue, Clair cried that he had shot in his foot, she tried to unlace his boots. I stabbed Alex's heart and punched the plunger.

He shot up. Alive. Gasping like a gelt, and punched me across my chin. He clawed my throat, damning me for ruining the best high he had in his miserable life.

Clair grabbed him by the hair and pulled him off, tearing a clump out and fell into the tub of puke and piss.

I rolled free and violence ended.

The three of us sat in shock, panting and drying our eyes. I on my knees against the vanity. Alex shaking in his own puke and blood. Clair sobbed in the doorway, still naked and too afraid to touch the liquids covering her shoulders and thighs.

Sav rubbed sleep from her eyes, she was wearing nothing but Alex's Kittie hoodie, her face disillusioned and numb like any waster after a long trip.

"What's the fuss about?" she asked.

Halfhearted, Alex laughed.

A l'intérieur.

My fingers bled on my fretboard during the last practise before our show at The Cellar. Band Only. My arms burned, lost their grip as my wrist limped on, barely able to keep time, thankful for no cheers and boos between songs. Alex wanted a professional moment before we tore up the stage. The right headspace he called it.

We spoke in song titles. I had come a long way since sounding like a beached whale. We were blood crazed sharks hunting leviathans. We smoked and drank and snorted until the damp Church was dry as Fundi Texas. I ignored hunger. Alex pacemaker. He refused to allow the weakness of his OD to slow his row. Matching sweat for sweat until Dev tapped from the pungent smell of onion poorly masked by body spray.

Alex wasn't even hoarse. His voice rang true after hours of shouting through feedback.

Breathless, tempo-slacked, blisters, our amps bled noise. I bailed.

Alex allowed us to rehydrate, before forcing us onwards through our 20-some-odd songs. There was a lack of definitive end to practise. A slow unwillingness to accept fatigue crept over Dev and I. We packed up our gear without a word. Arms shaking, I snapped shut my guitar case as Dev packed himself a final bowl, palms purpled. He called up Ryan. Alex, haunted the backroom. Shot up.

I forced myself to avoid creeping, pretended to read the collage of posters and scrawls lining the basement, hoping Alex would and wouldn't ask me to join him. I lied to myself about who was in control as the dire need to flee swelled into the evening sun. A panic attack crept its mean red hands around my skull.

I pinched some bud while Dev chatted up Ryan, rambling about hostility and keeping shit on the DL. Unable to catch my laboured breath, I cranked the grinder to force out my anxiety.

My stomach turned on itself when I opened the door to leave Church, wishing I had joined Alex, and not retreated into the chilled air rushing through the weeds and loose dirt of Skunktown. A cerebral overload of flashing lights, radio static, and pre-game upheaval flooded my senses. Trees whispered under the boom of gridlocked traffic on the overpass. The hometown hero's stadium roared with armchair experts.

Was it playoffs already?

Sav sat on the porch, her back to the door and rummaging through a backpack. She had stripped the rainbows and neon from her hair, stained her neck with drips and blotches. She hid under a cyan beanie. A sign she botched the metamorphosis.

When I stepped out, she turned to me, sunglasses like beetle eyes too large for her face. They sharpened her cheeks and chin. Behind them I saw the clean outline of a blackeye. She never said what happened and I was too much of a coward to confront it.

"There's a meteor shower tonight," she said, wiping the fragile skin hidden under her glasses. "Good for a hike, nitwit?"

The sombre hike along the escarpment became a sobering nuisance. The sun pierced through the bushes and cracks between tree branches quivering along the crest of the Devil's Punch Bowl. Leaves shone like emeralds dipped in amber. Sav hid from illumination. From me.

The closer we came to the overlook, the farther the sun fell, and the traffic faded as the stadium across town filled with sports cosplayers. As much as I wished to snap the silence, I couldn't. Not on the bus. Not as we cut across the baseball diamonds by Schwenger High. Not on our ascent. Each time I attempted words, I felt as if otherworldly slugs blocked my airway. I focused on the back of her cyan beanie bouncing in time with our melancholic footfalls.

I toyed with my lighter in my secret pocket to distract myself.

At the peak, we sought refuge on the opposite side of the glowing cross. Rested on the stone wall overlooking the escarpment. Green River beneath our feet. She swung her legs over the wall and I felt her desire to kick over the water tower. She traced the skyline, the streetlights burning like vigils on a grave. She hugged her backpack.

A white sedan peeled out as fast as it pulled into the gravel parking lot, leaving us alone to our private moment as the sun slept. We waited for the meteor storm.

"Try not to look so sad, nitwit." She removed her bug glasses. The darkness did little to hide the bruise. Even my father never swung at my face.

"I'm not."

"I think we're in too deep for these little lies of ours."

"I don't understand why you did this to yourself."

She adjusted the red bandanna that rested in the crook of her elbow hiding her track marks.

"I'll take 'Reasons we both keep playing this game,'" she said, without humour.

"I want out."

"Then jump." She nodded her chin at the pool below us where we swam a lifetime ago. How quickly lives change.

"And give them the satisfaction?"

Her labret piercing pulled her lower lip into a smile. A proclamation of sincerity I didn't know I missed.

"At least consider what we talked about." I tried to hide the uncertainty in my voice.

"You ever known me to quit anything?"

"Tuba. Sixth grade."

"Not funny."

"You're right. But your arms are nubby in contrast."

She snickered. Followed by a farseeing moment of silence. She slid her hands between her thighs, shivered. I removed my faded jacket, leaned close and draped it over her shoulders. It engulphed her. Save for her ragged tights and scarred Docs.

"There you go, poncho."

She bit her lip to fend off a grin. "You are a nitwit."

"Probably."

She placed her hand on my cheek and I rested mine on her bruised knee. Gave it a gentle squeeze.

"I'll leave him."

Despite the opening of the overlook, I felt her words echo. Reverberate off the cross casting long shadows over Green River.

There were so many things I wanted to say. I hunted through the darkness of my mind for them, but—How do you tell your best friend you care about them more than you should?

The slugs inside me took on an unnatural metamorphosis. I blamed bingeing on an empty stomach for screwing with my perception of reality, clogging the connection from head to heart.

An alarm went off on Sav's phone. A rotary briiiing. She silenced it and wordlessly carried her backpack to the cross. She fished out a pair of adjustable pliers and after a sharp crack, she snapped the lock on the disconnect switch under the glowing cross. She threw it with a clunk and the cross faded from existence.

Meteors exploded through the sky in stripes and tracers peeling through clouds as the alien elements crumbled in our atmosphere in zips and flashes.

The sight of something greater than myself unfurled the wad of wriggling slugs within me. They unfurled into butterflies and fluttered inside my ribs. A cage restraining them from open air.

Sav hugged me from behind. Her palm firm on my chest. With each breath I took, the butterflies soared towards her fingertips. Our cheeks touched and the things inside me rose higher, their wings strummed my heartstrings, plucking notes until our tunes matched. Souls ticked in tandem to the songs of our youth.

Lost together.

My hand found her neck, the soft chemical stain of her hair tickled my nose as I pulled her in.

As we kissed, the things inside us danced through our throats. I lifted her shirt, my fingers rolling over her ribs like they were piano keys, and then clouds parted and meteors rained on earth. We gave a piece of ourselves to each other. Explored each other's body with our hands and mouths. Found the answers most people search for their whole lives, but seldom learn. We attempted the hardest thing in the universe: love.

I adored her body in the taillights of meteors flickering over our heads, how she shone like the surface of the moon. Every bruise, every scar, was just another crater to cherish. We laughed, failing to find a perfect place in the dirt to match our locked bodies, and peeled sticks and brambles from our thighs and butts as we changed positions.

Her breath, stale from cancer, felt like morning mist. I heard my name. She moaned she was close. I was too. With eyes wide as an ocean, she looked into my hobgoblin face, and asked me to come inside her. I trusted her. We released each other at the same moment.

Our bodies convulsed. I collapsed on hers.

Our shouts melted to whispers.

Our names known only to the trees.

Oh, what could have been.

It is impossible to know what happens to characters after the curtain drops. It's hell to speculate. Trust me when I say I wish we could end here, pump this up with fluff, and close with how we abandoned Green River together, started new lives, married, had kids, retired, died next to each other at a ripe old age surrounded by worm babies. Blackholes are funny things.

I woke in Sav's bed, my shaggy hair damp from the shower and smelled like a fairy princess thanks to her shampoo. She slept peacefully next to me. My groin chaffed from overuse, so I clenched it between my thighs to dull the ache.

We had left the Devil's Punch Bowl shortly after banging, bought a midnight pizza for the bus ride back to her mom's place. We ate, screwed, and slept the rest of the night. Then the next day away. At this point in my life, it was the most fun I'd ever had sober. Sav gave me an over-the-counter cocktail and vitamins—she had perfected her system for dealing with withdrawal—to keep me lucid while I detoxed. It worked, for the most part, but we had smoked a lot of pot to dampen the jitters. We were dry by mid-afternoon, so I chewed ibuprofen like mints. Kidneys be damned.

Sav's landline rang around dinner. I was inside her and we both froze as dread and anxiousness suffocated our intimate thrill with each chime. As if the phone knew our crimes. We had powered down our cells to avoid this moment, wishing to live in our isolated world. But the landline, our last link to reality, ruined the moment, and if we answered its call, the whole world would know what had transpired between us.

The call went to the machine: "Hey Sav, it's Lisa. We still on to hang tonight? I called earlier, but no one answered. Your boy's wondering where you are, he says he wants to talk about 'that thing' before the show. Whatever that means. Anyway, if you need me I'll be with my Precious. See yah!"

I forgot that I promised Lisa I'd take her to see some garbage throwaway comedy, she was dying to see. I still can't remember the name.

Sav gave me a look. I tried to ignore her, and continue sex, but she pursed her lips and squinted.

"Don't." I looked away.

"Precious?"

"Don't ask." I tried to find the beat to *Little Bitch.*

"Precious." Despite her seriousness, she grew flush.

"Sav. Stop."

"Fuck me, PRECIO—"

I jammed my tongue in her open mouth. She pressed her body into mine.

We showered together. Again. Shared a mixing bowl of mac and cheese and watched Peeping Tom. Laughed at the absurdity of a murder camera. We kissed a lot. Played footsies a lot.

"When are you gonna tell him?" I asked, chasing pills with OJ to dull my chest pains, as Karlheinz Bohm monologued about his abusive father's snuff films.

"After the show," she said, scrubbing cheese dust from the bowl. She wore my jacket, hiding her self-conscious bones within. "I hate him, but I don't want to ruin everyone's night. We all looked forward to it for so long. It wouldn't be right."

I disliked her reasoning. It bothered the crap out of me. Left me feeling like she was ashamed and embarrassed.

"So what about us?" I tried to hide my desperation by sipping more OJ, knowing she despised neediness. But I did feel needy. I hadn't actualized how much I wanted to be with her until the night before, and the prospect of returning to a life without her filled me with an irrational fear. My inadequacy made me want to run away from Green River rather than face a timeline where I lost her.

"I will break things off," she said, rinsing the suds bubbling on the rim. "When the tension dies down, we'll let our friends know. If we have any left." She frowned at the bowl. "We might have to rethink your living situation."

A hurdle for later.

"Until then, we're what, a dirty little secret?"

"The dirtiest." She smiled a deviant smile and throttled the steel wool, scratched away at the cheesy pot. The scritching sound gave me tingles. "You need to dump Lisa. Probably soon. She really likes you. Precious."

"Oh eat a dick."

"Whip it out." She waved the pot at me.

I stood up, pulled out a fist full of my junk, and shook it at her.

"Why?" She cowered behind the pot.

"Embrace it!"

I gyrated my wiener like a windmill, called myself Der Dutchy.

It was late when we finally left the apartment for our first date. Sav had shaved my head because I kept trying to pull hair out. And she herself had straightened her bangs in an attempt to hide her black eye. We dressed fancy—which is a stretch for two gutter snipes who smelled of spit, sex, and cancers—and bussed uptown to eat a later dinner at one of those three-star chain restaurants a step above Wendy's. It was the best we could ever hope to afford.

We acted like we had pre-hookup. Friends hanging out. Talking shit. Comparing DOA to Forgotten Rebels, and blasting Billy Talent ringtones, and debated why Hardcore Logo disappeared into the background. I kept my phone off, but Sav occasionally went on hers. When I asked who she was talking to, she hastily grumbled something about mom stuff. We stole kisses when no one watched, rubbed against one another while we waited in line for a seat. No one knew us and would not care if we kissed openly, but there was an excitement about being a secret.

Mid-dinner we snuck off to the bathroom for a quickie. Our bodies were too sore to play for long and neither of us came. We did it because we could. Besides, no one has ever had satisfying sex in a bathroom stall. The awkwardness of the tiny space and differential in height made us howl at our ineptitude.

While I zipped up, careful not to irritate my swollen member, Sav insisted that she knew the best place down by the Bayfront wharf to explore our exhibitionist sides.

I laughed and asked her who she had gone there with, she deflected, and said we should call up Ryan for something laced, and find our own public place to play. When I reminded her we were sober she slapped her forehead and laughed. She was 'joking.'

We paid for overpriced dry burgers and swampy pasta in change and left no tip because, as Sav put it:

"If the waitress wanted a better living wage, she should unionize." I didn't agree with forcing socialism on capitalists, thought we should burn down Parliament, then change policy while spreading oligarch ashes across the oilsands.

She encouraged my outburst as we transferred downtown to the Number 5 to reach Sav's place.

Alone, at the back of the bus, Clair wept. Sobbing and keening something awful to the dismay of the wheelchaired man tied to a rail. Her mascara wings bled over her chubby cheeks and palms in a poor attempt to catch tears.

We sat with her. And Sav wrapped her thin ashen-yellow arms around Clair's pink and fleshy neck.

I didn't know how to handle Clair, or anyone emotional, even myself, so I just listened to Sav console her friend as the bus sped downtown.

"He's left muh muh muh meee," Clair said between glubs of snot. "Left me for Ryan. That slu slu sluh-uh-ut. What does she have that I don't?"

A personality.

Clair rubbed her makeup streaks with a crusty sleeve. "We were made for each other. I loved Devy so much, Sav. It hurts. I was gonna get Zoe to give me a tat of his name on my wrist to cover my—to cover my—"

"There will be others," Sav said, holding Clair's suicide lines to show her friends will carry you when you fall.

"No, there won't. I want to die! I hate how much I love him. Why would he do this—do this—to me? He was my everything. And after all we've been thr- he promised me he'd get clean for me."

"Trust me when I say you're better off without him. Take a week to gather yourself and then get back in the game. That's what I always do. Good riddance."

"You wouldn't be saying that if it was Alex that had cheated on you."

She hugged Clair, who wept harder for the simple act of compassion.

"If he did, I'd drop his ass and find someone better."

Sav made sure I heard.

Straw Dogs.

I spent another night at Sav's, enjoying our new routine of eating and sleeping and sexing. Avoiding others. I felt little guilt for ghosting Lisa, but failed to conjure an excuse that wouldn't trigger her into calling Sav.

Sav joked about starting a relationship complaints office and charge Lisa by the word to optimize capital and save herself the annoyance.

I asked if Lisa complained about me.

Sav laughed, said how much Lisa hated how I walked around the city alone, as if she were waiting for an invitation from me to wander in my company and plague my solitude. She didn't understand the concept of introversion.

By evening I was fiending for a shot, but Sav kept me distracted with *Battle Royale* as we placed bets with sexual favours on which students would die in which order. I had to eat her ass for 9 hours straight while she had to lick 3 measly boogers off my toes. I wasn't great at the game.

The night of the show, we took the Number 7 to The Cellar in silence. I thought about texting Jocelyn to come out, get her on the list, but decided against it. She was still pissed, no doubt. Sav thumbed her phone with poignant aggression. I tried to see who was stressing her out, but when she caught me birddogging, she said it was Clair crying about Dev and tucked her phone into her bra.

We escaped the bus a few stops early before we crossed paths with our friends, and stole kisses, elongating our fleeting moments together before facing reality. Somewhere between John and King and dry handjibbers in the Dirt Mall's bathroom, we lost an hour of time.

The crowd gathered outside The Cellar, wrapping around to the parking lot as Skippy, the middle-aged punk promoter who hid his balding head and grey hairs with vibrant red fauxhawk, worked the doors. Sav pulled me into the smoke shop next door, made sure no one was tripping within and kissed me for the last time.

"Listen, nitwit," she said, placing her hand against my chest. Her bruised eye looked puffy under a million layers of cover up. "We have to act like everything is normal. No one can know about us. When we survive the night, we'll celebrate our sobriety with a shot. Just the one. Withdrawal won't hit us as hard. Alright?"

I agreed. One shot. We had stayed clean for two whole days we deserved a reward. Besides, it would be suspicious if we both refused to consume anything all night.

Sav frowned.

I asked her what was wrong.

"I'm sorry if he kisses me in front of you."

The thought had never occurred to me. We were dating other people. I had to explain to Lisa why I ditched her without revealing I was having an unholy amount of unprotected sex with her best friend, who was also my singer's abused girl. The thought of Alex touching Sav twisted my guts like a kid tearing open a fish's eye with a bobby pin. I repressed the anxiety, told myself it'll be easier if it happens after I get high.

A thought: What if they screw? Animal raw. Violent, inhuman. I needed a cancer, a bump, a hit, hooks, anything. Was she meat to him, or was it organic and true like what she and I shared? Was I meat?

Sav wouldn't do that. She's not a slut. Right? She's not. Savisnotafuckingslut.

"You good?"

"No. Yeah. I mean yes." I lit a cancer. "I get it. Totally. Sorry if Lisa pulls anything."

"Be a good boy one more night. Precio—nitwit." She stuck out her tongue, so that her tongue ring sat beside her labret. I remembered the way it nestled against my tongue, against my cock.

"Har. Har." I leaned in to kiss her, taste the fruity punch of her lips, but she pulled back.

We kept a metre apart as we approached the riot of punks drifting from The Cellar, stumbling for the alley. We walked together but separate, feeling naked and cold. Distant. Zoe and Philip greeted us, told us how weak the opener was, but we bailed on them before the drugs came out. We were here to enjoy the show, but would party after Sick Sad World's set.

The crowd chattering inside the venue parted for the nobody band pulling out their gear. The drummer miraculously stuffed her kit into a Mini Cooper, like a Tetris wizard.

"What the fresh hell, dude," Dev shouted as he grabbed me by my face. "You missed the preshow sesh! Where were you?"

I could not think of a viable excuse.

"You missed the wild, wild hella bang fest," he said, pulling a baggy of pills from his Agoraphobic Nosebleed hoodie. PCP Tornado. Smoking gun. Mind blown.

"The what?"

"Hella bang fest! We pork roasted Ryan." He raised his hand for a high-five.

I was at a loss for words. So, I was honest. I gave him props, called it a turkey, and his stoned mind found the feint amazing.

"You're shittered, my guy," I said. "Save me a gunner?"

"Attaboy!" Dev grabbed my shirt and shook me, forgetting everything except the thrill of being a fully automatic rage machine. "To the alley!"

Dev herded a bunch of us over the cracked street and into our alley. The ground was stained with Rex's brown blood.

I found myself relieved for not thinking of a valid excuse to stay sober, but anxious as I joined the degenerates clogging the cramped alley like a calcified artery. I feared unleashing Crazy Dev.

The desire to partake faltered as I realized what a waste the shakes with Sav had been. Again. I reasoned I could survive another withdrawal regime with her, and searched the familiar crowd for signs of her. But recoiled when I found Lisa's straight platinum hair shimmering under the rusted fire escape.

"Thanks for the call," she said, falling in beside me. Her words weren't cold, and held a bored sense of notoriety I had come to expect when she was high. She wore a lowcut bleeding heart tee that showed her ribs. A sad chemical boys logo. Factory cut jeans.

"About that."

"Sav just filled me in."

"She what?"

"It's alright. I understand."

This. Is. A. Trap.

"What did she have to say about it?"

Lisa shrugged. Chagrin. Weak. "Everything, pretty much."

"Oh. And you're cool with it?"

"I totally get it." She threw her gaunt arms around me. I hadn't noticed before, but her face seemed covered in a fine fuzz. Like the powder had clung to her hair follicles. "My mom wigs out too. Mostly over little stuff. Sav's just so lucky you're always there for her, Precious. Like a big brother."

"Right. That's me. Always helping where I can."

"Yes Precious! I spazzed when you ditched me, but I forgive you. The last time her mom had a breakdown, she went all dark, it was so punk! Must be hard for Alannah, you know, raising a kid on your own, working two jobs, I *cannot* believe she hit Sav in the face this time, I thought parents were only allowed to hit you where you could hide the bruises—"

"People shouldn't hit people."

I counted myself lucky, and wanted to thank Sav for the lie. Dodging the argument my way would have been disastrous.

"I kind of told Sav I wouldn't talk about it. Not really into the whole gossip thing. I hope that's cool with you."

"Oh yeah. Totally! You can tell me all about it later back at my place after the show."

She gave me that look all girls give when they want you to kiss them. I tried to play it off, but after a century of her googling at me with those idiotic guppy eyes I panicked. I looked around the alley for Sav before quickly kissing Lisa's powdered cheek. Content, she led me by the hand towards Dev to score some pills. I wiped away the chalky coverup from my lips.

Tonight was all you can eat, snort, shoot, smoke. I took Dev up on his mix molly special. He started explaining how to balance the highs and lows, but I tuned him out. I was too worried about what lies Sav told to Alex.

I dry-swallowed the pills in twos and threes. Low doses of percs, oxy, and miscellaneous killers, I assumed. Unsure and uncaring about potency, I garbled a handful. I just wanted to get high. Have fun and celebrate my first real show. Besides, pills were easy to quit. Especially with Sav's help. We could get clean again. Detox over the weekend and by Monday tell the others we were starting over. Clean lives.

What? It was a good lie at the time.

While the other bands played, Lisa hung off my shoulders as she and Ryan tripped on lean.

Her voice slow and dronnnnnnning while my mind raced, trying to ignore Sav glued to Alex's lap, hoovering key bumps, she caught me watching and shrunk into Alex's neck, avoiding my orbits, Lisa floated to Sav asking if she could score and I feigned having to piss when Sav called Alex 'daddy' to coerce drugs from him, she blushed when he called her kitten, and I drifted beside

Philip, chest tightened, distilled from conversations—what's in the pills?—unable to hold Sav, having another girl wrapped around my arm—Valium? Nononononovocaine?—I want to leave, lay in bed with Sav and watch the way her nose crinkled when she laughs at Shrimplips, *The Creature from the Black Lagoon*, it's all I—lagoooned for—how'd Dev find Novocaine?—assholes, Alex and Lisa and Ryan- and who was on Philip's shoulders, Duck? not Philip, Rancid Jack, then, and all the posers and normals and lifers and blackhole kids—tarter sauce—impeded our next moment together and everyone who refused to leave us alone in this one-way train ride to get-off-my-nut-sack-ville, I just want to chill with Savannah Anne Moore—why is time slowing, how fast am I going—and watch lame movies and sing Gogol Bordello and diss crybaby conservatives and spineless liberals until Benji—

Benji.

A low levelled me.

I shifted gears. Regretted the pills. I should have listened to Dev about balancing highs and lows.

The third band, Barrow-Wights, was mid-set when Sav left the venue alone. I word vomited at Lisa that I was going to take a downer at one of the porcelain thrones. She kissed my neck, begged me to hurry back in that stoned drone of hers and I bounded the steps to the world above to catch Sav's dauntless shadow.

I felt like a fish's eye when I reached street level. That is to say: damp and haggard and teetering-on-the-void's-edge lit. An unnaturally cold wind hacked my skin like razorblades.

I'm coming down.

Sav struck her lighter furiously against the wind, unable to find the sweet spot to birth the spark. I took it from her, and lit her cancer, feeling nostalgia as I tasted her kiss on the filter and took a heartsick drag before passing it back.

"I can't do this."

I wrapped my arms around her before she could continue. Took in her scent of shampoo and hair dye. I missed the her I had known over the past two days, relived those intricate moments before sleep, how I watched her breathe next to me as the silver screen flickered to Rod Serling's speculative monologues as I shrugged off the shakes.

She kissed my neck on the same place Lisa had not even a minute ago. Lisa's was lifeless, careless, routine. Sav's warm and bright and goddamned clandestine. When she kissed me, she was kissing me. Specifically.

Sav let me kiss her mouth.

"What the fucking fuck is this?"

Alex slammed Sav to the pavement, lifted me off the ground by my jacket, and shoved me against the venue's wall. The studs on my jacket dug into my chin as he tried to mash my skull through spalling bricks.

"Let go!" Sav shouted, slapping at Alex's arms.

"I'll murder you," he said, raven face wild with nicotine-stained carrion between his crooked teeth.

"Do it." My voice without air.

The world stopped turning for an instant as Alex battered my head seven times with his fists. I didn't flinch. Didn't raise my hands in self-preservation. It was like how my father used to thump me on vacation.

Wailing on me for stoic defiance with singular goals: Make you cry.

Making me earn these tears, huh, boy? We'll learn you.

I wondered if that's why Cho bullied me. Did he smell the easy target my father had tried to pacify, or did I simply own the world's most punchable face?

At the time of Alex's beating, this wasn't what I thought of, my mind was blank. No Cho. No father. No mom begging in the distance. No teachers to pull us apart. Just Alex's fist and my hobgoblin face.

I gasped for breath while Sav tried to peel Alex away from me, taking her fair share of swings until she decided it was too dangerous to save me.

Blood stung my eyes. I thought of Jocelyn. Nothing specific. No emotion or memory. I just wondered where she was at this specific moment in time.

When the violence ended, I spat up a chipped tooth and missed Benji's melancholic smile, the times we rocked *Golden Eye* in his room when he skipped mass, our imaginary pirate ship made of crumpled boxes and chairs and a moth-eaten quilt. I missed how not alone he made me feel.

A waterfall of blood poured out of my nose and soaked my white Ed Gein shirt.

Sav cried in Ryan's arms. I knew Alex was going to kill her next. I tried to stand on my own, but toppled over, slumped against the wall. I spat. Thick. Metallic like an old spoon.

"Yo, guys," Dev said, indifferent to my suffering.

Alex whirled around, ready to unleash his fury onto Dev, who raised his hands in innocence. Brotherhood.

"We're up next."

Skippy, the butt-wipe promotor from The Cellar, announced our band like we were boxing champs. Welterweight challengers for the title for Best Breakup Since Yoko. Alex and I stepped on the stage from opposite ends, I tripped, woozy and overstimulated from the heat of the lights and chatter of the crowd. Lisa, worried sick, bless her, helped me up as she mothered me about the dried blood dribbling over my lip. Philip handed me his beer. I chugged.

We paced our cage like suicide bombers during soundcheck, waiting for the count, letting booze and drugs fill our existence and adrenaline fueled rage, waiting for the beat drop, for feedback to deafen and consume us. Death clocks. Midnight. Instruments turned machineguns. Poetic war cries.

I screamed.

I heard nothing.

Louder.

Wished for a missile to erupt over the crowd, soaking The Cellar in napalm.

The room went dark. I popped another unknown pill as Dev counted us in. Each drumstick crack counted down to Ragnarok.

One

Dev took a drag of cancer.

Two

Alex chased Oxy with a beer.

Three

I jumped as high as god allowed.

Four

Alex whipped his beer at the crowd.

We raged.

We never finished our last song. Alex screamed the second chorus of *Suburban Holocaust* when I snapped. He howled the lines 'You're not my brother/ not my friend./ We're not equal, your life's dead-end,' and I looked up from my fretboard. I didn't know the kid throwing horns at me. Young. Handsome. Nubile. Hell, it could have been his first show. Too clean to drift blackholes. That's how you know who's been in the scene the longest. Cleanliness. I hated his perfect spiked hair, dog collar, and anarchy patch bought from Hot Topic.

I wanted to officially welcome him to the horror show. I grabbed his dog collar and tried to force my battered skull through his. He went limp. Disappeared into the black mass. Lost forever to time and space.

Humans cheered. Others recoiled. I wanted to see if I could punch a hole through the stage with just my guitar, wondering how far I'd have to dig through the panelling until I hit the foundation.

I raged until Skippy turned on the house lights and killed the PA. Feedback faded over disgust.

The butt-wipe introduced me to the bouncer, but I threw my splintered neck at Dev's high-hat. Told them not to bother.

I booted open the heavy backdoor gouged from all the pathetic bastards like me, stuttered three steps, and dry heaved in the parking lot. Forced a finger down my throat. Euphoria.

"What the hell was that?" Sav said, slamming the heavy backdoor as I spat. "What has gotten into you? You're scaring me."

I said nothing.

"Don't stoop to his level," she said at a distance.

"I'm really tense right now." I tried to steady my breathing, like my old running coach, Hawthorn, had showed me after completing a race. "I'm tweaking out."

She hunted through her purse, pulled out her kit, and dug for tinfoil envelopes. My eyes melted when I counted it out. $200. Minimum. $200 she spent in an hour on shit she promised me we were done with.

She clawed at my face to see my pupils. "You've taken too many uppers. What were they? I think I can level you out. Alex told Benji it's about scales. Fine lines. Please don't OD. I can't handle—"

"I don't know." I really didn't. "Like five or six pills and a joint. Dev. I need to purge them. I feel sick. Sav. Can't. Breathe."

Lisa and Alex stormed out together, screaming noises erupted from their head holes as Sav shoved her kit at me. I stuffed it in my jacket's secret pocket, thankful for the freebees.

"What did you say to me?" Alex threw me at the ground. I caught concrete.

Sav begged him to stop. Lisa balled.

"See," he said, "I told you they were out here. Cheating."

"Precious?" Lisa said, looking more pathetic when she cried.

"I caught him just before our set. Scrote-stain is pissed he's busted." Alex spat on me. "You gonna cry?"

"Shut up, dickweed," Sav said, trying to pull me up.

"What'd you say?" He raised a fist to strike her, but Sav slapped him first.

"Don't you ever touch me again, you piece of shit."

"Precious, why did you do this?"

"Oh, shut up, Lisa, you fuckin poser."

"Don't you talk to me like that you slut."

"Loose legged whore."

"Limp dick."

"Why?"

"Cock sucking shit-stain."

"You would fuckin cry."

Nope.

Just. Nope.

I peeled myself off the ground as Skippy and the bouncer ran over, demanding reimbursement for the floor along, with half the venue who delighted at the prospect of blood. None noticed my departure.

A show within a show. Our lives were a distraction to these vultures. Artistic carrion. Music existed as a means to turn off their noise, forget their miserable existence. Afraid of silences between sentences. The realization that my art, my sick sad soul, meant nothing to them but social/personal/emotional/financial gain hollowed me as I staggered past the bus stop on John and King. I was a hobgoblin-faced stick boy who played guitar for drugs. Filler. A trophy to piss off parents between reruns of Buffy and ER.

Alex had poisoned Sav with the rot he carried within himself. I refused to pass it on. Sever the noose stringing Alex to Sav to me. Who had I infected? Lisa? Sarah?

Three blocks from The Cellar, along Embassy Road, outside a gay bar, Sav grabbed my arm. She panted, though appeared calmer than she had been when I peaced.

"Where are you going?" she said, wheezing. Makeup streaked. A cut along her boney knee, below a tattoo that declared 'contribute to the chaos', smiled back at me.

"I'm done," I said, dizzy with each syllable. Desperate to lay down on a cool floor, someplace quiet, without black mold choking my lungs. My childhood bed with Spider-man covers—

"Why?"

Because I want to punish myself for watching you sitting in his lap, kissing his neck for chems.

"I can't do this anymore."

"Let the pills wear off."

She tried to hold my hand, but I pulled away, afraid I'd cave at her touch, and continued drifting through the street. The glare of a normal hiding her purse while waiting for the University Line caused me to avert my eyes. Sav demanded to know what the normal was looking at, and the woman shuffled into traffic. Sav followed me, refusing to break the silence. When the beggars at the bingo hall asked her about picking up off Alex, She kept quiet. Then the distance between us grew. At the old post office I strayed from her footfalls to avoid a miserably unfortunate loner in his 30s and his bumbling googly-eyed mutt. Sav tried to close the gap, but I crossed Harvest indifferent to the clubbers and taxis. I needed to flee Sav's cloud of perfumed fruit polluting my lungs. I wanted to tell her to piss off, but was too angry to speak. My mind spiraling as I drowned in repetitious rage, reliving the moments at The Cellar and how I felt our relationship was a lie. I pictured her moaning daddy while Alex raw dogged her at the Bayfront wharf mocking me for falling in love with her.

If I died here and now, would she go back to him?

"This will all blow over," she said as she silenced the violence emanating from her cellphone. "Everyone needs a few to chill out. There's an afterparty at Church. Maybe that's what we all need. To smoke a bowl and relax. Talk this all out. Together. Philip is bringing his hookah."

I didn't want to. Why would I? The thought of continuing the facade turned my guts. I didn't hate myself enough to watch her flirt with Alex, even if it was just to score, nor did I want to be cuckolded, experience voyageurism, or get so blasted we three hate-fuck each other in an Eiffel Tower of debauchery just so I could lie to myself that I held a place—no matter how miniscule and pathetic—in her heart until I numbed myself substantially from the insecurity, and longing, and deprecation, waiting until the day I finally decided to kill myself.

"No."

"No?"

"No."

The vocal echo disorientated me. I had difficulty blinking away blinding streaks of traffic zipping past with indifference. The whoosh of cars washed over me like ornery waves. I swallowed diluted sick as she rubbed her forehead to force out a thought.

"What do you want? Why won't you talk to me about this?"

I flicked my cancer at a taxi, lit another as I waited for the traffic light to change.

I didn't know what I wanted. Her? Maybe. A re-do? Damn straight. But as she waited for me to respond and ignored her phone and the heckles of bros with popped collars mocking us for the holes in our pants at the intersection, I also knew what I didn't want. Uno: unfulfilled and unreciprocated devotion. Deux: live with myself as her second choice. A backup singer? Screw that. Drei: waste my time with another human I couldn't stand. I'd rather be alone than made to feel alone.

"If you want to talk, Sav, let's go right now. Hop on the next bus with me, and we'll go sit somewhere and talk this out."

"What about the party?"

"I don't want to get high so we can avoid our problem. I'm too goddamned—Listen. If you want to talk, then let's go now. We need to get on the same page about what the hell is going on between us. I'm not going to allow you to tell me how much you care about me, then watch you bang an abusive tit at the end of the night because you're too afraid to leave. It's messed up."

"Here we go. Mr. High and Mighty back at it again. You smashed up a kid's face, and your guitar like a baby throwing a tantrum because you couldn't wait. Shut up. You're violent, too. We all are! You didn't respect my choice. I'm not the only screw up, you cheated on Lisa and let her hang off you all night. What was I supposed to do?"

"So making me jealous—I was stoned! I couldn't deal seeing you—"

"I'm not some doomed princess that needs saving, asshole. Alright? Did you actually convince yourself I'm, what, the love of your life? Retard. Take me off the pedestal. Don't you dare fucking pout. Not everything is about your lonely fantasy. Perspective is a bitch, huh? Swallow your pride and get off your soapbox.

"I just. Fuck! I want a beer and to think. I'm not gonna screw Alex. I wanted you before you went nutters, but now I'm not so sure. Just give me my kit and I'll leave you to pout on your own."

It was decided then. Second choice. She wanted her drugs. Not me. It was never about me, hell, maybe it wasn't even about Alex. I pictured this as our future, an old junkie couple unable to commit to sobriety, freezing on the Torontonian streets, covered in scabies and birdshit.

"I tossed it." I ran my pockets to show her I held nothing. I hoped she didn't see the outline of her kit, resting in my secret pocket. It was bulky, and I hoped she was too stoned to see through the darkness. "Ditched it back on Emerald. We're supposed to be getting clean."

"You fucking asshole!"

"I keep my promises. I'm done with this noise."

I crossed the street, and she followed, cursing and screaming. She pulled at my arm to force me to show her where I ditched the drugs. A father honked at our disgraced parade and Sav kicked his sedan. She called me worthless.

"Do you know how much that cost me?"

"Leave me alone," I said, trying not to cry. I stuffed my hands back into my pockets to hide the kit. "You led me on for, I don't even know, like two years, and then you just happen to change your mind about me? Why? Because the King of the Junkies finally got around to your number and turned out exactly—He slaps you around! And you protect him. You always go for guys—"

"Don't you dare."

"—exactly like your father."

Certain things, no matter how hard you try, you cannot take back.

She told me she hated me.

"What do you want from me?" My words sounded pathetic.

"Nothing. I don't want a fucking thing from you. You don't do anything productive, and you're just a stupid kid with zero potential and Lisa was the only sorry bitch desperate enough to give you a chance because all you do is wander around the city stoned and lighting shit on fire. Alex at least has passion and drive for music. He has potential. Once he got clean, he was going to take Sick Sad World on the road and build us a better life. He was hoping to get signed tonight! Then you fucked everything up.

"Does he have issues? You bet. But he made me feel worth a damn. He was there for me when Benji died. Where were you? None of us knew! You cut yourself off and skulked about all 'woe is me' and only showed your face when we had drugs. Would it kill you to open up to another human being instead of writing lame ass notes to yourself all day and then burning them like a psycho? You can't keep living like this. No one is meant to be this alone.

"I'm so over this conversation," she said, pulling her hair from her eyes. "I'm gonna go back with my friends and have a beer, and deal with your mess another time."

"You are not listening," I said, finding my voice. "There won't be another time. If you want to get wasted, fine, all the best. As of right now I am done. Fully. We can talk this out now, or literally never. What's it going to be?"

Sav shrugged.

My last words to her: "I'm fucking done with you."

Begotten.

I wandered for two hours without a direction in mind before killing my pace. I just sort of hiked across town, past the train yards belching steel and coke, until I found myself on the far side of Green River, along the escarpment, patrolling Kiwo Road overlooking Schwenger High, and thinking about marching back to Sav's, hitting a shelter, going to Church, or swallowing my pride and waking my parents. Yeah. Great idea. Hey mom, hey dad. Don't mind my punched up face. I'm loaded on dirty pills and holding enough slump to pin a bull, sorta need a place to sketch. Until morning. These drugs and this life have levelled me. You. Were. Right. I am a failure. So, I'm cool to couch surf?

"No chance," I said to myself.

My face felt numb and clammy under the humid moonlight. I wanted to lay down on the side of the road. Sleep forever in a ditch. Swallow my tongue.

My hatred for how Sav reacted kept me in motion. Showed me where I belonged on her priority list. Below Alex. Below chems. Above tuba.

Was this the right thing to do?

I thumbed my lighter in my jacket pocket as I cut through an empty park. Thinking how I wished Lisa and Sav would recast themselves, change scripts written in hindsight.

When Lisa found me, a whole 7 seconds after Sav stormed off, she called me Precious and begged me to stay. I cut her off and told her the same thing I told Sav: I was done. She bawled, fell into my unopened arms and told me she was 'in love' with me. Being the douche I was, I told her 'love is nothing more than dopamine released over long periods of time and we're both sacks of complicated electric meat strung together by sinew and blood in Frankenstein's diabolical breeding machine. You meant nothing.' Her crying intensified.

She buried her head in my chest and said the most pathetic thing I had ever heard. 'I don't know what's worse, the fact that you're leaving me, or the fact that being in your arms feels so right.'

I had to actively resist laughing.

"What is wrong with you?" I said to myself after realizing I was in the middle of a forest.

Black leaves blotted out bruised clouds. Suffocating moonlight. Bush and toxic nothingness reverberated from slumbering woodland critters.

I replayed the arguments in my head as I romped through brambles and dirt. My head throbbed from the mind games I tortured myself with. Misery is all I'll have.

I drifted until the darkness drained the trail, hiking upwards and cutting across country roads until I found myself in a gravel parking lot with displaced mounds and gullies where car tires peeled out or stagnated. I hopped the chain barrier, walked on.

Devil's Punch Bowl overlook. Carpark. Where normals engaged in adolescent premarital sex in their parent's guzzlers. Something I missed out on because 1 I didn't have a license 2 parents could barely afford the Ultima 3 it was more practical to bang on a floor. Besides, Arielle put the fear of Jay Hova in me when she told me that Tyrone Belvin called emerge last summer because a stick shift climb up his butt.

I parted through the trees as a lonely white sedan rolled in behind me. No one got out. I was of no interest.

The glowing cross had resumed its titanic glow over Green River. The lock Sav had busted off had been replaced. The old one, snapped and rusted, lay discarded in a tussock of weeds with pale remember-mes. I chucked it over the edge. Jealous as it soundlessly fell, flicking into the void of the Lucifer's cup. I wondered how many drivers saw the sign from the highway. Did they enjoy the irony of Yeshua watching over where the Devil drinks?

I leaned on the stonewall where Sav and I had first-

You ever cry? No. Like real hard where your chest hurts and you choke on spit like your body's cool with killing you? Yeah. It was like that.

Nymphet leaves died in autumn's enchanted forest, lolling in the breeze. The waterfall dribbled into the calm pond peacefully surrounded by jagged boulders nesting in the shadows. Straight drop. 20 stories.

I texted Jocelyn. I know. I shouldn't have. Especially when I knew what the rot—

Especially after the way we left things. She took a piece of me when she walked away the night after the poetry slam at Saetia. Benji stole a lot of me when he decided to leave. My parents shattered and plundered. And the pieces I tried to give Sav, she rejected. The head rapist said this was why I hurt so much. Too many people lay claim to all my intangible parts. Use until numb. And now all I know is how to use others.

"I'm so sorry, Benji."

I swung my legs over the stonewall, feet dangled below, and wished he was here. He would have loved the view. It was dreamlike. Punch Bowl to one side, cross on the other. He would have told me to keep my chin up, dig in my heels, slug through.

"Sorry I don't visit."

I reached into my pocket for my lighter and cancers, but found Sav's kit.

I stared at the harmless needle and thought about how I smoked and snorted and shot my life away. I wanted change. I never wanted to kill myself slowly. That's too depressing. Each puff a gamble. Attempt at cancer number eighteen-thousand-and-twenty-six. Which is why, if you haven't guessed, I call them cancers.

What kind of sick bastard does this to themselves? Me. I do.

I decided to no longer do myself dirty. No slow death.

Benji had the right idea.

I dug through a garbage bin between the cross and found a half full water bottle. Dumped Sav's baggy of slump onto my lap. I cooked. Loaded the rig.

Humming a drunken lullaby, I plunged the syringe in the bottle cap. Usually Alex helped with a safe ratio, but right then, the rig was more welcome than a beer during wildfire season at an Armenian goat roast. I climbed back onto the stonewall, and thought about what that poet on stage at Saetia said about how throughout our lives we have conversations with people, that there was no such thing as a goodbye, only breaks in dialogue. No periods. Only commas,

A shame the one person I wished to talk with most no longer existed.

It'd be a long way to catch up with him.

I stuck the needle in my arm. As my veins caught fire, I slipped off the stonewall.

I told Benji I'd see him soon.

[second set]

Suspiria.

The raft reverberated with each passing wave. Rises met with screeching springs and riotous thunder. Ebbs with groans of sinners. Rot iron bars held the raft together. Failure. Fatal darkness surrounded me. Disoriented. Wotan waged war inside my skull. Drenched. Fumes. Cooked clay. I cried glass.

A fissure above revealed twin, honey-coloured moons reflectionless over inky waters. The longer I watched them duel, the fiercer Wotan's war inside me danced. I closed my eyes. Succumbed to the sea. I dreamt of swan children. My head cracked against the oak. Wooden Island. Rough, despite damp fingers. Hands traced oaks for golden apples. Razorblade leaves. Voicelessly, begging, popcorn clouds over an apricot tree. Undiscerned. Escape.

My raft drifted seaward.

The waves worsened, hastened and thrashed as I collapsed onto a straw bed. I clawed along the moonlit beach, trackless in ivory sands, slitting my knees. I climbed the oak tree, hands skyward, reaching for the twin moons. My hands stopped. Tapped on glass. I pulled myself over the trunk, face dragging over bark, knots goring my skin as my eyes levelled with the moons. Perched inside them, a robin taunted me with a ruckus of thunder snapping from its beak. Wotan's defeat.

Where am I?

A sonic boom emitted from the robin. I fell down the world tree. Crawled around the island for two days in outer darkness before noticing the island's sand stank of vinegar and bile. Everything hurt. Glass bones. Northwards, I gathered the strength to climb the oak. I passed foliage that caressed my cheeks—a puppy shrub kneaded my face with clumsy paws for leaves. Tar dribbled from my lungs.

I woke at the foot of a mountain resting atop the oak.

Each step revealed the summit. Light on the horizon. A village. My arms failed me twice, but I reached the peak. Village below.

Am I flying?

Before the answer came, the sky blazed, igniting my glass tears. Napalm retched over my skin. Liquified bowels. Two pillars stood before me. Pedestal of gods. I bowed. They morphed into a dress, distressed in winter fog.

Elohim?

"Not again."

On angel wings I flew from the mountain, down the oak, from the island and back to my raft. Marooned. Beg. Pray absolution.

The angel vomited on my skull.

Before I lost consciousness, I saw her in the sky.

Most of the time I screamed to a closed door, knowing she'd only open it if I was quiet, settled, docile, but

I needed my phone. Jocelyn was helping me to the toilet when I heard my cell go off. She abandoned me. I ralphed alone while she silenced the ruckus. A moment later another phone rang. She picked up. Argumentative tone. Told the caller to go to hell.

No sooner had she returned to helping me back into clean clothes than the phone rang again. She dragged me back to my bed in the basement when I heard the voicemail. Sav. My body kicked into overdrive. I tried fighting my way to her voice. Jocelyn barely held me back, dug her bitten fingers into my shoulders and begged for something to end this.

She pushed me onto the bed and rushed upstairs. Before the door slammed shut, I whipped a glass of apple juice at her. She managed to duck. It shattered in the living room. Scarred the hardwood floor.

"You need to calm down," she said, voice small, through the door.

A beacon lit inside my head. Vision tunneled and fuzzed. I tripped up the stairs. Cheeks hot, then numb as I screamed.

"Gimme my phone."

"I can't yet, you're still sick."

"This is your fault." Stop.

"Once your body finishes with-"

"I need it." No more.

"I can't."

My fist cracked the doorframe. "I'm not fucking around. Give me my fucking phone! I need to take the pain away." Make me stop.

"Lie down for a bit."

"Don't tell me what to do." I don't think I can survive this.

I rammed my fist through the wall. Pain jolted through my forearm where I hit the stud. A twig snapped. My vision blurred as I held my hand, screaming to numb my pain. Pinky dislocated at the knuckle. Hung parallel with my palm. I slid against the wall, smashed the back of my head against the panelling. The sensation loosened the grip of reality, I became manic, lost and wild as I drifted to the otherworld. I couldn't stop myself.

Is this how Benji felt?

"I hate you." I'm sorry.

"Why couldn't you let me die?" Forgive me.

"I'll fucking kill you." I'm so scared.

"Give it to me." I can't stop.

"I don't want your help." Don't let me go.

"I *hate* you, bitch. Cunt. Fucker."

Forgive me.

"I'm not him!"

The door opened. I stood, ready to rush through her. She buried my face in her chest, wrapped her delicate arms around my shaking body.

We cried.

My heart became light.

I don't remember passing out.

This is how my days, and nights, went for two weeks.

If I could take back all the things I said to her, I would. All hurtful words hurled her way.

Every. Single. One.

Abhartach: Orlok's Symphony of Horror.

On the thirteenth day I awoke to absolute silence. I drank the apple smoothie Jocelyn routinely placed on the stained nightstand, straining with effort to hold the cup to my dehydrated lips. She had tried to feed me other things, bread, tofu, salad, but they always came back up. Apples, for whatever reason, were the only things my stomach could handle during detox.

I lay, still as I could, noticing my fever had ended. I had focus. Clarity. A minor headache compared to the axe wound I carried for a fortnight. For the first time, I took in the 1960's basement loaded with veneer. Bowling alleys came to mind.

Zombie vibes. Wake. Eat. Puke. Sleep. Rage. Puke. Eat. Shit. Sleep. Repeat. I prayed to a god I didn't believe in that the last of the hallucinations ended. That I could return to living. That this was not the calm before the apocalypse. A false shift.

Sitting upright proved difficult. I rested a moment, then slouched in my hushed new world until my anxious breathing, laboured and forced like a great weight pressed into my chest, settled and the bowling lanes closed in. If I stayed, a turkey would drive a morningstar through my dome and spread grey matter over lane 12. I fled.

I climbed the stairs, stopping midway as the panic attack overtook me. When it passed, I was drained, sweating and shaking. I carefully opened the feeble door, hoping that shallow movements would stop the kettle-drum dancing in my chest.

The world above the bowling alley basement was overcast which shrivelled my virgin eyes in their crusted sockets. I knuckled tears in the clean air. Thankful to be rid of the putrid stench of the pit, I ascended.

Unable to find Jocelyn in the house, I grabbed a clean towel and searched for fresh clothes from her dresser. Nothing fit. It wasn't like I could squirm my way in and out of skin tight tees with my busted hand and it was too warm for a crew neck and her cardigans were too feminine. I settled on gym shorts and an undersized tie-dye shirt with thousands of paint stains hashing the stomach. Across the breast read Friendship Camp arching over infantile stick figures.

I drew a bath of lukewarm water. Soaked. Forever. Cried underwater.

When I tried on the clothes the Friendship Camp was at best a belly top and the green dazzle shorts exposed my thighs with a complementary crotch hole. Groovy.

I shaved my stubble, globbed toothpaste onto my finger and tried to scrape yellow stains from my teeth until I choked on the mint while scraping my molars.

Gums raw. Bleeding. My jaw ached from grinding my teeth dull during detox.

Static echoed in the tiny cottage. Drift fuzz. Music blasted through cheap headphones. The door was ajar revealing her imperfect hunch on the ground. One leg curled under her bum, the other knee supported her chin. Toes dancing to an upbeat song I had never heard before nor again after this moment.

She painted. What, I didn't know, but she appeared content with her work. Earnest. I feared ruining her flow, tarnishing her moment of creativity.

I pretended she painted this scene. Us. The here and now. The loneliness of early afternoons in autumn. Echo. Rain.

The world swayed and I reached for the doorframe for support. Accidentally kicked it open and cursed my bashed shin. She eyed me over her shoulder, wary. Resumed.

I stifled a guilty tear, then confused-rage tears. I hated how emotionally unstable the drain of detox was. As if my personality jolted to and from extremes. I clung to the lath and plaster walls until I calmed back to stoicism. Hoping not to bother her. Afraid to be alone.

Her studio led to an overgrown backyard and she used the natural, but dull, light to illuminate her canvas. I eased into a tackey green couch with pink flowers weeding over the cushions. I sunk on broken springs.

Watercolours stained her pale arms in blues and yellows veiling her freckles like campfire light in winter. A shrine of bottles and palettes surrounded her feet with more types of brushes than I thought existed in a haphazard circle on the carpet. At times she sat with the canvas no more than an inch from her face. Fragile strokes requiring the finest detail. The only time she stopped was to take a drag of cancer, or sip a beer that went flat hours ago.

A pause between songs revealed her growling stomach. She snorted. Disgusted with her body's need for fuel.

I peeled myself from the couch and went to the cramped kitchen at the front of the house. Hunted in her pantry. Stir fry. Tofu, rice, asparagus, carrots, green onions, and a little garlic. For myself I had a premade apple smoothie, which after sitting in the fridge for a day, was more like apple sauce.

When I plated the food, I had to continue to cover my nose with my good hand to dull the coarse aroma.

She waited at the table, lost in her thoughts beside the window with her flat beer watching ominous clouds. A darker grey consumed a lighter one. The watercolours had spread to her cheeks and forehead. Her tattered clothes loose around her boyish frame.

I set the table. We ate silent, avoided gazes.

I paced myself to appease my choosey stomach. I wanted to ask for an icepack for my knuckle, but was too embarrassed. I must have reagitated it while cooking.

When we finished, she wiped her lips with a cloth napkin.

"I'm sor—"

"Thank you." I interrupted.

Jocelyn nodded and boiled tea. Rinsed out her beer bottle while we waited with our thoughts. When she sat back down, she smiled tepidly. "Those are a bad fit, huh?"

"I know, right?" I said pulling at my Camp Friendship shirt.

"If those shorts were any shorter, your butt would tumble out."

"It was the only thing you had that would fit."

"There's a purple dress," she said, "in the back of the closet from my chubbier days. I can fish it out, if you'd like."

"If it's not a problem for you."

"Not at all." She smiled more naturally. Hid behind her Daria mug. "Seriously though, I want my hobo clothes back with all holes accounted for."

"So that's why there is a pee-hole in the shorts."

"Be nice. I use those when I'm stabbing canvas with camel pubes."

"Your paintbrushes are made from camel pubes?"

"The softest."

"This explains the gigantic pharaoh crab that stole my wallet."

"You're so funny, aren't you?" She sipped her tea.

"I really am." I lied.

A moment passed. Nothing with substance came to mind.

"So, what are those clothes?" I gestured to her tattered men's Crash Bandicoot tee. "Hobo reserves?"

She folded her arms, leaned in. "All hobos are on active duty, storming the borders of the United States of Terrorism, thank you."

I welcomed her belligerent remark. It eased me out of anxiety. I'd do anything to avoid the looming discussion of what a horrible human I was to her. I'd eat my own dick to keep the peace. Hell, I'd carve out my ribs with a spatula to do it too.

The humble kitchen grew dark and the amber glow of streetlights illuminated the dirty pans steeping in the sink. Neither of us minded the lowlight. Jocelyn's face crept into chiaroscuro until all I could discern was the yellow paint hugging her pale neck rising out of the blackness.

"She called you every day, you know," Jocelyn said, suddenly changing subjects. She fingered the brim of her mug. "Until your phone died, anyway. Took me a while to find a matching charger at the Discount Emporium."

Sav.

"I respected your privacy," she said, blowing away the last of the steam, before taking a sip of her tea. "I knew from the number. I still remember it."

"Vincent Price's birthday," we said in unison.

"Such a dork. Anyway. The voicemails are still saved. She hasn't left one in a while, so I'm guessing she filled your mailbox."

She pulled my phone out from her pocket. Bitten fingernails picked at the broken plastic. I had no memory of cracking it, but inside me I knew I had in a fit. Hysteria. Yeah I said it. I could feel the ghost memory. I lashed out at Jocelyn for—I couldn't remember.

"I didn't want her to"—she thought for a moment—"ruin your chances. I was afraid you'd start using again. You're better than that. You don't know it, though. I can't and shouldn't dictate your life, and you are your own person, but I couldn't lose another friend like that. It'd put me over the edge and I can't—It's selfish of me."

"Not at all."

She gave my phone a second glance as if she remembered it existed. I heard it slide across the table. I almost dove at it as it skittered away from her soft hand. My instinct was to call Dev to pick up, go on a bender, call Sav and run to her, kiss her, screw our brains out while we tripped.

But I didn't.

I sat still. Watched Jocelyn's delicate nose, freckled and pale, as it gleamed in the twilight. An earthy steam danced from her mug. Her nose wrinkled as she contemplated something inside her.

"It can wait," I said, leaving the phone between us. "How'd you find me?"

I gulped the last of my apple sauce, trying not to gag on the sweetness. Some dribbled down my chin as my throat rebelled. I haphazardly tried to discreetly clean myself, unsure if she could see me.

"He used to bring me there." She looked outside the window. Streetlights betrayed her profile as she stared at a place farther away than her neighbour's bushes. "We'd go there to escape the hectic blurbs of the city. Most couples go there to hook up, but we would sit on the hood of my dad's Civic and chat. About nothing in particular. Trying to make each other laugh. This one time we left the engine running, windows down, listening to a mixtape. All his favourite songs that reminded him of me. We killed the battery. I know. We had to beg this hick couple to boost us. I became hyperaware of battery drain after that. And thanks to my dad's lectures.

"It's embarrassing, but since he passed away, I go up to the Devil's Punch Bowl to cry. Couldn't tell you why. We shared other spots. Better ones engrained with more of our history, but up there next to those stupid blinding lights, I feel closer to him. Neither of us cared for religion—I don't know. I feel so dumb trying to explain it out loud."

I told her she wasn't dumb.

"The night I found you I had just pulled in as you walked through the trees to the overlook. I didn't know it was specifically you at the time. I assumed you were some random out for a stroll, or a party creep coming home from the gristmill, or a lonely kid who couldn't sleep. A girl sneaking out to see a boy.

"I cried for a while before I got a text. Your text. I was pissed. Not about how we left things, I got over that. It's just—I didn't even read it. I believed that the text violated my time to reflect about him. As if it poisoned my peaceful place. Discouraged, I decided to stretch my legs and left my phone in the console in case another text came. Sorry."

"Don't be."

"I am," she said, brushing away my apology. "Not just in retrospect. I have this fear that some people can't take hints when I don't respond right away. I couldn't deal with some pathetic 'nice guy' while I was emotionally fragile.

"You were on the ground when I found you. Slumped atop the overlook, half hanging over the edge of the escarpment like you had been trying to crawl—If it weren't for the way your foot caught—I ran over, cursing myself for leaving my phone in the car, thinking I should call 911, but decided leaving you would be worse because you could tumble—I pulled you back over and then I saw that it was you." Jocelyn released a quivering breath before continuing. "Your eyes were dead. I couldn't tell if you were breathing, and there was this gurgling, and I was too frightened to call for help, and I could see his face in yours when they asked me to identify—"

"You don't have to go on," I said. "I'm so sorry, Joce."

"My landlord hates when I smoke inside. Want to come nervously chainsmoke with me?"

The weeds in the backyard were so thick they appeared like a Lovecraftian Old One seething through a portal on the lichenous fence. I told Jocelyn this and she forced out a laugh. Told me the landlord said there used to be a natural pool under all that thick brush.

"I'd like to clean it out one day," she said, picking at hangnails as she tried to resist another cancer. Scabs picked. Puffy and pink. I felt responsible. "I'd at least like to see what lies beneath. Before I move out, you know? He said he'd help clean it. He said he would get it done before autumn. But look where we are."

"What was he like?" I asked. Knowing she switched from her landlord to Benji.

"You know what he is like," she said, sitting on her hands.

"Not what he was really like. I knew him when we played toy wars with Transformers. Stole his pop's beers at 13. Somewhere in the between we changed. I didn't know he was shooting. I realized after he—I realized he changed. That people take different lanes depending on which road they travel."

"In the intimate moments that people share when they are truly alone."

I nodded once.

"He had a habit of kneading his head into my clavicle when overtired. And when I left in the morning for the Youth Centre to help with those painting classes, he would watch me get dressed. I pretended I didn't notice him peeking while I applied makeup. I'd make a point to adjust my bra several times, admire myself in the mirror and be certain my outfit sat just right, then touchup my warpaint. In reality I was posing for him. And he would wait until I was fully dressed and ready to walk out the door to grab me by the hand and in a hoarse hush he'd say my name. It's funny, you know, thinking back on it. It was like a reverse strip-tease. Who does that?"

I wondered what ran through Benji's mind while he watched her dress. The version of Benji I knew would puke at the sentimentality, but in this version, Jocelyn's version, he was just a boy. Simple.

I wondered if there were other moments, other people he considered worthy of this alien behaviour.

"He texted me his goodbye note," she said suddenly.

I knew better than to speak. If I uttered a wrong word, she would close up once more, or worse, our fragile friendship would smash upon the rocks. I sat still, apprehension filling my guts as I cautiously sucked harsh nicotine from my cancer while she spoke.

"They say he had a heart attack. But he sent me the truth. That night. He went to Alex for one last hit. I was here. Right here, on this porch arguing with my mother about where to put that ratty couch, when my phone went off.

"I didn't read the first text. Or the second. I assumed he was telling me another elaborate anecdote, or a goofy rant, or something outlandish you said to him. On the fourth text I checked. I couldn't read them as fast as they were coming in. There were forty-two in total and each one vibrated my shaking hand.

"He was sorry he couldn't give me the world I deserved. He thought he failed me. I didn't understand, I kept thinking why is he telling me this, are we breaking up, what had I done? I tried calling but he declined and kept texting. When he told me that the doctors couldn't help, I knew it was coming. He had been in the hospital a lot after being arrested. Mental health stuff. Rehab meetings. He had told me he had a chest infection he caught from a guy in the cell, but it was a lie. The doctors gave him a week to live if he didn't get treatment.

"He took his life after the third day. Bacteria spread to his heart from dirty needles. Endocarditis. I should have known by his splintered fingernails, but he told me it was too much guitar or injuries from cleaning crew. His body quit on him. His heart was too weak to fend off the infection in his heart valves. They deteriorated. The doctors called him lucky for living this long without medication. He was sick of hurting and knew he would never stay clean, so to him there was only one logical choice.

"They found his body north of Toronto along Cherry Creek, I'm sure you know. He climbed up a boulder, swung his feet over the edge and took his last hit. I saw the picture they took when they found him. He looked identical to his pretended sleep as I dressed up for him."

She closed herself to the world, and whispered to her heart. "Was my name the last thing you said?" She peeled at the puffy pink scabs in the crooks of her thumb before slipping her hands under her bum again. "After me, they called his parents to formally ID him. A courtesy since his dad hadn't seen him since he ran away. His mom lied about the suicide. Some Catholics they are, lying to their god, living in separate beds instead of divorcing. Ugh! Hell doesn't even exist. It's Bible fanfiction.

"I'd like to think when we're done here, we all just wait at a train station for old friends. No baggage packed. Well rested. Reunion Station.

"I still can't believe Alex sold to him. Knowing what he intended to do. They all refuse to address it. They knew! They fucking knew. You can't go back to all that noise. Do it for him. If you can't do it for yourself. Do it for Benji."

I cried when she said his name. We both did. When our faces dried we went back inside, said goodnight with a short hug. I told her I cared about Sav, a lot.

"I know," she said, drained of emotion and malice. She let go. "I'm not saying don't be with her. Live for you. Don't let her fire kill yours."

Dead Alive.

Flakes of white paint peeled off the dingy shed nested in the weeds of Jocelyn's backyard. It needed a solid sanding, I knew and so did the robins, but we lacked time and money and skill and obligation. I fought the bush with a broom. Single-handed with swollen pink knuckles. Once the door was liberated from the wild, I found sleeping gardening tools rusting on carpenter spikes. Like me, they'd have to do.

Jocelyn was out for the day with Carmen, her new sigo who worked at Saetia. I had met her once. Apparently. Jocelyn said they had gotten friendly during Green River's Art Crawl—something I had missed during a binge—and she said they had bonded over Japanese sex pervert cartoons.

I was glad Jocelyn was finding her footing again. She couldn't live in a depressive sexless rut her whole life and it wasn't like being with Carmen made what she and Benji had less meaningful. She deserved happiness. Someone worthy of holding her heavy heart.

While I cleared the yard, I wondered how their road trip to Prince Edward County was going. They sought the mysterious fresh water anomaly, Onokenoga. The

Lake on the Mountain. Jocelyn said the lake fills itself with the spirits of the Mohawks dwelling within the bottomless waters. I told her she was nutters. She smirked.

With her away, I felt less guilty about freeloading, but I was happy for her. Honest.

I took the long weekend to get my head and heart aligned. Looking for jobs and a place to live. Housework after noon. Chainsmoking cancers and crushing apples until I cleared the backyard. The bane was the massive thorn bush consuming the back corner of the lot like the Greenman's Sequoia Throne. It shredded my arms and shins, but thanks to the shovels and sheers in the shed, I conquered it.

If I'm honest, I found peace in physical labour. No. Not that way. What I mean to say is sweating out lingering toxins felt freeing because I kept myself too tired for depression. Distracted. It procrastinated my obligation to speak with Sav. I knew I shouldn't avoid her, but, like I said before, I was dope at running away.

By dinner I had cleared the yard and found the pond, but it looked more like a possum hovel filled with bog water. Nonetheless I celebrated. Starved for protein I fired up a hotdog—classic caker meal—thinking I could stomach raccoon meat and boot leather. The sizzling stank of meat sweat made me gag. I puked after biting off the ends, picked at the bun before switching back to apples and decided, as the moon crept over my bed in the bowling alley basement, to finally listen to my messages. End my avoidance. If not for the exhaustion, I wouldn't have been able to listen to them all in a single sitting. I ran on fumes for so long my engine would have seized up as I ran into the night looking for the blackhole kids.

"I hate you."

"Alex is looking for you. Says he wants to talk. I still hate you."

"Hey. Just wondering where you've been. I'm not mad anymore. You good to talk?"

"Did you run away without me?"

"I keep picturing you on one of your long walks. Surrounded by strangers in parts of the city most normals have forgotten. Are you thinking of me? I'd like to think so."

"I get it. You're pissed. But I know you're too sentimental to ignore these messages. I'm just going to talk—

—I know you'll keep these. Even when the phone's battery gives, you'll keep these. On a disc, maybe, listening to it after you've escaped Green River, gotten married, and farted out a worm baby or six. I'll still be on this little phone, won't I? Am I dead? Am I haunting you, nitwit? Or am I sitting next to you, plump and blushing at how foolish all this was?"

"I miss you."

"Phil and Mexican Dan said they saw you with her. I'm glad you're alive."

"Something happened. Don't be mad."

"I iced my jaw yesterday. It's getting harder to say this isn't the worse I've been. Why do I lie to myself about how one day I'll laugh at all of this? Did you ever find me funny? I'm leaving them behind. Our friends, I mean."

"I'm so trashed right now. Can't you tell? I think I'm growing out of shows, they aren't as fun

as they used to be, scene's dead, and I've been thinking about me lately, how I lie about who I am—who knows me?—This happy-go-lucky facade hasn't been honest in what, eight years? Maybe I'm holding onto the remnants of wild youth as adolescence falters. Is this what dying feels like? Trapped inside a box, or refusing to step out? I should come clean. Sellout. Do parents dream their kids grow into junkies? I feel sick. Screw it! From now on I'll step on toes. Sav the toe crusher. I like it. Time to make tall leaps and- and ditch this despair. Yeah. I mean, sure, maybe it was good for drinking, but it never wished me well and that's the whole point. Isn't it? You'd send me a Get Well card, right? Oh, what the hell am I talking about? You're not even really here."

"I miss you, bastard."

"Can you come get me?"

"Hello? This is Alannah Moore, Savannah's mom. Could you call me when you have a chance? It's about my daughter."

Event Horizon.

Steady pulsing whines sounded from the nurse's station, pulling my attention from my novel, *Battle Royale*, and tried to keep my eyes from scanning darkly as Yoshi lay on the classroom floor. It was no use. The high note sounded as the green LED flashed on the station board. Low note timed with a polyrhythm in red.

It reminded me of turn signals. I have this memory as a kid, in my dad's dog of a station wagon as we're leaving the public pool, bodies ripe with chlorine. I'm in the front seat, a place for big boys, stuck in traffic. Benji is in the back, wiping boogers on the window. My dad's trying to turn left along with every other normal leaving the community centre. Everyone's turn signal flashes at random and dimwitted me is hung up on the lights, hoping to catch them synced with ours as it clicks while my dad grumbles about Mike Harris and his 'bullshit common sense regression.' I almost quit for fear he would catch me 'screwing around' while I squirm to see all the blinkers. A miracle happens. The advance green illuminates as if divinely ordered and all the cars in row blink in time. Once. Then they all immediately fell back out of time. For that one click we were all in tune.

Is that not what we're all hoping for? For our lights to click on at the same moment.

I returned the book to my backpack, set it beside my gift for Sav, careful as to not rip the jet black wrapping paper. I wished I had come to the hospital sooner.

"Leave with me?"

The man who spoke to me in the patient care area wore a blue striped hospital gown. Dishevelled goatee. Ear tussocks. Silver with age and trampish. A cracked out homeless owl from NIMH.

"What?" I asked, wishing I had music to drown him out.

"They got their trackers in my blood," the homeless owl said. "Told me it was an aspirin, but I can feel smelting with my bones. Don't let them take your pulse, it's how they mark you for processing. I didn't believe in Abby. My left shoe hurts. Quiet! Do you smell crickets?"

I scanned the cream hall for an orderly, but found nothing. "Maybe you should sit for a bit," I said.

"Ask me where I'm going."

I paused, hid my backpack with Sav's gift between my legs. "Where are you going?"

He turned his back to me, squatted, and shoved his head between his legs. Old man butt. Wrinkled and free. The tip of his ballsack rested on his chin.

"I'm going to the moon," he said.

"Is your son a walrus?"

"We're descendants of lobsters who owe me twenty bucks," he said, before stomping away, nards swaying as he screamed at clouds to 'come here.'

Sav's mother came into the hallway as a nurse ushered the homeless owl away from ward doors.

Alannah Moore used both hands to pull back her frizzled hair from her cheeks, faked a smile. She looked worse than she sounded on the phone. Unwashed hair with greasy roots from sleepless nights. Eyes glazed with weariness. Spicy pits. She was proof humans could erode into nothingness.

"Your daughter is in the best hands," said a top-heavy and soft-spoken doctor who smelled of savoury curry. He looked at me, frowned. "Think about what I suggested. It's best for Savannah's recovery. Marie at reception will have pamphlets you may find helpful. Programs run very frequently at St. Josephine's and there are local sponsors on the inverse that I'm sure will agree with your concerns."

"Hello, Missus Moore," I said, shrinking away from the doctor as he went into the next room.

"Thank you for coming," she said, hugging me tightly in her lilac arms. "I knew it would do her good to see someone who cares about her."

"Anything to help," I said, feeling useless.

"She's been sleeping a lot. It's that damned medication they have her on. I thought she'd be more awake today. I'm sorry."

I understood.

"When she wakes up, you'll be the first person I call."

"Actually, if it's all the same to you, I brought her something." I pulled out the crudely wrapped Vincent Price biography I stole from the library. "Would it be alright if I left it in her room?"

"Take your time," she said. "Just don't wake her. She needs rest. I'm late for my shift. Again. If anything happens call the nurse, will you?"

"One hundred percent," I said, giving her an awkward thumbs up like a toddler. "They're making you work?"

"I've reached the 'accepted maximum' at both jobs." She splayed her fingers to distract from her tears. "But because it's not me in the hospital and because she's an adult, both say she doesn't need me there. What child doesn't need their mother? Can you name one? They couldn't either. 'My child wouldn't end up at the General.' Bitch. Sorry, dear. I can't bear thinking about her going through this alone. One place has already written me up for 'failure to notify.'

"How is this legal?"

"They told me if I try to fight it, there will be a lack of floors to clean next season."

"That's messed."

"That's life," she said, defeated. "When Layton takes over, things will be different."

He didn't. They weren't.

I sat by Sav's side for the better part of the day. She didn't stir during my visit, nor did I attempt to wake her. When I wasn't mumbling to her, I cried. The specifics of what I talked to her about do not matter. Not to you. Those moments alone in the cramped hospital room with her during early recovery are my memories and mine alone. I do not wish to dilute them, or tarnish them by giving them voice. When I tried to type them out, I broke down. Cried in my car at work. Refused to touch this book for many months. I owe her to get these out. Some things don't heal with time.

After visiting hours, a nurse asked me to leave while she cleaned Sav. I was baffled that I had been so bemused to lose track of time. Not minutes, but scores of hours. I nodded to the nurse, thanked her for caring for Sav. I left Price's biography next to my dollar store greeting card. I almost forgot to sign my name.

In the elevator, I texted my ride as a physio with bleached hair got on at the second floor. She checked her anti-stoic counter, proud with her gains.

I had expected the main foyer to be as bustling as it had when I came in but it was abandoned. The sound of a tile polisher hummed as it judged a man with a toilet seat stuck around his waist and another with a drill bit screwed into his palm who shouted at his son with Balkan grunts. The former stunk of still water.

As I exited the hospital and stepped into the chilly air, two jacked security guards dragged a girl, kicking and screaming, outside. I mustn't have heard the commotion over the noise in my head or the polisher. I knew who she was by the curly blue hair and 'Kick Me' hoodie.

"Fascist pigs!"

"Ryan?" I asked, holding the door for security.

She was thinner with gullies hollowing her cheeks. Eyes like glazed almonds. She had picked scabs off her neck.

"Hey longtimer, gotta smoke?"

I handed her a cancer without much thought.

"Dope! They kick you out too?"

"Something like that."

"Fascists." She spat a wad on the window. "I've been trying to see Sav for days." She yelled at the glass doors. "We just want to see our friend! Fucking rent-a-cops."

She kicked the glass, and one of the guards threatened her with a finger wag. She stuck out her tongue and called him racist.

"Why won't they let you in?"

"Damned if I know. Alex came on the first day. Booted! Lisa on the second. She missed Zoe's going away party. Worse than bouncers. Lisa called Sav's mom, but she gets screened and when we pop by the apartment? Nothing! Think she's living in the hospital? I guess you need to like 'be approved' or someshit to visit certain wards. I have no idea."

"Probably."

"You heading home?" She picked absently at a scab on her forehead, focusing intensely on my reaction. "We can ride the bus back together because there's supposed to be a party tonight for this guy Chico. I don't think you met him, he's a bit older than us, he's back in town for a bit and smuggled up some peyote, he plays in this band, I forget the name, it was Spanish or some shit, Taladro de Carne, I think? Whatever. He's back so we're throwing him a party and everyone is gonna be there, even Lisa, she's real torn up, my dude, it's bogus, but we all think you two should like get back together or whatever and I can tell her—"

"Thanks, Ryan," I said, heeling my cancer on the curb, "but I have plans. I'm waiting for my ride."

"Oh. Right on. He can come too. No worries."

"I don't think that's a good idea."

"Alex says he's over it," she said, but when I refused to indulge her, she raised her hands, balancing her cancer between her lips. "Your boy's not down to party, huh? Lame. He's not a sellout, is he? Oh! Can I bum a ride back?"

A white sedan pulled into the parking lot and flashed its high beams at me.

"Sorry, we're not heading that way," I said, walking to my ride.

"But I didn't tell you where the party is!"

I slipped into the car, thanked the driver as we pulled out.

"No problem. Who was that you were talking to? You're sexually advancing on the disabled again, aren't you?"

"Nobody," I said. "I'm starving. Want to watch me fail at eating?"

"Always."

Jocelyn cranked her stereo. The Postal Service panned between us as she pulled onto East 7th. I found the strength to sing along with her.

Perfect Blue.

The first real job I ever had—which didn't require me to run drugs, panhandle, or steal—was at a tiny fish and chip joint called Goldens. The owner, a big sloppy Dutch doughboy named Gustav Ardaplemot, liked to brag that it was family owned and operated for over forty years. Being a potato monkey was the best job I ever had.

Gus's rules were: 1 start work any time after close, 2 no outsiders inside, 3 cut and blanche potatoes.

The only rule I ever broke was 2 when Jocelyn tricked me into drinking with her after a screening of some arthouse dud called *The Freelancer*. I got wrecked and woke up entangled under a table while she teased me for being a lightweight space cadet.

Listen: the reason why I said it was the best job I ever had was because of how ideal it was for me at the time. You must understand, my body was cadaverous. What normals found stimulating—stock boy, cashier, bottle boy, dishwasher, labourer—I found enraging or horrifying. Physical strain robbed me of endurance and I needed frequent rest. Move at my own pace. Hell, if I walked too long my head spun like a teacup ride which ignited my anxiety. I became afraid of becoming afraid. I hyperventilated a lot. Large groups were worse. They assaulted my senses. Rattled my core with overstimulation. I feared collapse and convulsion. I spent an evening in Saetia once, pacing in the handicap stall while Jocelyn argued with Carmen about stages of clinginess. I thought I was suffocating because the green tea was too hot.

And there you have it. The reason why I loved my job as a remedial night shift potato-slave.

I took it out of necessity, too. I polluted Jocelyn's space for too long. Decided to rid her of myself and found a place to live. It was a modest apartment in the building of a friend of a friend of my mom's coworker's kid's hairdresser barber kind of deal. It was ghetto. Cheap.

I spent my nights at Goldens and my days feigning sleep. I made regular trips to see Sav—who would tease me for smelling like a grease trap—when I felt strong enough to walk to the bus stop and resolved to handle the commotion of commuters.

Several times I guilted Jocelyn into driving me home, too afraid of losing consciousness on the bus, because I ate my emergency apple in the bottom of my bag because what if I died from lack of sugar? I didn't know if I was diabetic and was too afraid to get tested because needles put the fear of god into me.

Jocelyn would always smile, and lightly say 'alright, but you owe me one.'

On a miserable night, she cashed in. I was blasting a burned disc, *Punk in Drublic*, on a CD player I scored at a yard sale on West Avenue North. I was covered in itchy starch, trying to force a plain baked potato into my stomach as the music skipped. It went berserk when I turned on the rattling peeler. Lacked anti-shock. I made a mental note to buy a new guitar and play it at work instead. Determined it was the logical and only place I could play.

An urgent clack echoed through the dining area. I peered over the fryers at the front window. Found Jocelyn tapping on the glass with a nickel. She waved. Cheeks blushed from the early autumn chill. I pointed behind me and mouthed 'back door' in that overexaggerated way normals do when they forget how to speak. Hushed whisper-yell. All vowels. Nose.

She pointed at the door handle. I wagged my finger, remembering how last time she tricked me into getting dickard. She made a heart with her hands. Puppy-eyed. I made a crude gesture and she flipped me off with a smile and headed to the back lot.

I stepped outside, cancer already lit, wishing I had more than my yellow dad hat and grimy apron to fend off the chill.

"Please don't tell me you're wearing that because you want to," she said, rounding the corner.

"If I wore what I usually wear people would think I broke in." I discharged cancer into the frigid midnight air. "What's your excuse for wearing blankets in public?"

"Blankets can be clothes," she said, spinning her oversized green shawl around her body. "Besides, I can't wander the streets naked, can I?"

"Don't joke about traumatizing old bitties at this hour. I hear they hunt in packs."

"I blame the hip hop and your complicated shoes." She quivered involuntarily from the wind. "It's the real reason Canadialand is losing its wholesome fundi values. Gosh dang over-privileged poors with their single mothers and fear of guns. So. You gonna invite me in?"

I told her fat chance after what she pulled last time.

"It was a joke! Geeze. If you can't sexually assault your friends, then who can you?"

"Ma'am this is a family establishment."

"Alright mister potato slave who follows rules now, have it your way. I came by to tell you I'm cashing in on all those rides."

"I'll do anything but anal."

"I'm rubbing off on you, huh? You're faster with those than you should be."

I shot her with finger guns and she rolled her eyes as if that was going too far.

"I have tickets to a gala," she said. "High scale event. Balcony seats. Fully catered and black tie. It's tomorrow. I know. I know. Last minute. But I thought it'd be cool if we went somewhere outside Green River."

"Lies," I said, and her nose scrunched. "I'm down. But I have to be back here to continue the potato genocide."

"I'll make sure to get you back to the frontlines, soldier." She threw the salute from Spaceballs. "Dismissed." She snapped on her heel and marched away to her car.

"Where and when though?" I shouted after her, flicking away my cancer butt.

"Afternoon. And you're right, I am a liar. I just wanted to keep the surprise a little longer."

▬ There are three ways to tell when you've reached Toronto from Green River. Onest: the density of product placement on the highway. Twond: the waterfront, however this accounts for The Ex and is only a stone's throw from the core, thus discounting the burbs orbiting the Six. Threerd: My preference, the edge of Etobicoke at the huge graffiti sign, along the side of the pedestrian overpass crossing the highway that reads 'have a nice day <3.' From the train, you can make it out for only a second before skyscrapers consume it.

Canada's blessing and curse is the honour system. Especially for transit. You're morally obligated to pay for tickets. Conductor monkeys only patrol the trains hunting for freeloaders during big events. Jays. Leafs. Expos and concerts. Like in Toiletpaper USA, you can buy tickets beside the tracks, or you can buy tickets in-person last minute. Or you can be like Jocelyn. Simply walk on and sit on the glorified dust sponges stinking of white-collar BO.

The best thing to do when cheating the system is to act like it's normal to get on without paying. Nobody gives a second glance. They're all too polite and cowardly to speak up. Too Canadian.

The other option is you could be like Benji and me when we went to the Docks for Punks Dead Fest. At Mapleview Station, there's an overhang where the normals wait for the train with a key design flaw. The roof can be reached from the 3rd floor of the parking garage. We climbed onto the overhang, timed the jump as the train pulled out. gg ez.

The last time we used this lifehack was during a Bosstones tour. Sav and Benji and I were running late because Benji wanted to pick up before the concert. The train screeched out of the station as we made the jump onto the overhang. Benji leapt first, landed flawless and golden like everything he touched. I was running out of cars when I went next, twisted my ankle under me and starfished onto the train car. Adrenalin and hash dulled the jolt of pain. Before I got my bearings, Sav leapt after me and rolled over my legs. Her momentum carried her the width of the car and I scrambled after her, grasping at her hands, barely caught her backpack before she tumbled over the edge. After a moment staring at Green River rushing past us, she rolled to her knees, threw her hands into the air and yelled 'Nailed it.' I told her she was bonkers. Benji laughed, hoping she didn't shatter our hash pipe.

With Jocelyn, who still insisted on the secrecy of our destination, we simply walked on. Found empty seats. No antics.

The greenbelt and Devil's Punch Bowl faded away until Green River's landscape dissolved into an urban wonderland. The steady dakka-dakka of tracks guided us closer to Jocelyn's secret place.

Union Station; a human beehive humming a special type of hell. Jocelyn emptied her purse of coins in a clatter for an old bluesman with red suspenders and kind eyes. His sax trilled. Noon rush peaked and I battled with the urge to hyperventilate, used my hand to cover my mouth as I sucked in steady breaths. Lungs too nervous to fully expand, tricking my mind they were out of breath. If Jocelyn noticed me struggle, she decided best to ignore it.

I joined the long line snaking around the ticket booth to purchase a subway token. My brain rioted from the overwhelming city sounds and noise clusters orbiting around me.

Jocelyn motioned me away from the line as I defended myself. I wanted to offer to pay, assuming she had bought tickets to some hipster event, but before words came, she hopped the turnstile.

No one cared. Not the Italian berating his daughter for straying from his reach. Nor the Punjabi in a crisp button down going full Super Saiyan to the delight of his friends. A young scrawny Hong Konger, paced like an elder with his hands folded behind his back as he and his busty Jamaican girlfriend flirted, sharing headphones. The commuters were all lost in their singular ecosystems, focused on their own worlds.

As with most of our wandering adventures together, Jocelyn and I did not talk. As we walked through the hordes of humans in the underground tunnels, we didn't exchange glances. We stayed separate, yet together. Caged by the strangers encircling us with their chatter and the groans of subway cars. If the normals paid us an iota of attention they would never have guessed we were together. We became two more faceless pedestrians roaming TO. I was thankful for it. I'm sure she knew from my clammy skin and wiry eyes I was always in a state of anxiety when in public. Useless and unfocused. Unworthy of public conversation.

We got off at Museum Station. She adored the sarcophagi-meet-totem-poles-meet-terra-cottas support pillars. Ran her fingers over the carved surfaces as we passed them.

Some board of directors thought they were a real neato design, but to me they felt tacky inside the urine stenched platform.

On the escalator we fell into single file like the other normals returning from their midday feeding break. My body lulled into a false sense of security and I was able to chill now that the worst of the panic attack was over. I wanted to joke with Jocelyn about how if we brought a time traveller from past to present and showed them the escalator, they would stroke out on the spot. 'What madness is this?' they'd ask, clutching their chest. 'Stairs whence walk for thee? Tis d'evil marked! Witchbreed pox. A blight on thine house and ye poor souls misfortunated to meet thee!'

But I never spoke up. Kept the foolish words in my chest as I followed Jocelyn's regal blue cardigan as she ascended into the bright sky.

I asked her if we were going to the ROM.

"Not even close," she said. "I only enter museums when held at musket point. I'm still traumatized from the buddy system. I blame babysitting Bert, the local autistic kid. I mean. Don't get me wrong, B, was a sweetheart, but I get flashbacks of nine-hour lectures about Sonic the Hedgehog every time I see modern art. I shouldn't know things like all ten of Princess Sally Acorn's nicknames. Or how Thatcher's Yellow Peril changed the Ninja Turtles to Mutant Hero Turtles."

"Makes withdrawal sound not half bad."

"I bet that sounded funnier in your head."

It had.

We ate street meat for lunch. I chose Billy Dogs, paid cash to the toothless hippy with a skullet who smelled of cut grass. He had four types of wieners: pork, beef, chicken, meat. We are still unsure what 'meat' is. We doubted lamb and decided best not to ask. My chicken dog was greasier than a nerd at a comic convention, and I sipped off-brand OJ to chase it down my gullet. Jocelyn crushed a box of poutine with gravy slopes and cheese curd snow caps. I teased her about laxing on her vegetarianism. She tried to force me to deepthroat my Billy Dog.

I managed three whole bites before quitting. New record.

She led me through various streets at random, trading main drags for sides, dodging pedestrians, veering over subway grates, and leaning off my shoulder like a bored child while we waited for crosswalk lights to change.

My back ached, but I didn't fuss. Let her do most of the talking while I panted from exertion. Storage space of Subaru Crosscheck vs Scion TC. Benefits of being alone in a new city. Where the best doughnuts in Ontario are. She told me about the controversial Yakuza skins displayed in a Japanese museum. The notorious gangsters were skinned after death so normals could gawk at their ink.

"Each piece tells the story of the individual," she said, when I asked her if we could sit and rest so I could get in some electrolytes. She wriggled her toes as she bent over to stretch her back. "Imagine if they did that here? See this kid, he listened to heavily distorted and riotous nonsense, called the punk. This is an Operation Ivy logo, standard, and nicely compliments the hallmark anarchy tat on his left calf. To your right, you will see our female."

"Excellent breeding stock," I said like a zealous tourist, willing to diss Alex's ink and feeling rejuvenated for the rest. "Look at the pierced nips, clit, and tongue—Purely for sexual enhancement. If you rotate your view you may even catch a glimpse of her tramp stamp. High fashion. Legend has it, it's a cover up of her totally custom unique tribal which, as an easter egg, resembles her lover's name. Spike. Tres original.

"Lastly, we would like you to see this strapping young lad," I said, pointing at a nine-to-fiver in a niche cafe across the busy street. "Classic hipster trash. The proto scene kid with hallmark birds, anchors, compasses, and the Madonna. Though free and unique, it must be noted that he never actually left his hometown. Never flew, sailed, nor owned a bike. He excelled at pretending he did things."

I laughed at my own joke, coughing hard from the excitement and lost my breath. She tried to comfort me, but I waved her off.

"We're close," she said, wincing at the cafe sweeper as if she now pitied him somehow. "Once we get where we're going, you can rest again. We'll hail a cab back to Union."

I told her I was fine, and stood when I caught my breath. It could have been anxiety from the coughing fit, but from the way my whole body burned, I was convinced we walked for an eternity. I was about to cave and beg her for another rest when she stopped at an uninspiring cul de sac.

"This is the part where one of us gets violated, isn't it?" I said, wheezing, before chugging and spilling tart electrolytes down my chin and throat.

"It was a joke!" she said. "Yeesh. Just go." She gestured with her eyes.

I leaned against the stained brick wall to hide my stomach pains stabbing my guts. I wished I had more time to hide my weakness. I tried to delay.

"Draw straws?"

Unaware of my pain—and thanks to my constant downplaying—Jocelyn pretended to think it over before blurting out a nope. "You go first. That's been the plan all day. Nine out of ten doctors recommend it."

I cursed the outlier. Though I did trust her. I pretended to move cautiously.

The tight and musky alley had a path cut through of crushed cans and broken glass which piled higher than my knees along spalling bricks. It was like entering an urban cornucopia. Missteps met with crunched and cracked shards and rusted steel and riven iron. I swept my hand along eroded mortar for balance. Graffiti blossomed towards the shaded building tops. Painted in bright red block letters which read 'For Marlon' and just after those words, there it sat. A single playground swing secretly suspended in the centre of this forgotten cul de sac. The chains showed no sign of rust on the zinc coating and were drilled to either side of the buildings, protecting it from the cool sun.

"Sit," she said, her discombobulated voice sounded clear as if next to my ear. Though I knew it was impossible. She only came to my chest. Even on her toes, she couldn't reach my neck.

I stepped over the swing, sat with my back to her, and let her push me.

It was peculiar. Being pushed like that. Not knowing

what lay behind me, each thrust sending my gaze father down the endless trash piles. At the end lay a door. Metal. Unremarkable with an etching of two anthropomorphic foxes with ram's horns holding teeth under an archway which resembled a harp. It was signed Lucia Trent.

When it was Jocelyn's turn, she asked me not to push. Said not to make it weird. "I just kind of want to sit. If that's cool."

I told her it was. I lacked the strength.

She spoke softly to the bricks and piled garbage and pigeons roosting above a fire escape.

"Don't leave yet. I won't be long."

I watched her back, same as she watched mine when she pushed me. Her red hair was tucked under her beanie, feet fondling one another centimetres above the battered concrete, fragmented from winter, as she swayed on her secret swing.

I lost myself in the cadence of the city. Distant traffic. Damp footfalls of pedestrians. Faint coos from the pigeons. Blunted by these two close walls.

"You're strange," she said at last.

"Probably."

"You love her, don't you?"

I didn't know what to say.

"Be honest with me," she said, over her shoulder. There was something about the angle of her cheek, how regal her nose seemed. I hastily inspected the bolts anchoring the swing to the brick walls. "Even after all you've been through, you still feel that way about her?"

"I don't know what to tell you."

"Benji used to joke that you two should date. That's always how it is with girls like Savannah."

"What do you mean?" My face warmed as I blushed.

She considered her words for a moment, went to chew her thumb, before catching herself and hiding her hands in her cardigan.

"Boys like you will always want girls like her."

"She's pretty dope. We have a lot in common. Lotta trauma, too."

It was meant to be lighthearted. A layup for witty banter, but she ignored it.

"While you were detoxing in the basement, I couldn't wrap my head around why." She started to rock the swing, pumping her feet gently as she spoke. "Is it codependency? Do you think you can change her? Or are you so lost in your own self-loathing you believe you don't deserve a decent sigo?"

"I wish I knew," I said. "Honestly, I just want her. The whole her. Every imperfection. I like how she makes me feel, the way she swears, how she knows what she wants and is fearless. She's alive."

"She's rotting." Jocelyn's toe kissed the ground, bringing her minor swings to a still. "I don't want her to spread that rot."

I wrapped my arms around her. I can't say why I showed her that gesture of affection. It seemed like the appropriate thing to do. Shit. Other than the night my detox ended and my awkward gesture in Enrico's after Benji died, we never touched.

"I know you hate her," I said. "I wish you both could make up. It's the drugs you should hate. Alex. Besides, I'm a big boy, Joce. I can manage a little bit of rot."

She nuzzled my arm, pressed her cheek into my chest. "I don't think you can." She leaned back. A dim smell of mango filled my ribcage and her green and hazel forests she had for eyes met my hobgoblin stare.

"I'm glad you care about me, dude," I said. "Besides if I fall, or whatever, you're gonna help me back up again, right?"

"I might not be around—"

"Then I'll find you. The world's not so big."

"I'm leaving for B.C. this winter. Semester starts in January. Fast track."

"I'll hop on a train. Duh."

"Is that a promise?"

I held her freckled hand which grasped the swing's cold chain.

"It's not that far. I will come out to see you. Pinky swear and all that crap."

"Push me," she said in a faint voice.

And so, I did.

She told me more about her plans for school. Her flat on Vancouver Island. She joked that one day she would have an exhibit ready for when I came out for a visit. She called it her Doodle Tour. I could chauffeur and repay her in all the gas she burnt shuttling me around. I promised to sell sexual souvenirs online to private investors to repay the debt quicker lest she try to turn me into a butt slave.

When she asked what my plans were, I told her I was taking life one day at a time, that I put zero thought into anything long-term. Then she asked what I wanted out of life.

I had no answer.

The sun retreated behind foreboding clouds and we sought shelter from the chill, and dinner, in a bar called The Library. Standard coffee house. Shelves lined the walls with novels and zines for customers to peruse. The lack of dollar store art left me heartbroken. Jocelyn found that wonderful.

I ordered a turkey club and a craft beer called Cthulhu's Brew which was thick and tasted of burnt barley. I made it halfway through the turkey club before retching my guts into the bathroom sink. Jocelyn plucked out the bird and finished the rest.

It was good and dark when we hopped on the train back to Green River. We put our haggard feet on the seats in front of us, and Jocelyn nestled against my shoulder, quickly falling asleep.

I thought about texting Sav and bringing her to the secret swing when she was healthy. And then I realized some memories should be kept personal.

I rested my head on Jocelyn's lush citrus hair. The tang of sweat and hairspray clung to her beanie. Not the crude odour of crusty punks. Hers was a faint sweet savoury smell of-

My chest warmed and I found her hand wrapped in mine. It was then that I knew what I wanted out of life. I wanted to wake her and tell her, but knew better. I took in her aroma once again, letting the train's steady dakka-dakka carry me away before succumbing to dreamless sleep.

Creepshow.

By late October the rains finally came. Violent chords overwhelmed the hushed patter of droplets on Sav's hospital room window. Every Time I Die thrashed *Hot Damn!* as we hung Halloween decorations around her hospital bed, drew crude creatures with black ballpoint pens on rolls of toilet paper stolen from the nurse's bathroom.

Sav couldn't believe how cushy it was compared to the tissue paper they forced her to wipe with. 'Feels like rubbing my vagina on a whetstone'—her words.

We used the bleeding ink to our advantage, scrawled winged gargoyles and ghosts of Tnugdalus' otherworld, then sticky tacked them to the eggshell walls. When we finished, Sav's room resembled a Hieronymus Bosch acid trip.

We fit too easily, side by side, in the pre-op bed. It's surprising how much weight we had lost since I detoxed and she was admitted.

Her baby toe pocked through her ankle sock. Nail painted black. Pulp of dead leaves coated my scuffed boots. Unlaced. Hung over the bed. Tapped in time, crinkling the unspoilt blue spill sheet. Floater.

When the CD died, Sav leaned over me, her armpit smelled like my runners shirt after I bog trotted in Oakville's '5k for Colin Miyazaki,' and she popped in a new disc from a case that demanding we *Steal This Album!* System's groove was incredible.

The charge nurse told us to cut out the racket and Sav changed it out during the third boom and put on *Drunk Enough to Dance.*

She closed her eyes and listened to a pining riff. I gave her a look when she opened her eyes.

"Lisa brought me it. Pre-op emo—What?"

My look intensified.

"You've been missing. We made up, but she really hates you."

"Probably." I asked if she had seen any of the others.

"You know how it is." She turned over and pulled my arm around her like a comforter. "My mom has a ban list. Only 'approved' guests."

Her mom had a point. Keeping her daughter at a distance from that world. I didn't tell her what I thought about that noise.

"You're like the prime minister," I said.

"Or a spineless liberal."

"Can I be your first lady?"

Her devilish smile widened as she looked back at me and stuck out her tongue between her butter yellow teeth. She had removed the stud.

"You just want to wear a dress again."

"Those little shower robots made a convincing argument," I said, gesturing my surrender.

"What were you on that night? All I remember is one minute you're screaming at the soap about sea labs and scorpions then the next you're tearing through Ryan's closet. Refusing to go to bed, and then you pranced away like a dandy fairy boy, until Alex found you naked except for a cream tutu. Chanting 'I've got the ivory, bro!'"

"I think that was the night I ate all those mushrooms with Ronnie Two."

"Ronnie Two! I forgot about him!"

Our laughter died. I asked her why he was called Ronnie Two and who was Ronnie One? She had no clue.

"I'll ask him," she said smiling to herself, her hands clasping mine as I held her, "when I get out."

Her smile waned. Grip loosened.

When.

The word stagnated between our bodies, wedged us apart despite my chin pressed to her hair. She had been on this ward longer than anyone else. The doctors constantly ran blood tests, chest X-rays, CTs, and MRIs. She told me they recently tried a transesophageal echocardiogram and something called an electrocardiogram.

I had no idea what any of that meant, just that it had something to do with her heart. It's why they were pushing her for surgery.

Sav never told me outright how she got admitted here. Or why her stay was so unusually long. I didn't want to press. Especially so close to surgery. I just tried to be there for her, make her laugh when I could, keep her comfortable. Several times when I visited, I walked in on her weeping. On those days, I'd sit at her bedside. Waiting for it to end.

One day it didn't. I remained reverently beside her, the room sharp with antiseptic, until the nurse gave me the five-minute warning to leave. I kissed Sav's hand.

Lips dried from the hand sanitizer. Doctor forbade spit swapping. Because of the infection. Bacteria could spread through me to her. Her dampened eyes were bathed in sorrow when I gathered my bag. She texted me while I was in the lobby, waiting for Jocelyn to collect me. Sav asked not to come by unannounced anymore. She didn't want me to see her this way. The day we decorated her hospital room was the first time I had seen her since.

I don't blame her. There's little to do in the hospital. They aren't practical for fun. Especially for two aged-out blackhole kids. Mostly we lay in bed, talked about the old times, listened to albums, talked shit, and walked the floor. We couldn't leave unless a nurse buzzed us out, or had a key card to swipe the card readers. It was for flight risks, patients getting lost, or becoming hurt without staff supervision. It's apparently important.

'Hospitals treat people like animals,' she thought, 'how can you expect a person to heal if they waste their lives inside a cage?'

I agreed. Health equates freedom. Not enslavement.

Anarcho punk truths.

A-wing's eighth floor was a clammy, sundried, egg-shell, neighbourhood. It stunk of bleach. And when old Dagmar Haggle kicked the bucket, it stunk sour. I noticed the workers taped flowers on the doors to indicate discreetly to staff she died. Penguins meant someone was physically restrained. Sparrows a contagion. Ballsack Guy's door had a sunset. I didn't know what that meant.

Sav was by far the youngest on her floor. The others were geriatrics with heart disease, attacks, and clots. I discovered this on those days when all Sav could do was hold a vacuous stare while I noiselessly pushed her wheelchair, chewing spearmint to control my need of cancer knowing I'd smoke more to catch up what I missed.

Like I said before my word wandering, today was one of Sav's good days. She was more talkative and after lunch—teriyaki salmon with mixed vegetables, a Greek yogurt, and Pocky from a plug Jocelyn knew—she said I had to meet the ward newcomer.

I help Sav into her wheelchair, which she stubbornly used herself. Watching her strain caused a turmoil inside me. I wanted to help, but knew it was something she had to do herself. Prove self-sufficiency. Control.

She pulled up at the room beside the ward doors separating A-Wing from the rest of the hospital. Sav knocked the patient's room, rolling backwards with each thump. I locked the brakes for her and she batted me away, saying she could do it herself.

"Who is it?" cackled a hoarse voice that sounded how cancers taste.

"Yo, Dodes! It's the kid. Open up, bitch."

"Hey, girly!" Dodes, a fifty-something-year-old woman with skin rougher than sandstone, said. Baby blue mascara arched below her pencil thin eyebrows. Dark roots pushed through her cropped bleached hair. She wore a tank with a vintage Bugs Bunny done up like 2Pac. Her toothy smile, with fissures and knots like driftwood, told me she hit the pipe hard at some point despite the tattooed cross behind her ear.

"Look at you wheeling about," Dodes said, hugging Sav. "How've you been?"

"Tired. But I'm feeling better today."

"You would be after playing with thunder—Oh. Is this—You look different. We met? Boy toy?"

Sav went red.

I introduced myself and Dodes latched onto me in a deep embrace. I froze as she gave me an inappropriate squeeze.

"The gentleman! A real cutie too, girly. Sorry, love. I'm always like this 'too friendly' for most, I'm told. If you're not careful, Savvy, I'm gonna pinch this one up. His butt's tighter than the last one. Huh? You ever enjoy an older woman? I'll teach him a thing or two, if you'd like."

My face flushed hot with embarrassment and the two women laughed at my discomfort. The blatant sexual harassment dulled my mood, but I tried not to be a buzzkill. Kept mostly to myself as Dodes pulled out a chair into the hallway. I leaned against a wall, day dreaming how in a different life we'd be chilling on a porch during a barbeque. Bong rips. Pony bottles. Complaining about who forgot the ice.

I cleaned my cuticles as they spoke like two old friends who let the distances of cities wedge them apart before reuniting at a funeral. Nostalgic melancholy.

Sav noticed my lack of interest, how I was playing with my lighter in my secret pocket, and tried to pull me into a conversation about how the world changed after you could no longer smoke cancer in food courts. Dodes explained how she was one of the original pioneers of the punk movement. Bra burner.

"It went up faster than a priest's prick during Christmas mass."

The flames then jumped to her head, attracted to her hairspray. She clawed at her pixie cut to show us her melted skin under her scalp. Her eyebrows never grew back.

My attention waned from the two generations of riot grrrl beside me as they gossiped about some TV show and I fixated on Ballsack Guy.

He walked up and down the same two metres of linoleum, attention fixed on the nurse's station and the double doors beside us. Normals would have been worried by his erratic movements and self-conversation about the aerodynamics of staplers, but I wasn't. Shit I had lived in Skunktown where that behaviour was expected. I was too curious about what he was planning to consider him dangerous.

Sav and Dodes stopped speaking, enthralled by the man's strangeness.

"Fire chief's back," Dodes said.

"He's gonna do another," Sav said through the side of her mouth.

"Has it been two weeks already?"

"About."

"I heard last time he made it all the way to B2 North before they caught him."

"I heard his wife was down there for a stroke."

"Here's what you're gonna do, girly," Dodes said, returning her chair quietly to her room. Eyes locked on Ballsack Guy. "When he splits, I'll join him. You take your boy toy to the green door in the back of the ward. Do it slow-like. Dante will catch on if you bolt."

"Wait," I said, too late.

Ballsack Guy threw off his gown, charged at the double doors, genitals flapping and romping between cantankerous knees. He was graceful. Majestic. Vercingetorix in a storm of warp spasms, vaulting a wall of Roman centurions. He pirouetted past us and threw his hand against the fire alarm pull station. I saw butthole. It was amazing. When he landed, he horse-kicked the doors open, then scampered down the hallway as the fire alarm sang his victory.

I was in awe. How did the foreign terror know about the built-in safeguard that unlocked all magnetic locks? If he had a thought bubble above his head, it would show the hum of a microwave.

Ballsack Guy danced and skipped to Kaiser's grave as Dodes stood up and blocked the pull station from Nurse Dante and snuck out behind him. I carted Sav to the back stairwell. The emergency door opened with ease. I pulled her out of her wheelchair, supporting her as we carefully climbed the stairs. I asked her how far, and she panted 'to the top.'

I was lightheaded when we ran out of risers. Six flights. Saliva thick. My body craved ralfing. Lungs struggled for breath. I couldn't believe I used to climb the Mountainview Access. Twice. Every Wednesday. Downtown to uptown.

Sav sweated torrents. Her eyes glowed with hopes of open air. She jostled the rooftop door. Sighed with relief as she stepped outside for the first time in months. The sky greeted her with overcast clouds and the scent of petrichor. Drizzle spattered our heaving chests.

Using the HVAC units for support, we navigated the mechanical maze of rooftop units and conduit and cable runs. I slipped on the slick membrane, drenching my left butt cheek and Sav wheezed behind her faint smile. At the front of the building, which towered over East 7th Street, we stood eleven stories high while a riotous wind rushed a welcoming gust. Sav tilted, and held my arm for support. She peeled off her ratty socks, dipped her bare toes in mossy puddles, spread them wide across the white membrane.

Below us, the tops of umbrellas caught the soft rain spilling from our cheeks.

"Do you remember," she said, her hair matting from the rain, "that time we nearly ran away?"

"It was just after I dropped out."

"It was the reason you dropped out." She leaned into me for warmth.

She was not wrong. But not totally correct. Mrs. Fink, my guidance counsellor, had called me into her office after the coffee house to talk about exposing my bony ass to Andrew Cho.

Her office was the type of clean perfected by serial killers. Everything in her cubicle-kingdom had a specific place. Benji had mastered the art of moving around her knickknacks. He would adjust them—paperclips, family photos, printer, once he reordered her entire bookshelf—ever so slightly. Offsets so minute she would spend their whole session scanning the room, distracted like a mouse aware of an unseen hawk. Insanity of the void.

In my last session with Fink, I was loaded on purple. Burrowed deep within a K-hole, tunnel vision. You get it. Fink, whose fat fake smile and blonde swooping combover encircled her plump face, wanted to 'have a chat.' Gave me the obligatory 'you're a good kid,' 'I'm worried about your future,' and 'you've fallen in with a bad crowd,' and had the audacity to imply I actually had friends at Schwenger High.

After her speech, she told me I could not take the guitar class I wanted to next semester. She told me—hand on my heart, no word of a lie, for once—that 'it was a waste of everyone's time.' If I was not speechless from the purple, I sure as hell was after that. She went on telling me 'some people aren't a good fit for the educational system.' And with my track record of suspensions, skipped classes, and obvious drug use, I was better off 'mopping floors.' She had my best interests in mind. If I dropped out, I would open up a 'spot not just in classes, but maybe one in the whole school, for someone who deserves it.' I 'would be doing Green River a favour.'

I think two of the worst things you can say to another human is: 1 you are not good enough, two you *are* stupid. Never punish kids for dreaming their dreams. Especially with a smile.

Fink asked me what I thought. I told her I wanted a Pepsi. I walked.

"I was so angry at my mom," Sav said as my memory of Fink faded. She looked out at the cars passing under the rain, the sound of tires splashing sidewalks as they chased yellows. "She found my stash and chewed into me. I was supposed to go to college. I'm not built for Big Brother's cubicle life. Looking back, I know what she was trying to communicate through her shouting. She wanted me to take the opportunities she had missed.

"I was just so pissed off. I called Phil first to see if he wanted in on running away. He had always wanted to train hop to Cape Breton. But he had just been accepted into university and needed his parent's help with tuition. He baked me salty bread as a goodbye present. Who does that?

"When I got to your place, your parents had already left for work and had you under house arrest for dropping out. What messed me up was when we packed, you kept looking at me. Sorry. Not at. What I mean is you saw me. You knew I'd be back at my mom's within a week, but this was *your* out. A real out. You loaded my pockets with jewellery and told me not to look so fucking sad. And then you punched her mirror."

"You can still see the faint scars when I'm tanned," I said, pulling my hair from my eyes. "I should stop picking scabs."

"You need to stop wrecking that hand. You could lose it."

"Probably."

"Bloody knuckles will never stop you, will they? Nothing will. You went as far to create a new identity. Marched right downtown to Toronto and got a new Health Card."

I chortled. "Marine was a sweetheart," I said, remembering back to the desk monkey who pitied me. "Still feel bad for lying to her."

"They weren't lies. You *were* abused by your father and you *were* a runaway."

"But I wasn't looking to better myself. I just needed paperwork to say I was 19 to make it easier to get booze."

"You still got a SIN and a Birth Certificate without anything other than your word."

"Cheaper than getting fakes. Shame I lost them when that Stoney Creek gang crashed the Church. Douche nozzles."

"Do you regret it?"

"No."

"I do."

"Look, Sav, I know this sounds arrogant, or naive and that's fine. But I have accepted my life for what it is. Every heartache, every loss, the broken knuckle and black eyes, chipped teeth, the nights I barely remember. Addiction, withdrawals, attempts at ending—My days rotting in hell. I'd do it all again. Besides all roads lead home. To this moment. Hard times made me into the hurricane I am today. I'm only going to grow.

"Those days taught me to hold onto those fleeting moments shared with others at 4 a.m. Yeah I'm weary, but I've lived more in one day than most do in a lifetime. I became a better version of myself. On my grave you can be sure it'll say he lived how he died: standing, swinging, screaming."

"But did you find the importance of joy?"

"Duh," I said, "even after all I've been through, the outcome outweighs the cost."

"You've been seeing Jocelyn again, haven't you?"

"She's decent," I said, rubbing my neck, feeling dumb for slipping up, but felt the need to defend my friend. "Her snarky hippie attitude is chill. You two should reconnect—"

"I'm cold. We should go back inside."

We walked back to the eighth floor, noses running, feet trailing squeaky puddles over the lifeless linoleum sheets.

Order inside had been restored. No one noticed our escape and instead were too focused on finding Dodes. We never heard from her again, or wherever she wound up. Ballsack Guy, though, was clothed and lolling in his room, obviously doped out of his dome. Sedatives. I wondered if storming Rome was a worthwhile high. Probably. But that was something I'd experience in a decade or so while trapped in the bughouse, but back then, seeing Ballsack Guy's bliss, I was desperate for a shot.

Sav stopped me outside her room, half inside the doorway with a damp and defiant frown.

"I'm dying."

"What do you mean?" I asked, confused at the cruel joke. I thought it was punishment for galivanting with a woman who accused her of murdering one of her best friends.

"It's called infective endocarditis."

I didn't know what that meant.

"My heart is killing itself."

"I'm not following you."

"It means you and her have another thing in common. I'm your Benji."

[interlude]

It is here, I suppose I should expand on home life. Give insight into the inner workings of teen angst, temper tantrums, in a chapter where I prove I disappointed my mother, and deserved my father's beatings. But I won't. I am an embarrassment. What good would proving it bring? Like many things in here, it's been redacted. For no reason other than this paper doesn't concern them or my follies in youth. In short, this isn't about them. It's not even about me. But you knew that already. No?

Man with the Screaming Brain.

Maybe I'll catch fire, I thought, staring at myself in a stranger's mirror, fighting the urge to call up Dev. I was on the second last show of what Keith called my mini tour. Like mini putt. Not really golf, not really a tour. Seven shows over six days. Kitchener to Oshawa.

I hid from drunks and wasters and Eli during a basement show somewhere in Etobicoke, fiending for a shot. A bump. Pill. Tabs. Dabs. I had smoked two whole packs in under six hours.

The Staircase, which was the venue's official unofficial name, was run by a young boho couple with a passion for music who occasionally opened their doors to unknown indie act such as myself. It was a clean house. Bummer.

When you've been to as many house parties as I have, you reach a point where every building is interchangeable. Memories and trips blur. You swear there was a dude who called himself the Beer Walrus chilling in the garage, but, no, wait, that was in the Six, or Green

River, Scarborough, Hammertown. Didn't I just party here with a Croat and Serb? Didn't I steal lightbulbs out of the McDicks around the corner? Whose house is this again?

I dreaded returning to Green River. Leaving Keith and Eli made me feel—

I quit my job, for shit's sake. Gus was heartbroken he'd never find a potato-slave as dedicated as I was. But I needed the nights off for the mini tour. I would have to go back to my minimalist apartment alone and jobless with no plans and little hope of surviving through winter without eviction.

Getting high to cope seemed the best solution.

Don't misunderstand me, it wasn't living in stranger's ecosystems that bothered me. Keith still maintains his spot of raddest dude I've ever met, but I literally feared returning to a life without playing music. Sav had her first surgery the day I left and would still be recovering when I returned. I knew I would go stir crazy waiting to see her again. My nerves couldn't handle it. The mini tour with Keith kept me distracted. Worry-less. More importantly, if I came back and lost my apartment it meant failure. I'd spiral on my own anyway. At least if I got high here, I'd have a support system. I couldn't put Jocelyn—

She said I was welcome to stay at her place if I ever relapsed. But I knew I wouldn't swallow my pride and bother her for help. Besides, she would be out of province by x-mas.

Yup. Catching fire seemed the better alternative.

I stared at myself in the mirror. Confused and upset. I didn't know what I wanted. I just knew it was easier to get high and forget. Hobgoblin eyes judged me as I nervously chewed and peeled hangnails along bloodied fingers, unsure what to do while Keith's nasally voice drifted under the bathroom door. His grandpa's guitar rang through the basement as hipsters belted the chorus to *After Sedation*.

I wondered if he'd lend me one of his bi-polar pills, or if I should lick my phone battery.

Wondering how I got here? I'll explain:

Before I had moved out of Jocelyn's I spent my days playing songs on a half-sized guitar I scored off the internet. A disgruntled father who equated music with his rebellious preteen. I wrote songs, covered my favourites, and even played some Sick Sad World tunes, while Jocelyn worked, and at Goldens after I chopped up fries for the next day.

It never felt right existing in her space, so again, I moved out, and stashed money for a proper guitar.

I took to wandering Green River much like I used to when my fingers needed a break to grow calluses. One night, after drifting until my foot blisters popped and desperate for a place to sit, I found a crusty bar near the factories. Open mic. I listened to a kid without eyebrows lament over a piano girl. Felt envy. I went to the library the next morning and asked Jeeves about open mic nights around the Green River area.

Inside every bar lived washed-up has-beens dying for drink tickets, and playing 'the classics' that had gone out of style despite their nostalgic buzz, and teenagers hoping for a break that would never come but fawned over dreams of getting their dicks sucked by half-drunk coeds. Pleasant ignorance. Both types believed some jerk in a suit would sign them. Thus turns the ouroboros.

As for me, I lived in the between. Mostly wanted a place to turn off my brain. Avoid pumping black tar in my veins. A place to cease existing.

After a few weeks of being on the open mic circuit one of the bar owners asked me to open for larger shows and if I was willing to sell tickets, since it would make me, and him, more coin. I lied and said I was new to the city, that I came from a small town in New Brunswick. I didn't know a single soul.

Most owners and promoters were understanding of my lies. Some put me on the bill anyway.

When I made enough money at Goldens for first and lasts—a little before Jocelyn and I went to Toronto to that sacred swing secretly tucked away in a cul de sac—I found an apartment building on Napier and Caroline. No more mother's sister's hair dresser's niece, clusterfuck. Nothing to be said about it other than it had a floor to sleep on, and a place to poop with a door that closed. I furnished via online shopping forums, and buy and sells, and Myspace mom groups. Roadside 'Free Stuff.' Bare necessities: a foldout table with a janky leg, suitcases instead of a chest of drawers, two chairs—one steel, the other a folding lawn chair—and lastly a mattress for my floor. Complete with grandma's salmon duvet that flowed like a princess's gown.

Neither Jocelyn nor Sav came to the embarrassment that was my sleeping hovel. And I sure as shit never mentioned the shows to them. Not to distance myself, but because I needed autonomy. A just-for-me. I would hyperventilate thinking of them, or the blackhole kids, coming out to watch my set. Selfish in my self-therapy, I needed a part of me unadulterated by ex-lives. A place without worries of people decoding the messages in sad-boy lyrics like Ryan and Clair and Lisa had. I wanted to rip out my own heart and stare at it for twenty-two minutes. See the soft murmur pulse. Was it as rotted as I thought? Probably.

After I played a set at Dodger's, a taco slash metal bar in Green River which stank of armpits thanks to Dodger's chilli mix, Keith approached me. Offered a spot as the 'local act' on his tour.

He was a soloist like myself. Plump where I was scrawny and covered in stick and pokes—mostly acquired when drunk—and a thick lumberjack beard he always fussed with.

He told me he dug my set, that I sounded like 'Bob Dylan after losing a fist fight to Ian MacKaye.' He said he appreciated my ability to switch rhythm and time signatures mid song. It kept it 'interesting.' I admitted I knew nothing of theory. I played what sounded right. Raw. Keith loved that.

He played after my set, called himself Honest Hearts. And every show he introduced himself by saying 'Hello, world. We are Honest Hearts.' Everyone got a real kick out of the joke. He had another bit where before each tune, he always said 'This next one is a protest song.' I heard he stole that one though. Me too.

After his set we bonded over punk music and I agreed to join his tour. He called it an adoption. We settled to seven shows over six days. He introduced me as his son to the other band, Les. When I asked where he was from, he called himself the last true train hopper and left it at that.

On the second night on tour, in a little bar called Pearl's, he told me between beers he was Christian, just not a good one. Because he bummed cancers. Each time he apologized to his god, to me as well, for catching him in sin.

The cancers and his lack thereof are what drew us into conversations between sets when I opened for him at Dodger's.

I'll admit, I thought Keith was nutters at first. Abducting a young man from his hometown and living in a beater van with curtains was hella sketch. But despite my apprehension and unwillingness to get swept away in the music scene and world of parties and untrustworthy friends, everything was impossibly chill. Keith always asked my opinion about stuff, even things that didn't affect me like his set order. Stark contrast to Alex who ruled like a warlord. Who made me feel inadvertently threatened by his presence despite my desire to please the bastard.

The members of Les were also chill. On guitars were Mato and Salali—Mat was a large, caring man about my age and Sal was a twitchy prankster going through a quarter-life crisis—and Eli on keys/percussion. Fuckin' Eli, man. A spunky collage-aged woman with a bob cut who grew into a quick friend because of our unfaltering love of *The Twilight Zone*. Her real name was Elisi. Translated to Grandmother in Cherokee. She hated it.

"Imagine," Eli said outside of Pearl's while Keith played his set, "the psychological damage done to lovers if I stayed on the Res. Brothers would be all 'Oh, grandmother, eat my ass!' Yeah, you laugh it up. I'm serious. It's bugged."

When I asked how they got roped in with Keith, Sal insisted it wasn't unusual to whisk away randoms. They had all met in Montreal, Les's hometown.

Over the tour Eli had shown a great interest in my lyrical style. After our show in Guelph, the two of us went back to the van, while the others drank in a Tim's parking lot, and I played her a riff I was working on. She helped me knead the knots and smooth kinks until it was a damned near perfect tune. She was brilliant for bouncing ideas off, always attacked from an angle I never thought of.

When we first hooked up, we stopped once our pants came off. I felt guilt. I did the unthinkable, I expressed my concerns. Knowing that telling her about the other woman back home, was the right thing to do.

She told me it was her fault. She was trapped in a dingy van with three dudes—four including myself—all autumn. We made a pact to keep our relationship strictly physical. She thought emotional cheating was despicable. I couldn't say I ever heard of such a thing, but she promised me all women hated it infinitely more than physical cheating. I rationalized that the person who I really wanted to be with was unavailable, and practically so.

We never had sex. By which I mean penetrative. We only used hands.

She didn't want to give me the wrong impression about the kind of woman she was. Eli viewed what she called 'true sex' as a deep and meaningful connection between two consenting adults. My excuse was more complex. After I recklessly led Lisa on screwed with my own self-worth, I swore I would never a bang someone I did not truly adore. And because, well let's be real, I've made it clear where my heart lay hidden.

Yes. I cared deeply for Sav, but I'm only human. Albeit a weak one. It was hard to care for her while I watched her drift away. Withering. Her emotional heart was dying in tandem with her physical one. I needed validation. To feel warm. It's what the flesh is good for. Besides, Eli and I both swore on our instruments that what we were doing was strictly mutual masturbation with kissing and pillow talk. Hardly romantic. Hooking up in a van that stank of 5 unwashed bodies in a parking lot and cuddling between three dudes was far from idyllic.

Eli and I spoke frequently before and after our sessions about how temporary we were, affirmed how the logistics were out of whack.

I'd have to be insane to drive 8 hours to Montreal for a woman when I was so obviously in love with one in my hometown. And her parents would lose their minds if she came home with whitey. And an English-speaking one at that.

And what? You're thinking, now that you're up to speed about how I arrived in a bathroom in Etobicoke in some boho basement show while Keith strummed a cover of Boys Night Out.

I put my last cancer out on my reflection's forehead, cursed Dev and Alex and my unwillingness to throw away my hard work, my promise to Jocelyn.

I almost flushed my phone down the toilet because I couldn't be trusted. But decided to go for a walk instead, hoping overworking my body would bleed the addiction from my meat, or I'd faint from lack of energy fighting it. Again.

I was too afraid to leave the bathroom.

Eli had been furious when she found me last time after my set. Unconscious outside the Eastside Theatre between a dumpster and chainlink fence. I 'needed to eat more,' I told her. I didn't have the heart to explain why I couldn't. How my body viewed food as poison. I still can't explain it. I was told in the bughouse my biggest problem was naming the anorexia. Whoops.

When I mustered the courage to abandon the boho bathroom, a man was waiting for me. Tall as a Dane, flat-nosed, lesbian hair, and his flannel coat smelled suspiciously of dryer sheets. He stretched out his tissue hand. I took it.

He was a normal. Even had a normal name to go with his normal smile. Tim or Tom, or another generic one like his fashionable chapeaux and ripped girl jeans. It was difficult to hear him over Keith's banter.

TimTom explained he worked for an e-zine which spotlighted 'aspiring artists.' Nameless. Nobodies. He dredged on about great opportunities he was providing me with before getting to the goddamned point.

"I could sell comics to a blind man," he boasted, as he handed me a card stamped with his name.

He insisted I review his propaganda films on YouTube, which sounded like nothing more than exploitation of art.

If Benji were here, if I had been my old-self, we would have taken a swing at him.

I played humble. Told him that I could not—in reality would not—come to Parkdale and allow him to film me playing in the aesthetic alley behind his apartment. Had I been a woman, this offer would be sketch.

"Come to Oshawa," I said to him, as a homie in a Turkish shawl pushed past us belting the chorus to Keith's *Baby I'm a Regular Mess.* "It's my last show on the circuit. Film my set."

He agreed to come, but we were in an unspoken understanding with reality: he had zero intention of showing up.

He persisted throughout the night for an interview when he found me alone. Went as far as to stalk me in the crowd, cornered me in the bathroom, again, when I needed to hide due to a panic attack, and followed me quite aways when I ran to the Big Bear for more cancers. Hell, he joined in a conversation Keith and I were having about Dimebag's murder and if Canada's Toilet was going to reignite another Satanic Panic.

TimTom finally wore me down near the end of the night in front of Eli. I caved to shut him up and because she teased me about too reclusive.

We crossed the street and I gave uninterested answers as Les took the stage. Eli's elaborate floral intro cascaded past the parked cars lining the hollow street. Partway through the interrogation, which lasted an eternity, Les finished their set and the venue was clearing out.

Eli interrupted and TimTom appeared more content to speak with her since she was more willing to interact.

I took a backseat to my own interview, painfully picking at scabs, while he flirted with her.

I wanted to tell him to shut up, piss off, and move on, but then what? What would I do? Go back to thinking about getting high all night and masturbating myself into numbness while thinking gingerly about a certain someone's naked body, or count the minutes until Sav's discharge and worry about her relapse along with my own? Great plan. I wanted to slap TimTom across his normal face. Find drugs. Kill myself.

"So when's the LP coming out?" TimTom said, crinkled notepad in hand, waiting eagerly for my response.

"Whenever the monkeys with their phones upload it."

"LOL, what?"

Who says lol irl? Assholes. That's who.

"I dislike the permanence of the music industry," I said, arms crossed and obviously over the charade. "Once it's burned into a disc, it exists. Materialized. To me, what I am doing will one day disappear, just like me. Or at least the me that created it. For right now, I intend to live in the moment. Same with my tunes."

"That's so deep," TimTom said, scribbling away.

I resisted the urge to roll my eyes and my fist over his chin. Instead I gave Eli an unimpressed look.

"One last question," he said. "I noticed you don't have a stage name. You're not even on the ticket, but you're making a name for yourself. Heh. What do you call, well, you?"

Nitwit.

"Red Oak."

"Red Oak. Interesting. A primordial vibe and connected with the World Tree, no doubt. True?"

I pointed to the street sign above TimTom's ugly hat. He frowned, misunderstanding the joke. Eli hid her laughter in her armpit.

The last show I played with Honest Hearts and Les was at a pub called the Mockingbird in Oshawa. Eli convinced me to play the song she helped me workshop. I told her that I had reworked the lyrics that morning. It was far from complete. She didn't mind. She just wanted to hear it before we parted.

I saved it for last, explained to the crowd that it was a work in progress, and if it sucked they should take it out on Eli. Mat and Sal pointed her out in the sea of flannel and ripped jeans. She pushed her way to the front, where she always stood when I played.

Normally my songs remained nameless, but in my head, I named them after horror films that reminded me of the people who they were about. I normally went on stage without introducing them and played until I was out of riffs or the sound guy gave me a warning when I was about to go over my set time. I would only stop strumming for a drink or a cancer drag between ringouts.

I titled this one Perfect Blue.

Eli's eyes lit up when I introduced it, even sung along the parts she remembered as my blistered fingers danced over an F chord. When the final verse came, where I made changes, I watched her excitement wane. I knew why. Looked away. She had developed feelings even when she had fought so hard to deny herself romantic attachment. The lyrics hurt to sing to her, and I choked for a moment, voice catching in a lump.

'We're only temporary,' after all. Weren't we, Eli?

It was in the crowded room of strangers that I realized she had hoped that this song would end up being about her, that she had thought our fleeting moments together meant the world to me. It became clear to us both in that final refrain, how little she meant. As we both intended. What broke her was the name of the other woman in the song. One I had hidden from her during the short tour.

The crowd cheered. Keith whistled from a barstool, sin on his lips. Eli left.

I found myself in Montreal in the middle of winter, many years later, sitting in a poutine shop that Eli had recommended. Vos Hommes. My soon to be wife was on the phone arguing with a client about prices of original compositions while I, beside myself, watched cheese curds melt to Brian Fallon and Chuck Ragan strumming *Great Expectations*, wondering if Eli forgave me.

Funny Games.

The worm baby smooshed his face against the glass. A mashed scowl that greeted customers as they entered the store. Well-dressed mannequins guarded him from the strangers in the mall while his organic parents, too involved in their shopping, failed to notice their missing spawn. I hoped the deal they got on khakis was worth the abandonment issues.

The boy glared at me as he chewed the glass, rubbing his chin against it for larger mouthfuls. Boogers painted the display window, smeared over his cheeks. He pulled away and giggled at his Rorschach blot.

I saw the devil.

I flipped him off.

The kid cackled.

“Excuse me, young man.” Her voice startled me. Jocelyn stood with her hands on her hips, a tacky plastic bag hung from her wrist “Some people’s kids. Where’s your holiday spirit?”

“Right here.” I pointed to my guts and tried to eek out a fart.

She gave me a look. “Really?”

"The spirit lives in my lower intestines. It's digestible."

"It's a miracle you've had sex."

I made a face. She made one back.

The mall's floor tiles were slick with rotted snow, trailing in a film of grey slush and salt stains into the stores. The kind normals trudge in, then pout at. Blame the man with the mop! No need to wipe your own shoes.

Jocelyn led us to a clothing store with neon pink letters reflecting the level of elegance they demanded from their customers. I tried not to puke. An RFID stand outside the store was ripped apart. A dutiful soldier with one leg bleeding cables. Capitalist casualty.

"All hail consumption," Jocelyn said, stepping over the cables. Her rubber tall boots faintly squeaking. She looked cosy in her pullover coat and Nordic socks up to her boney knees.

"For king and capitalism." I said, aware of how wet and cold my toes were in my converse. They were all I could afford with the money from the mini tour. Docs were too steep and my steel toes had rusted and threatened to dislodge.

Stores are filled with things I will never understand: deals on last season's fashion, signs with 75% off items no one will ever buy. Clunkety bracelets. Wide-load earrings. Things dubbed rad, swag, bro, drip. I watched a man of twenty-one try on a sweater that said 'SELF MADE.' He asked the clerk monkey if it had any in the backroom. Large. Black.

As a rule, I avoided consumer pits, but Sav said her clothes no longer fit since her surgery. Jeans hung from her sharp hips, her unisex shirts swallowed her whole, and tanks did little to hide her bones. She was going to try to be a normal. Force a shift. Abandon safety pins, patches, band logos, anarcho black, and even stripped the dye from her hair. Something Dodes had taught her before she bailed from the cardiac ward.

When I told Jocelyn about the wardrobe change, to my surprise, she offered to help pick out clothes. She needed new sweaters for B.C. I was just thrilled she was less hostile towards Sav since I came back from my mini tour. Glad to have someone with taste and style similar to Sav's. Who better to employ than the girl who used to share clothes with her in middle school until Sav's growth spurt?

Jocelyn hovered over displays like a red hummingbird, prodding the occasional article, holding some to her slender body to see the cut. If she disliked what she took, she folded it neatly, resting it back in its place. A rarity, I quickly learned after seeing the state of the shops, in the women's section. I've done drugs in cleaner places.

"You know the drill," she said with her arms full.

"See you in ten."

"I'll wail ever so fierce if any of this is decent."

I waited for her on another bench made of wood substitute, poked the faux-grain patterned skin with stiff cardboard innards with my lighter. A woman who stunk of expensive irradiated lillies drifted past me. I buried my mouth in my shoulder to dampen the nausea, thankful for my deodorant, which smelled similar to a UHU stick.

When Jocelyn returned, I thought she had been body snatched. She usually wore something loose, casual, comfortable, to hide inside but she stood in a turquoise circle skirt and a tight cream long-sleeved button up sweater. She still wore her self-knitted scarf draped over her boyish breasts.

I said nothing. Feeling stupid in my threadbare flannel and faded Moneen tee.

"Something for spring." Her cheeks matched her hair. "I look like a potato."

"Get mashed?" I stuttered, and instantly regretted my reaction.

She had caught me off guard. I was used to seeing her drowning in baggy sweaters and layers of soft hand-knitted threads, I forgot that under those layers there was, well, a girl. Of course I didn't know what to say.

She told me to get bent and huffed back to the change room.

We left the store with two sets of blue jeans, black washed jeans, and a grey factory-stitched toque for Sav. Nothing for Jocelyn.

"Hungry?" she asked, without looking at me.

"If you want," I said, trying to pretend everything between us was normal. "That'll bleed out the last of my cash.

"Fine."

The cafeteria was on our side of the mall, and brimmed with a roaring herd of shoppers cackling and shouting in an echoing chamber of soggy food and cockroach paste while Mariah screeched on about snow-daddy issues.

We split up. I found the cheapest thing I could find with protein. A burger that suffered from depression and onion rings with an identity crisis. Jocelyn ordered tofu pad Thai. We ate in silence, or what silence the cacophony offered us. The indiscriminate chatter of the feasting mob deafening my mind, flooded my chest with oppression.

Jocelyn's cold hands hid inside her cardigan while she took quick bites off her chopsticks. She finished half her box, folded it closed, and rested her head on her hands.

"Still can't eat?"

I had taken two bites of my burger, enough for the cabbage leaf and mayo to spill out in a glomp on my tray. I surrendered.

"My brain wants the food, tells my body it's good, but when I try to eat it, my throat says no."

"What did your doctor say?"

"I have to force myself to stretch my stomach."

"In other words—"

"I'm screwed."

Her frown was sincere.

"Luckily for me, my new coworkers don't notice. So long as I keep punching window vinyl. How's what's her name?"

I sipped watered-down lemonade, hoping the sweetness would purge the taste of pickle. I felt stupid talking about me.

"Carmen," she said with a grudge.

"Sorry. My memory is still kind of a fog."

"I know."

A family sat at the table next to us. They looked like a 70s propaganda photo. Children of God types. I hated the nuclear way they enjoyed each other's company. The way the boy keenly licked his ice cream, indifferent to the heavy snowfall outside.

"Carmen was great," Jocelyn said, a little bothered, "to have after he passed, but there's been this ..." She stared at the father feeding his daughter in her stroller as if he guarded the words she wanted to say. "Remember when you played guitar?"

"In Sick Sad World?" I caught myself from exposing my mini tour. I still hadn't told her about it. "Barely. I remember feelings more than actual events. I was really, really high. Like a lot."

"Do you remember what you told me about when you played live?"

I nodded. I had told her that being in front of all those strangers was like I was driving a stake through my guts. Like each wound was on display. A bloody aura flowing out of me and into those around me. Keith had told me how beautiful my songs sounded. Flawed but earnest. All I heard was the pain of my piece, and the memories associated with them.

"It's like that with Carmen," Jocelyn said. "She knows about how I was after he passed. I felt so exposed. She knows I'm leaving for B.C. before Yule. She thinks it's the right thing for me. Start clean. She wants to keep contact after but—I know this sounds crazy—but she reminds me of him. Supportive. Unwavering. Selfless. I don't think we'll stay together. I don't want to. I should tell her sooner, huh?"

"Sounds like things are working themselves out for you," I said, watching the boy bite his ice cream. With his teeth!

"How's Sav doing?"

"Her mom says she's getting better every day. Stable. But Sav sounds worse than before. I'm hoping to see her in person tonight. Instead of a discombobulated voice on the phone."

"Oh right," she said, then added: "Didn't you say something about another surgery?"

"Next, next Thursday." I rubbed my forehead to pinch out what the doctor had said. The memory failed me. "I don't think they got all of it the first time. The bad heart tissue, I mean. They say she will have a limp from being bedridden for so long. Some physio will correct it if she puts in the work, but she's too stubborn. Too depressed for mobility. Alannah hopes Sav will lose the big sad when she returns home."

"Well, if it keeps snowing the way it is, we'll have to put skis on her wheels."

I smiled. "Last time I saw her I called her Hot Wheels. She did *not* laugh."

"Oh, jah?"

"She chased me through the ward, rolling with one hand, shaking her bedpan in the other. I darted past two interns pushing a gurney and she crashed into it. The cloth covering the cadaver wrapped itself in her wheels and the naked old man flew face first into Nurse Molly's ass."

Jocelyn chuckled at my flailing exaggerations, covered her mouth as she laughed.

Despite the oncoming snowstorm, the sound warmed my heart.

We had one more stop before we called it quits. Jocelyn needed to go to One Dollar Dave's Discount Drug Mart for a box of brandless chocolate. Early x-mas gift for her dad. When I asked why she wanted to waste money on crappy chocolate, she replied that it was because he hated it.

"You told me that Noam said x-mas was for capitalist swine," I said teasing, as we turned around to find the drug mart on the other side of the mall.

"Yule is punk," she said. "We murder trees and parade their bodies in our windows for the whole town to gawk at. Some people keep them alive for weeks, denying them sweet release as they bleed into a dingy bowl. To go further, I know a sick puppy who replants the tree after dressing it up like a drag queen. Been using the same log for six years."

"Buybacks exist solely to screw over the consumer and weighing your love on a dollar scale to show how much you value someone is messed up."

"But I only buy crap people don't use," she said, all snark. "Like tea bags with no leaves, meat mallets for vegetarians, the foulest scented soap I can get me nubs on."

"Where do you find these?"

"Discount bins. Duh."

"The gods of punk would be proud."

"That's not why," she said, making way for a single father and his daughter before entering the Drug Mart. "All that stuff gets tossed or rots on the shelves for decades. The objects are made, but are never used and without a task they become meaningless. I give them to people who don't need them. Everyone says they hate it, but I think they'd be disappointed if I got them real gifts. I have it on good authority that they all chuckle when they're reminded how useless my gifts are. Then they go out and buy something to give that item a purpose. They buy tea leaves, use the meat mallets to crack walnuts, and prank their friends with the rank soap. No matter how brief that may be, the item serves a purposeful function."

That's what I adored about her. She had her own mental plane where only she belonged. Seldom let others tread.

We split up in the store. Jocelyn to ruminate over chalky chocolate, I to the hair dye to cross off the ones I and Sav had used. I tallied two full rows and took a photo of the neon pink for Sav. Asked if she remembered when Benji had tried it and ended up looking like a melted popsicle.

I had to sneeze, but it refused to come. I forced myself to stare into the buzzing tube lighting, wincing as I concentrated. I sneezed. Four times. Booger machinegun.

My eyes opened to darkness. I was blind.

My parents used to say if you didn't close your eyes when you sneezed, they'd pop out of your skull.

I touched my cheeks. Nothing hanging down my face like ornaments. I tried my eye sockets.

"Ouch."

I could still feel so I wasn't dead.

Using the shelves as a guide, I traversed the length of the aisle, arms dragging me forwards, product smashing to the floor as I stomped in the darkness.

There was a firm mechanical slap, and the world flickered into existence.

I found myself entangled in the shelf with a box of Chestnut Brown in my face. The model's puckered lips threatened my own. I pulled away from the pseudo-kiss and rose to find that only the emergency lighting had come on.

A slow murmur swelled from the aisles. A child screamed. A parent shushed it.

I followed the other customers to the cash registers where I met Jocelyn. The head stock monkey, a burnout with a Martian tattoo, told us the storm had cut the power. We needed to leave the mall in an orderly fashion through the nearest exit and get home safely, or whatever.

A few people insisted they needed to pay, but the stock monkey reasoned he couldn't open the register. A group of high schoolers complained that their ride wasn't coming until 9.

Jocelyn pushed through a couple complaining about bus rides and slapped a blue note on the register's belt. Walked out. Paying more than triple the price for garbage chocolate.

I chased after her through the mob towards an exit. She stopped.

"We're not parked that way," she said with a suddenness that made me question her memory. She spun around and walked against the organic tide.

I was too fixated on my make-out session with the box of hair dye to protest, found myself missing the ammonia scent of fresh colour and wondered if I was ever going to change my hair colour again. Aware for the first time what a dishevelled mess I must appear.

It wasn't until she opened two worn doors hidden between a bookstore and a maternity boutique that I realized what she was doing. There was a good chance that the security systems were still rebooting.

"Thus begins another thrilling chapter of potato girl and her goblin boy," she said, sneaking through.

"Hobgoblin," I said, correcting her, as she descended the poorly lit corridor.

I craned my neck to see if any mallrats or clerk monkeys lurked behind us before running after her. Shoes squeaking and echoing in the red lighting.

We wandered through the gullet of a great worm. Each light passed was a rib that held the beastly mall together. We followed stairs snaking to a basement filled with abandoned skids and Easter decorations poorly packed with clear wrap, waiting for x-mas to end. They mimicked frozen carcasses. Poised to snatch those foolish enough to venture the true north alone.

She led me to the end of the maze. A single room lined with computer servers on either wall, blinking static and grumbling machine cant as we tip-toed through the center past a rusted chair and a foldout table guarding an ancient laptop belching lines of DOS fueling the nervous system of the mall.

I wondered if the cameras were back online, if security would detain us, or ban us forever.

Jocelyn, unconcerned with our fate, opened a closet door and disappeared. Absorbed by a red glow.

"Mr. Tumnus?" I whispered at the glow. "Lolita Liddle? Come out to play-ay."

Jocelyn screamed.

I charged for the closet, wrenched open the door, fearing she'd been abducted by molemen, and found a huge storage room twenty feet tall and filled with ancient rooftop displays.

Jocelyn dragged an F-7 fighter plane from between an inflatable snow boy and an ornery gorilla.

"Help me!" Her eyes crazed.

I grabbed a wing as she guided our way. She pulled, pushed, kicked the plane to where she needed it, then used it as a ladder to climb something I thought only existed in Sunday cartoons. A place where she used to plant her diapered butt before her parents' love lives crumbled over stale cereal and runny eggs.

She climbed it. All ten feet. Once at the top, she steadied herself with its huge black ears, her thighs wrapped around its chunky neck. She mimicked his pose, fist flying through the air in triumph.

She mounted Mighty Mouse!

She whooped like a child, sung the theme song a cappella, deepening her voice for gusto. I cheered her on, begging her to save me from the evil bulldog's army of lollipops and fighter planes.

"Here I come to save the day," she said, throwing her beanie at a fire truck. She missed, but we pretended it exploded like a grenade, saving our lives.

Out of breath, she dismounted, bowed. I applauded. Handed her back her beanie with a dainty curtsey of thanks. She kissed the back of my hand.

We rested on Mighty Mouse's daring cape, our bodies melted in its crevasses as if it waited for us, for this specific moment in time. Almost entwined, we shared a cancer and earbuds. Her shuffle: Alkaline Trio, Arch Enemy, Story of the Year, Daniel Johnston, Yeah Yeah Yeahs to name a few.

"I needed that," she said, sucking the cancer then handing it to me as Evanescence came on.

I could taste her lip-gloss on the filter. Mango. Refreshing.

"After all that's happened, we both did."

"How are you holding up?" She pulled a loose hair from her thigh and draped it on Mighty Mouse's cape.

I wanted to tease her for her radical taste in music, but decided not to risk ruining the moment.

"Fine," I said, and passed her the cancer.

"No. I mean how are you really holding up?"

"Rough," I said, before word vomiting. "I'm sorry for everything I put you through. Especially all those things I said. A friend of mine said I should make sure you know how I feel. And I uh—I've been avoiding. Because of how guilty I feel. That friend said I should—We should have gone to a professional for my withdrawal and that thing with the apple juice, I'm sorry I scarred the floor—"

"That landlord was an asshole." Her forgiving smile put me at ease. "He cried about an indentation on the toilet bowl and blamed my pee stream. Cleaning the backyard saved my deposit. Thank you. But hey! At least we know you have a striking career as a pitcher."

"I wasn't myself," I said, disregarding her attempts to minimalize my episode.

"None of us are." She took a drag. Smoke framed her face. "Life is a slow-motion car crash. You hope against hope that you'll veer and miss, but it always ends the same. Head-on, charging, until there's nothing left but pancaked metal and ghost treads where a car used to be. You can only change your fate, not the fate of others."

"What if you could?" I asked, refusing the cancer. "What if you could go back, before Benji's suicide, before Sav's overdose, or your parents' split, or my breakdown? What would you tell us? Tell him?"

Her brow furled as she strained with pained memories. She took a drag.

"Get out of the car." Her eyes glossed over. Dew formed in the cool browns and greens of her eyes, and shone in contrast with her red hair and the grey burn of cancer smoke. She was a sunset. "I'd kiss him one last time, tell him how much I fucking love him."

I put my arm around her.

We sat motionless like Mighty Mouse's fibreglass cape until the cancer smouldered to a tube of ash. Speechless. I crushed it on the slab floor. I never realized until years later, but that was my last cancer.

"I'm going to miss you when I'm gone," she said.

"Me too. Tell me how your doodle exhibit goes."

"No doubt. But only if you start playing guitar again. You were dece."

I forced a smile and thought about telling her I hadn't stopped, about my mini tour, the friends I made and TimTom and his stupid hat. But the guilt over what happened with Eli kept me from speaking. I couldn't muster the courage to tell Jocelyn about the song. I feared ruining the moment. It was our last day together. And. Well. Friends don't write love songs about friends. In another life, or another universe, perhaps. Just not here.

We leaned in closer.

If the world's end happened that night, we never would have noticed. All I could see were the holes left by our grief. How light shone through our punctures and into the room around us. Our lights merged into a single luminescence.

I could smell her mango lips and for the first time since getting sober I was hungry.

The power came back on with a clunk. Vents groaned, spewed recycled air. We rose without a word in the illuminated storage room, said our heartfelt goodbyes to Mighty Mouse and returned the way we came.

At the mall's entrance, I asked her if she really had to go into the west. She did. She needed to grow and there was too much hurt in Green River.

Our footprints crunched perfect holes in the virgin snow and our cheeks and chins were weather-beaten when we reached her car. We listened to the Mountain Goats fill the space between the four doors of her white sedan as she carefully drove me to the hospital to see Sav and drop off our clothing haul.

I opened the door, hugged Jocelyn goodbye. She pressed her lips against my cheek.

"I'm going to miss you Jocelyn Daye," I said, blushing as the innocent gesture swelled in my chest.

"More than you'll ever know," she whispered in my ear. Her breath reminded me of autumn's wind skirting through an alley.

I tasted her mango lips, felt her tongue slide against my own. Neither of us wanted to break away. It was the only thing we could do. All roads.

The brief kiss faded and we rested our foreheads against each other's. I left carpark and watched her taillights fare the dying storm. Pulled my collar over my cheeks to hide my blush. I waited in the cold until the white veil consumed her car.

I was late to see Sav, and I thought it had been worth it.

No. I never told Sav and Jocelyn never told Carmen. It was one of those moments you never speak of. Not because of shame or regret, but because we both knew it would dilute the beauty of what we meant to each other.

Some cars are meant to crash, but not this one.

Eraserhead.

Savannah Anne Moore died at 21. She passed before her second surgery. The infection had returned. Spread to her brain and liver. Endocarditis forced her heart to work more than physically possible. Failed to pump adequate amounts of blood throughout her dying body.

"It's like a fungus growing in my heart," she had said after our excursion on the rooftop of Green River General Hospital. "If the first surgery fails, they will replace my heart valves with artificial ones. I'll be a bionic woman."

The first surgery was a success, but she worsened. The rot, soundless, unimpeded, spread throughout her body. Baffling doctors. They scheduled a second procedure to make certain they had removed the thin layer of fungi encapsulating her heart. The universe wanted her dead.

On paper it was a stroke.

'Nothing we could do.'

Yes, I was there when it happened. I held her mother back while the doctors and nurses tried to save her life.

Alannah Moore denied the others from attending the funeral. Went as far to post on the obituary: By invitation only. Out of all her friends, I was the only one accepted.

The blackhole kids stood across the street during the service like tourists gawking at exotic creatures from alien ecosystems. Mouthbreathers.

That's life, isn't it? Stand on the edge of the abyss, from the comfort of our orbits, leering into other worlds. People watching. Television. Books. Cliques. Clubs. Concerts. Mass. Therapy. Bingeing online and in line. On the bus, on the way to bars, movies, hell, passing persons in a crowd. We are all guilty. Background characters.

The songs of our youth, wasted, at the edge of the otherworld.

She would have hated the photo they used at her wake. Her at fifteen. Brown hair, not pink, or green, or rainbow, or black, without her piercings—her battle armour—and stick and pokes—warpaint—staining her skin. The her before the violence. Savannah Anne Moore. Not Sav.

After the service, I hugged Missus Moore goodbye. She said I was always welcome to stop by her apartment. But I never did. She cried in my arms before moving onto the next person and cried into theirs'.

I wanted to join her. Release the hurt bottled inside, but the streams were frozen deep within me. I walked the 10 kilometres back to my apartment through the snow. Feet numb. White. Thankful to be alone. Happy Holidays, you bastard.

My body showed up for work at the factory, but I was disconnected. Physically alive. Mentally another headspace. Emotionally unavailable. All day I punched window vinyl and doorframes. No education required. I thought it'd be a good thing to keep me occupied while she healed.

In my state of catatonia, I never once strayed farther than my nose. I took breaks alone. Punched vinyl alone. If I ran out, I just stood still. Silently between whirring assembly lines and raging forklifts. Waiting. At times, hours. Eventually the lead hand offered me a better paying job in the paint shop because I was 'productive.' I airbrushed the same four colours on the vinyl I had punched weeks earlier. Never spoke. Only worked. There was always something to paint. Tape to peel. Brushes to clean. Hoses to unclog.

After my shifts I rode the Number 12, factory route, along the lake with broke working-class Joes like me who smelled of steel and sweat and coke. Misery. Reeking of sleepless nights. Broken homes. Hands thick with grime.

Some days I wouldn't get off at my stop. Still like a gargoyle until the bus went out of service and repeated when the next Number 12 came. Most nights, I waited until the last bus before going home. 1:15.

On the coldest nights, I returned to my apartment by sundown to sit and watch my wall. The spider, a daddy long leg, weaved a short web where the skirting boards met imperfectly in the corner before wrapping around the apartment like a snake devouring itself. The web never grew. The spider never moved. There were no flies. Nothing more.

I was forced to stop this ritual one weekend morning. I say weekend because my sense of time fled from me that winter and it was daytime, yet I wasn't at work. Therefore weekend.

I received a buzz on my intercom.

"It's Alannah. Can we speak?"

The open-door buzzer never worked in my apartment. The landlord promised he'd repair it, but never did. I never complained. I had no visitors.

I pressed the talk button, but said nothing, just watched the holes in the steel protecting the speaker, listening to feedback clip, wondering if this was how the spider got in.

I left barefoot to let in Missus Moore, but found Ryan's smiling face greeting me through a plate glass window. Her dark skin was covered in sores. She rolled up her hoodie revealing scars slashing up her dark arms. Burn marks smiling at me from Bic lighter kisses. Her face warped and gaunt in the oblong double glass and wire mesh that split her toothy smile. Four stairs above ground level, I stopped. My toes hung ten over concrete steps.

She motioned to someone out of view. Alex pushed past her. Screaming. A prized dogfighter. He thrashed against the door. Undecipherable. Muffled from the fortification separating him and his army of my old friends and another thug with the uncanny resemblance to my old bully, Andrew Cho, who laughed with glee as he smashed my face in, swirlied me, chucked oranges, and spit in my hair.

Alex smashed his knuckles into the glass. It fissured.

Why did I, the deserter, get to say goodbye to her? His rage seemed to say.

I was answerless.

I sat on steps and viewed Alex the same way I did the spider. Feeling nothing. Wanting nothing. Can spiders hate? Did they feel pain when I used to rive their legs from their hairy bodies? If Alex got in, would he make me feel something when he ripped apart my limbs?

I stood to let him in.

He smashed his face into the glass. Again. Again. Again. His words became feral slurs. Alien and savage sounds hidden between curses and cries and poetry. Blood welled inside the cracked glass. His restlessness thundered. Boomed. I lost his face, hidden behind a web of blood and the thin flakes of flesh flayed from his knuckles and forehead and palms.

They left.

Alone once more with the sound of my heart beating dully inside my chest. My soul told each pulse pulverized against my ribcage, that I was feeling fear and excitement. But I felt none of it.

After that incident, I resumed my old walks to the pier, sitting on snow-covered benches, watching the grizzled sky. I went straight from work to weather the cold. Once I spent the night on a boulder at the Bayfront, watching dead trees creak in the wind. Fully conscious yet totally toneless, waiting until I had to go back into work. I got frostnip on my nose. But didn't know it at the time. The hunger, the cold, the insomnia never registered.

My torturous rituals became the purpose of my existence. Months alone. Punishing myself. Bleeding. I blamed myself for her death, for not doing more. For kissing—choosing Jocelyn. Hooking up with Eli.

Putting myself first while a person I loved slowly rotted away in the hell of her dying body. All the times I got high. Tarnished her flesh.

I hated me.

I was too depressed to end my suffering. Hell, I deserved hurt.

Once, after a 12-hour shift, I saw Ryan and Dev cleaning car windshields at Dundas Park. I watched them at a red light from inside the Number 12. It reminded me how truly abandoned and lonely I was. When they recognized me through the sleet, they attacked the bus. Hurled their squeegees. Kicked the propaganda sign on the bus's side, racking steel toes. As if denting the realtor's photoshopped smile slighted me. Dev tried to pry open the side door, causing a child to cry. The bus monkey dialed John Law. My former friends chased after the bus until turning wheels outdrove their strides.

Most people have a pile of shoes at their door, I had a lake of white envelopes with islands of junk mail. The only bill I paid was for rent and always got paid on time because it was directly withdrawn from my bank account. The receipts were immediately consumed by Mail Lake.

The phone company removed my phone from their network, which became my glorified alarm clock. I carried it with me to pretend I was important enough for others to message. A means to do something with my hands when I grew cold outside and wanted to punish each finger for touching her. I doom scrolled old photos of my dead friends to make myself more miserable.

Jocelyn sent me letters, which also remained unopened. They were not sent as tribute to Mail Lake, and instead hibernated on a nightstand within arm's reach. Much like my bed beers I used to rock every night until my life went ass up. She sent a baker's dozen in total. I meant to open them, hell, I wanted to. But depression drained me of the strength needed to confront them.

The letters meant that Jocelyn survived her flight west. It also meant that after thirteen attempts she stopped trying to contact me.

She must have seen the obituary online. Missus Moore had shared it everywhere. Jocelyn hated me, no doubt, for cutting her out. I had to. The last thing I wanted was to drag her back into this cesspool. Besides, if I found the courage to kill myself, I wanted her to hurt less. And I sure as shit didn't want codependency if she tried to save me again.

I met with a head rapist—therapist to normals. Stuck it out for a whole single session and was something I'd regret skimping out on after my vacation to the bughouse when my wife miscarried. I dreaded social interaction, but after returning to the dark place, I toughed it out in hopes that a professional would bring me back to life.

He gave me confirmation bias. Product of poor upbringing. Chemical imbalance. If my mother loved me more, if my father touched me with his hands not fists, then my rot might not exist. These factors 'forced' me to seek drugs, booze, associate meaningless sex with validation, and accelerate suicidal tendencies thanks to a lack oxytocin. What a sick sad world I lived in, huh?

The head rapist offered me pills, which I refused.

When asked why, I told him I was worried about losing my sense of self, returning to dependency. That I would be unable to create my sad songs for sad boys. I would rather hate myself and be free, than tolerate mental slavery.

He told me there was a strange sense of nobility in suffering for one's art.

I told him, calmly, to violently insert his pills into his anus. We didn't book a second session.

▬ As I grow old, and watch my daughter, who we named after Savannah Anne Moore, I think of my wild youth. Realized I was worth losing. Unlike her.

When I first attempted to write this, I was manic in my garage at two in the morning in late July, before my wife had me admitted for trying to suffocate myself with her car's exhaust fumes. I found myself begging my mother's god to put these old ghosts of mine to rest as the smog filled the cab. And if my poor mother is correct, and there is a heaven in which wretched souls like mine congregate, I will find Sav. Waiting for me beside Benji, my pup, and unborn child. Surrounded by other blackhole kids whose faces I cannot unremember. I hope they can forgive me. Because I still have yet to forgive myself.

Last Man on Earth.

The day I finally woke I sat on my bench along the pier, watching sparrows honour killing rivals as hens twittered from their perches. The snow had blackened, slushed, and melted a lifetime ago. Spring rain slowed to remnants of showers in the thinning grey veil of clouds inevitably losing their battle with the blooming summer sun. I traded my long johns and winter coat for a crewneck and flat cap, marvelling at the violence of songbirds.

Fishermen, and yacht club elites tested blueing waters. It felt like moments ago there were couples skating in front of me. I wondered if they were now in the motorboats scuttling across the lake, splitting perfect V's until rhythms of the waves retained order.

"I said: How's it going?"

The beggar's black hair thinned on the top of his wide wrinkled forehead. Tan skin, weather beaten from the blizzard we had moments ago. No. Months ago. His varsity hoodie resembled sour milk and caked with stains attributed to filth, sweat, booze, and bile. He stunk of vinegar balls.

"It's going," I said, returning to the motorboats humming into the expanse.

"You don't recognize me?" the beggar said.

"Cho."

Andrew goddamned Cho.

"Your beard's worse than mine," he said, pulling at his patchy whiskers. "What I mean to say is, you look real different without that whacky hair."

"And?"

"I was shit to you."

"Yeah."

"I was looking for butts by the fountain when I saw you." He held a baggy full of cancer filters. "Hope you don't mind. Wanted to say I'm sorry."

I wanted to drown him. Drag him to the lake, hold his head under the blue algae, feel my muscles resist his squirms as mutated fish feasted on his—

"I had a drug problem back then." He appeared earnest, voice like crushed gravel, and not the strong basso of masculinity it had been when he tormented me. "I was slinging blow for these playboys from the Six. Social worker says it's mashed my brains up. I got these pills now." He showed me the capsule, jiggled the chicklets inside. "They keep me calm. Psychosis is bugged. Want one? The others say time slows down. I don't feel that, though."

I shook my head, wishing he'd take more and overdose and vanish from my life as he crunched a pill between his molars. Chalk formed on his lips as he spoke, caked like custard between brown teeth. I hoped it clogged his airways.

"I was rotten back then." He sniffed through his single nostril.

"No shit. You were a chicken fucker. You feeling nostalgic and want to whale on me again? I still have a chipped tooth from when you and your jockstraps dunked me. Learn to walk."

"What I did to you defined what happened to me."

"What the fresh fuck is that supposed to mean, asshole?"

"I want to make amends, homie. Hatchet bury! I was hometown hero, you feel. I had a different low-self esteem whore for every night of the week and rode into Uni on a basketball scholarship. I had dreams of making captain, but couldn't slow my roll with the gunners. Failed my drug test. One semester and pops curbed me when he learned I slung."

"And I was what? An outlet for misguided aggression? Poor you."

"Screw you," he said. "I OD'd for the second time about a month ago. My case worker told me to hunt down everyone I ever wronged, and ask for their forgiveness. Paige fuckin hates my guts for sellingout, but I couldn't find you online so I skipped and lied to Judy, even though she said it's alright that some people can't let go of the past."

"You're half the reason I don't go online! That page you made where—"

"Chill, fam. When I saw you here, I was like 'oh shit, it's my boy.' It's some savage voodoo fate type stuff. You are real, right?"

I gave my best white guy smile. Lips pursed, eyebrows up, avoidant eyes. It was difficult to bite back my anger at the years he spent torturing me all to apologize. Absolve guilt. I hated him more.

"Groovy! If you're not real totes have to tell me." Cho emptied his bag of half-smoked cancers. He dissected them on his fecal covered khakis, ground out the nicotine and threw away the filters before rolling. He offered me a drag, but I waved it away. "What ever happened to that smoke show you were always running around with? What was her name? You know the one."

"Savannah."

"Tight little ginger, right? What's she saying these days?"

I said nothing.

He finished his cancer, burned his finger tips and swore when the embers reached the end. "My boy's hung up on his ex, too. Siv, I think. What is that, Swedish? Anyway, she died last year before I met her. Fucked him up."

"How'd you meet?"

"Sold sticky hash back in the day." Cho lit another cancer. "He lets me crash at his place sometimes. They say some kid left a free bed so I snatched it. Church, they call it. Lame, huh? Anyway, so my boy Alex is always spaced out on hard junk since his girl died. Really hitting that oxy shit, you know? Dude looks like a praying mantis. I think he cuts with dust, but I'm never around when he is conscious anymore. Plugs man.

"His baby mama, Ryan—who gives their daughter a boy name?—said he's been that way since his bottom bitch died. I think it's a terrible environment to raise a kid. Homies should know better. I hope she gets into a shelter or something when she farts it out. Kids shouldn't watch their parents get high. This guy, Jeremy—Philly?—said Alex lost it when he learned Siv was pregnant. Two kids with two women. Damn, son. What if the kids met?"

"How did she die?"

"No one knows." Cho leaned in, looked about for prying eyes and licked his dehydrated lips as a fat man struggled to contain his Australian Shepherd from mauling Canadian Geese. "Ryan says one day a few of them snuck into the hospital to see her. Everything was legit, blood. They were getting high on morphine they stole from the nurse's station and then the next day, the day of the big blizzard, bitch up and died. No clue why.

"We made decent money off the product, though. Bought some sparkly China White with it. What gets me, is that Alex and his buddy, Crazy Danny, were banging Ryan on the side the entire time. Which is how she got preggers. I mean I've had her myself and she's a rad lay, but everyone makes the dead chick to be Queen Shiva or some other biblical broad. Feel me? If you're with a goddess, why bang a hoe like Ryan?

"Church is a soap opera, fam. You're lucky to avoid all that."

"Probably."

"Oh. Sorry, fam. I didn't mean to ramble." Cho used his fingers to kill his cancer and began rolling a third. "Real talk. My bad for picking on you. You sure you don't want a hit, Poop-eye? Heh. What? Too soon?"

I stood, offered my hand to Cho, though I still hated him, but I wanted him gone. He shook it, wishing me his best, what little it was worth, and thanked me for forgiving him.

"Where're you off to?" he asked, lighting another cancer.

"Home. Heading home."

As I unlocked the door to my building, I noticed, for the first time, that my landlord had fixed the window Alex had smashed. Blood web removed. I saw my translucent reflection in the new glass. I looked as haggard as Cho. Dishevelled and gaunt behind my patchy beard, eyes half hidden under a mop of hair, fried ends with greasy roots hung past my chin, cracked lips. I tongued them, surprised at their coppery taste.

I showered and shaved for the first time in my life. Pattering water trailed my back as I used a soapstone to peel off rotten flesh. Clumsy hands held the razor blade as it tore away frail tissue paper skin. It was the first time I saw my hobgoblin face, really saw it, since Benji died. I looked beautiful. Broken, and sad, and pathetic. A mauled skunk gutted by buzzards. I appreciated me.

When I finished in the shower, I tried to dry off but collapsed on the bath mat. I cried. I cried for Sav. For myself. For everyone stuck in the between.

I mustered the courage to open Jocelyn's letters in May. Took the day off work. My supervisor told me in a thick Portuguese accent it was alright to be sick. Don't feel bad and rest well so I could come back to work.

I chipped away at Laundry Mountain and mopped dead skin cells off my floor before draining Mail Lake. After lunch, I lifted the daddy long leg and relocated it to my window overlooking a florist and Max Milk. I cracked the window a sliver to allow flies or aphids or whatever the hell it had survived off of inside. The spider did not seem to harbour hostility towards the eviction. Periodically I checked in, delighted to see it weaving a new home.

My procrastination ended when the stomps of children in the hall boomed past my apartment. They skipped and laughed to their homes, filled with wonderment and joy as they smelled their mother's roasting dinners. I heard snippets of the mythos they sang to their fathers about their day. A mysticism reserved for the young. Pure.

The nightstand holding Jocelyn's letters was a flimsy and frail secondhand piece of garbage like everything I owned. The corner guard had peeled off when I lifted it from the dumpster outside Green River High.

Sitting cross-legged on the floor, back to the mattress, I opened all thirteen letters she sent. On each envelope was a doodle. Most were simple avant-garde linework in black ink of rivers and trees, or depicted detailed landmarks and cityscapes. My favourite was a fox head. Every line lay exactly where she wanted. I pretended that together her doodles told a story of her adventures. I envisioned her drawing in coffee shops between classes behind sips of green tea, bored at a desk while her profs rambled about the holiness of the Renaissance, or content in her new home, curled on the floor after a house party like when I had watched her paint. A slender sketching pen clenched between finger-bitten nails.

In one letter, she mentioned learning of the German Romanticists of the nineteenth century, and had scribbled a coastline. Sombre and wanting. She sent several photographs consisting of unnamed trails and landmarks with her smiling beside strangers she called friends.

I was overjoyed, truly, to see her in her element. In these letters she let me deeper into her heart. Spoke of fears, hopes, and experiences during those first few weeks of her new life. Dorm life. Communal cohabitation. Art scene. She asked me to add her to 'the social medias' so we could keep in contact.

The last letter she sent, and I knew it was the last because there was no art on the envelope. Not even my name. It contained no photos, nor doodles in the margin I had come to expect. This was the letter of a woman who had given up.

She wrote:

> *I don't know where we stand, anymore. I don't know why I bother. I thought you felt I had abandoned you and this silence was your way to childishly punish me. But you're punishing yourself.*
>
> *I know Sav died, but you're not the only one who feels like they could have done more. I wish I was there for her. Just like I wish I could have been there more for him. I wish she and I had buried the hatchet.*
>
> *You could have told me what happened instead of leaving me in the dark. Again. My parents told me after Yule. After you got to bury her. I didn't bring it up before for your sake. And then I thought, why am I protecting you?*

I should have come to the funeral. Gone together. But you had to keep it to yourself. Do you have any idea how selfish that is? I get the anxiety of opening up, but you did this to yourself. Congrats on keeping me at a distance. I shouldn't be the one saying goodbye. After having all this time without contact, I feel like you robbed me.

And as much as I hate you for snubbing me out of your life, I do hope that you're okay. I can't go anywhere in this city without being reminded of you and hoping you're still fighting. If you're hurt and bleeding that's alright. It's what being alive is about. It's a sure sign of hope. I believe in you. Just not in being around you.

Don't get me wrong. I care about you—always have. Although it was brief, I enjoyed our moment together. I should have told you sooner, but part of me romanticized the idea of bringing you out here, or that you'd follow me to the airport, or chase after me on a train. Start over. Fantasy can never coexist with reality, can it?

I fell in love with you. You don't know it, but I realized it when I was planning to leave Carmen. Even though you loved Sav, I decided to tell you how I felt. But then you disappeared. Wandered off for weeks to avoid me without explanation. I actualized how I felt that afternoon at the secret swing. Each arch brought you further into my heart because you trusted me. Our hands felt so right entwined as we slept on the train ride home. When I woke in Aldershot and saw your hand in mine, your thumb fit perfectly on the freckle on my hand.

I was a puzzle with too many missing pieces after he died. But when I was around you, you filled those holes. When I was with Carmen, both physically, and sexually, and in those hours of night where normal people sleep, I always thought of you. That's the real reason I broke it off with her. I should have said so at the mall. She wasn't you. I wondered what it would be like to let you have me. I know witches aren't supposed to allow men to treat them like objects, it disgusts me when I see it, but I wanted you to have me. But you never made a move. And it made me want you even more. You were comfortable being friends.

That night we slept at the fish and chip shop meant the world to me. I hadn't been that drunk in forever and it was your first beer since that night at the Devil's Punch Bowl. Your hangover was the worst, you said. It was your final send off into sobriety, remember? We should have kissed then.

I wiped my eyes with my sheets. Remember? Of course, I remembered. In the morning I couldn't find my pants and asked her what happened as I scrambled away from the table we slept under. I cracked my head on the seat when I noticed Jocelyn wore my sweater, her bare legs tucked into her belly. Her bra on the chair next to me.

She gave a tired smile, curled into a tighter ball, her hair brushed over her eyes.

"Did I rape you in your alcohol induced state, you mean?" she said and my face flushed with embarrassment and I stammered a response, but she cut me off in a sly voice fried from singing and drinking the night before. "Did I ravage you? Tie you up? Stick foreign objects in your butt? No. It was the other way around." She rolled over, back of her hand to forehead like a silver screen starlet. "You threw yourself at me, I begged you to stop, *dar*ling, and told you I was *saving* myself for marriage, but *you* wouldn't listen, you 'needed to *have* me now!'" She pulled down the hoodie zipper and rubbed her exposed belly. "It's a boy. What do you think of the name Kevin?"

My mouth dropped.

She leaned in, her breath sour from coolers and said she was messing with me. I had puked all over myself and Table 9 before passing out. She had cleaned our clothes in the sink and left them to dry beside the fryers.

"You're really nice when you're wasted, you know. You even helped me mop up. Sort of." She gestured to the puddle on the carpet.

I told her she was literally the worst person on the planet.

She stuck out her tongue. I tried to grab it. She pulled me under the table and, while I struggled to pinch her soft pink smile, she called to the locals for help, telling them that it was happening again and send for the Mounties. I doubled my efforts.

> *It was moments like those that made me fall for you. But you're also a damned stubborn fool. I used to think you were so in love with Sav that I didn't register. Maybe you were just too enthralled playing Lancelot, or addicted to your own misery to give a damn about anyone else.*

I know that the last time I wrote you I said when you were done drowning yourself in loneliness to call me. I take it back. Please. Don't call. If you care about me, truly care, like I used to hope you did, then listen. I would rather keep you as a forlorn memory. There I can still have hope and dream of what could have been.

The version of you I adored would respect this. Don't prove me wrong.

You still run through my head every night when I lay in bed.

Once yours, Joce x

I reread this letter countless times, pontificated until the light of day vanished and I could no longer discern ink and page. Alone, surrounded by umbra, I dreamt of my mistakes.

Would I ever be worthy of Jocelyn? Fuck no. Never. I'm not that daft. In another life, or another universe perhaps. Just not here.

Right?

Right.

The Evil Dead. Versus. Brain Dead.

Mapleview Station resembled a disorganized circle pit as 9-to-5ers rushed platform to platform. Same rules apply: elbows out, toes stomps, zero eye contact, if someone falls pick them up. I pretended that the commuters waited for the headliner—Pain Train. Restless.

I paid damn good money for this, says the man in the blue overcoat. Traffic will be a nightmare, says Davey Super-fan in his risers. Seeing YYZ will be worth being grounded. I've seen the Lakeshore at least a dozen times this month alone, says the pregnant woman with yellow hands.

I wanted to scream from the overhang, 'Open up the pit!' Complete the daydream. But reality was nothing would happen. A few might snicker, walk on. I'd liked to think if I was ever blessed enough to be part of a spontaneous pit, I would get my slam on. Two minutes of hate. Purge my dwindling angst and rage. Mentos and Coke. An epic explosion like a virgin busted with stolen panties.

After growing painfully bored waiting for my train, I descended to the tunnels and paid the kiosk clerk for a science fiction magazine, orange juice, a cinnamon bun, and a soggy sandwich with smoked ham—which I crushed before the climb back to the platform. I thanked the clerk for the eats and slipped back in my earbuds to catch the end of *Hey, It's Your Funeral Mamma.* I upgraded. Making the plunge from CD to MP3 was a no brainer for an audiophile.

I sat on the platform, under the shade of the schedule screen blipping in the morning sun, picked at Peanut's tag sitting next to me on the bench, and wondered how he got on in prison, if he was out soon. Could you reform an artist? Would they suffer miserably?

I distracted myself from the heat and my past lives with the magazine and forced myself to relax. That's what normals do on vacation. Relax.

"You earned this," I reminded myself as the commuters abandoned me for their grind.

This vacation was to celebrate one full year sober. I survived the blackhole. I deserved it. I planned the trip when I came to my senses in May, worked twelve hour shifts at the window factory, gobbling overtime landed me a position as Warehouse Nine's lead hand. Sorry. Lead monkey. The pay difference plus the money earned doing gigs on the weekend covered the trip. Easy.

Lacking friends and no addictions has perks. Do not misunderstand me. The people I met and shared that brief part of my life with were good people. Decent for normals. But they were never the family I left behind in Skunktown. They were people I killed time with. Benji would have called them seasonal friends.

When I saved enough money for my vacation I went back to school. Night classes. Acquiring my GED sucked, but so did swallowing my pride for a piece of paper Ms. Fink bull guarded from me. But the idea of having it, actually holding it, meant I didn't quit. I just took my time.

They called it an 'Adult Learning Facility'—which to me sounds like a BDSM dungeon. A bunch of pencil moustache perverts in melted latex watching gangbang instructional videos. Cucks. You can only learn so much from watching smut gauntlets. It's all about participation.

It was there that I learned I was good with my hands. Sorry. Building things. After my vacation I decided to pick up a trade. Plumbing seemed easy enough and I didn't mind the smell. Couldn't be worse than punching vinyl.

My luggage consisted of a week's worth of underwear, a pair of jeans, and my guitar—which was my most expensive possession. A whopping buck fifty. Lovingly used. Hidden in my unmentionables were sandwiches for surviving the gruelling train ride. When the conductor at Mapleview searched my backpack, he allowed me to keep my food but asked what the jar of peanut butter was for. Assassination. Not. I told him I had a loaf of bread in my guitar case. He chuckled at that one.

As I read my sci-fi magazine, I wished for someone to share this joke with, but instead I giggled like a child, totally alone on Platform 2.

Alex came up from the tunnel and shuffled onto the platform on the other side of the tracks, unaware I was watching him. The bleach in his stringy hair faded, revealing an inch of roots on his scabbed scalp. His grown out mohawk had lost its erection but maintained a crusty appearance. He twitched and spazzed, rapidly phased in and out of reality, scrounging for crushed cancers and garbage food muttering to himself through wooden teeth.

He was inspecting a coffee cup when his head jerked up like an irate vulture. He saw me. My guts turned to Greek fire. Even in the apex of his trip, he recognized me.

The metallic groan of an oncoming train provided a perfect cadential beat. It tore between us. Screaming as it slowed. Each passing car blinked Alex's furious stare into existence. As the train slowed, he disappeared longer and longer. Dilated eyes above his hooked nose. Seething hatred. Wielding rage like Lucifer's morningstar. Carving a scissure in my chest. I wore the wound with pride.

The train rolled slower. A gap.

I envisioned myself killing him.

He knew. He was killing me too.

The train stopped. A car blocked Alex as a gaggle of pedestrians hurried to the main terminal.

"Please stand clear of the doors," the conductor's jaded voice called from rusted speakers hidden in the rafters like birds in row.

It startled me. I moved to see if Alex waited on the other side. He had vanished.

The announcer repeated himself and I jumped at the pneumatic hiss. That distraction was all Alex needed. He charged through the nearest train car and swung. I couldn't get my hands up in time.

I lost myself in the blows. Wordlessly we punched, kicked, bit each other. He pinned my neck to the hard ground and caught my cheek between his stained fingers. He wrenched me upwards by my hair, kicked my chest and back and threw me at the ground. I reeled him over me, found myself above him as I clawed for his neck, I slammed him into the platform, knees digging into his forearms.

I separated from my body. Watched myself pummel him, endlessly screaming, crying, swinging.

"You were supposed to love her."

His cheek bone collapsed. I heard my glass knuckle shatter. I refused to stop. Killing wasn't enough. I needed to scrub him from existence. The self-loathing in his eyes begged me to end him. Release his misery.

As I battered him around, I wondered if living with the pain of her was his way of keeping her alive. It's not like either of us believed we'd all be reunited once our hearts stopped beating. It was better to suffer. Remember her through grief.

I dragged Alex to the tracks as the grind of an approaching train shook the platform. He could barely lift his vulturine head. I held his starved frame over the rails, watched his blood drip along my broken fist. A klaxon blared.

"Please." His voice was soft. Infantile. "What did she say before she died?"

Sav.

I let him go. The train rushed past. I slumped onto the platform, wishing for a redo.

Alex rolled away pathetically, weeping gore and grit from his face. I couldn't kill him. He should have lost consciousness, but he was too lit.

I understood him in that moment. He was too much of a coward to kill himself. He abused hard drugs to experience her touch. Chase her with highs and lows to relive and unlive their brief moments together.

"Please." He wept. "Tell me."

Memories of that night in the hospital came back. I remembered the softness of Jocelyn's lips. The brisk smell of falling snow cut with mango. The chatter of the lobby. Patients at the windows, watching the blizzard as I rounded the elevators. Alex's face. The big shit-eating-grin he had when he stumbled off the elevator, morphine glaze. He winked as we passed.

If I had known what was going to happen, I would have killed him right there.

"Screw you, Alex," I said, picking up my suitcase and guitar as my train squealed to a halt.

"Don't."

"I hope you live forever," I said, leaning in close so he could feel my wrath. "I hope you never learn. And you'll chase after her, won't you? Chase her like she's the best high you've ever had. You'll do everything to relive that day. Just like me, you'll wish you could have done something different, maybe if you tried harder, forced yourself to care less, loved her the way she was meant to be loved. It won't do either of us any good. We stole too many pieces. We took and took and took and fucking took until there was nothing left. It's not tragic she died without you. It was a fucking service. She had two people who truly cared about her in this world, two, and we had to watch her die.

"You killed her. You fucking killed her, Alex. I hope you always remember it."

I left him at the station, slumped over himself, spine gnarled from drug use. Delirious. Weeping. Broken. Smelling of cat piss in the sun. He's poised eternally in my memory like this. The last time I saw him.

Many years later, shortly after my daughter finished Uni, I learned that Alex finally died. He succeeded in overdosing in late October.

Ryan and Dev had passed away long before then. Dev was stabbed in a bar in Halifax over counterfeit credit cards by a man from Bridgewater named Rexington Windsor. The same Rex we assaulted in our alley outside The Cellar during Rock Against Racism.

Being the tough bastard he was, Crazy Dev drove himself to the hospital. He was loaded on so much blow, that he stayed conscious. Papers called it a miracle. He held his guts in his hands as he walked into the ER. He collapsed. Passed in the lobby. Blood loss.

Ryan started selling her body shortly after her child died, Everald, who passed at four. The police found her in the basement of Church. Someone had cut her body down from the rafters, had the decency to veil her face before taking her wallet. She left no note. After her death, Green River demolished the building. No one remembers Skunktown, but the weeds and broken bricks are proof it existed.

I learned all this when I returned to Green River to visit Benji's grave, after my mother returned to her god. I paid my respects to my lost friends and said so long to mom.

Those summer years of my youth were the best I ever had. We dragged ourselves through hell, but we made the most of it.

We were young. Nihilistic. Overlooked. Blackhole kids. Longevity wasn't on the setlist. We knew this. Every high, every low, brought us closer to death. We relished in self-destruction. To quote Philip: Just kids playing games for the thrill.

And ain't that the truth.

My friends died how they lived: Reckless and wild.

If my adolescent counterpart heard that I lived to my forties, he would take a swing at me. Spit in my face and call me a sellout. On my old battle jacket I had a poorly stitched patch Benji made for me that said 'Live Fast/Die Numb.' I lived fast, but I didn't die. I won't for a while, probably, for my daughter's sake.

My wife held my hand at each gravestone we visited. I cried a lot. Told our dead friends how sorry I was while she held her tongue. When I visited Alex's burial plot—this side of Hamilton, and a Mormon if you can believe that—my wife waited in the car. I told him about my life since that day at Mapleview Station. I forgave him. Hoped he had forgiven himself.

Before I departed, I emptied a beer onto his weedy grave, left him a pack of cancers. In a reverent voice I whispered to him what Sav said to me before she died. The single word that haunted me for decades. In those ephemeral moments before I fall asleep I relive that moment beside her hospital bed.

There is shouting over erratic sirens telling me something is wrong as I rush to her room. Her mother is here, screaming. Doctors and nurses frantically fighting for a solution. It's noise. Loud and horrid. I focus on Sav's terrified face as she slips into another seizure. I hold her mom. 'My baby. My baby.' An endless loop. A skipping CD of terms mothers use when they know their child is never coming home.

For a sliver of a second, Sav regains consciousness. Her eyes no longer glazed, now bright and sober, lock onto mine. Confusion. Asking me why. Her still small voice echoes inside my chest. She cries my name. Flatlines.

Zombies Ate My Neighbours.

Lethargic from the four-day train ride, I sprawled out on an empty bench in Pacific Central Station. Settled into miserable steel. Face clammy, shirt twisted. I missed my rickety sponge bed aboard the train. When I closed my eyes, the world around me still rocked as gently as it had during the long ride. Like the spins, but not nearly as entertaining.

It was six in the morning when we pulled in. Too early to call, too late for sleep. I waited until 9.

Public phones out here were cleaner than the ones in Green River, but I still felt the ghost touch of perma-crust. Frowned at the Nimbles tag along the handle.

I held the receiver with my good hand, and punched the number with my busted one. I bought a bandanna, red, when I transferred in Winnipeg. The cuts on my knuckles from Alex had yet to heal. I grew tired of receiving unwanted stares. I covered the ugly.

I left a message with an operator. Then an answering machine for good measure. I waited in the station, people watching. A group of teenagers said heartfelt goodbyes.

They were young. Going away to college, I decided, though I wasn't sure when or if the semester had started. They appeared normal, untainted, virginal. Their whole mungy lives ahead of them. I envied it.

If our lives had played out differently, would that have been us?

Hugs and kisses exchanged. One of the boys called a girl his angel. I gagged.

Jocelyn had once snapped at a douche bro dumb enough to try his pickup artistry in Saetia who had made the same mistake. She snapped his head off. I'd never seen her so worked up. An adorable ball of tiny rage.

"I'm not some pedestal mounted fairy godmother," she belted, as Carmen tried to calm her down. "I'm a flawed human and my purpose in life isn't to wipe smegma out of your foreskin."

I loved it. The douche bro skulked out in shame. I bought her a round for upholding the sacred tradition of public crucifixion.

Noon rush came and went as I huddled beside an outlet to charge my MP3 player. Evening rush came and also went. Again, I had to recharge. I remained on my bench with a pile of fast-food wrappers strewn around me as I fought the urge to make another phone call.

It was nine at night when I started to search tourist maps for a motel. Tomorrow, perhaps. I finally found a place I could afford when the nightlife rush was at its height. Thick crowds of college kids with fermented breath weaved in and out of the invisible bubbles humans use to distance themselves from each other. I tried to measure their comfort zones in French fries. Wondered who gave more space. Vancouverites or Torontonians.

I hung up the phone, didn't leave a message this time, and went about collecting my junk.

A flicker of red weaved in and out of the crowd near the turnstiles. I lost sight of it as warm tears stung my eyes. My vision battled the blur, but nonetheless I followed her outline in the undertow of the clubbers and drunks and blackhole kids and art freaks and uptown shoppers.

I hoped to find the familiar scent of mangos.

Is it so wrong to dream?

Sitting and starving myself from anxiety seemed the better option now that my guts twisted with apprehension and hope. It was easier to survive on fumes. Gave me a reason for feeling helpless. Weak.

Had I gained the weight back? Am I too fat?

My knees gave out when I stood. Chest tightening. I steadied myself with my guitar, panting hard. The cold case absorbed into my calloused fingers. The last time I felt this weary I had just gotten clean. Surviving off apples and dream-walking in the daylight. Addicted to self loathing.

I'm better. I'm better.

Pleasegodiwanttobebetter.

I tried to shoulder my guitar, quell my hopes with reality, knowing I was mistaken, delusional. She told me to stay away. My hands lost their grip, fell to my sides. My guitar clattered on the ground. No one helped me. They walked around, my bubble growing wider with each wave of humans surrounding me, swallowing me as I cursed myself for my foolish—

Her voice. Gentle and kind over the crowd. She used the same questioning tone Sav had that night at the hospital as she died under mechanical cries. Pleading. Confused. Sincerity.

My head was too heavy to lift. Ashamed for breaking an unspoken promise.

Her quivering smile assured me I was wanted. Missed.

We lost control. She repeated herself and I tried to lift my arms but could only hold my face, hiding my hobgoblin tears as she spoke that single word which haunted me during my nights of catatonia, as I watched the motionless spider in my hollow apartment, while Mail Lake flooded over worn floorboards, the same abominable slur I denied Alex in life.

Her perfume of sweet mangos, of earth and rain and graveyard dirt, swelled in my chest as she veered towards me.

I broke. Sobbing in response to her still small voice drifting through the oblivious crowd like an echoing rain. Just as I had in the hospital when Sav spoke the same worthless word before she died.

Jocelyn crashed into me. Held me close.

"Bastion?"

Acknowledgements

Mr. John Murphy, J.S. Veter, Jaclyn Desforges, Jennifer Jones, Jeffrey Griffiths, and the groovy people at Guernica Editions who took a chance on this unabashed story. Thanks to everyone who sacrificed five minutes of their lives to natter about music and folklore, or who shared a stage, a beer, a joint, a couch, or a laugh. Thanks, h, for being my stinky. And all those people between Tino and Razum who kept me grounded when my brain turned electric. The real world blackhole kids: E, Z, J, P, C, E, J, K, J, V, M, & R, I wish you were all still kicking. After I visit the House of Donn, I'll join you for shots. Until then, give my dogs a scratch. Lastly, I'll acknowledge the councillor who convinced me I'd never be a writer and that my education was a waste of everyone's time: look at all these people whose time I've wasted with this book!

I'll close with something our Billy taught me which helps with surviving these long horrible stretches of sobriety: Plead insanity for the craic.

About the Author

First generation Irish-Canadian, **j.l.oneill** dropped out of high school after completing a grade 10 education. It wasn't until graduating college that a high school diploma was considered worth the bother. Daylighting as an electrician and moonlighting as a writer, the horribly elusive author resides in a busted bungalow somewhere in Southern Ontario. *The Blackhole Kids* is j.l.oneill's first novel.

Check out jloneill.com for more.

Printed by Imprimerie Gauvin
Gatineau, Québec